rogue wave

ISABEL JOLIE

ISABEL JOLIE

❀ Created with Vellum

To Jake's Watch… and our family beach days on Killegray Ridge

one

TATE

The screen flapped loose in the ocean's wind. Rotten wood surrounded the windows and doorframe. The dark and weathered cedar shakes cried out for a coat of fresh paint. The house before me stood as a shadow of childhood memories, of past summers spent on Haven Island.

Back then, light gray paint covered the cedar shake siding, and white Adirondack rocking chairs with clean, colorful pillows filled the porch. Surfboards hung from hooks on the far back wall. A yellow bucket with seashell remnants rested near the outside water hose.

"Are you Pearl's?" The voice carried over the distant sound of crashing surf and pulled me back to the present. An older woman, with weathered chocolate-brown skin and kind eyes, sat in a golf cart, watching me.

"Yes." The wood board I stood on cracked beneath my

weight, decayed and splintering. I mumbled, more to myself than to her, "I was."

"You're still hers. Always will be."

I stopped looking at my feet and examined the woman behind the wheel. Her hair. The thick, woven braids pulled back. I remembered her. I used to debate with the other kids whether she wore dreadlocks or braids.

She stood and came around to me. In her palm, she offered a key. I stood staring, and she raised her arm. "Take it. It's yours."

"What is it?" The woman's name eluded me.

"It's the key to this place. Your grandmother asked me to hold on to it for you. She was a dear friend of mine, you know."

"How did you know I'd be here?" I'd landed on the ferry less than an hour ago, then walked up Long Wynd, the one long road from the marina along the south side of the island. Golf carts whizzed by me, although I earned a few second glances. The long-haired, scruffy guy hauling a massive backpack didn't blend in with the resort beach scene.

"Pearl asked me to keep an eye out. I've got your golf cart too. Been keeping it at my place. Your cottage took a hit in the last hurricane. Not too much damage, but the floorboards need to be replaced. You'll need to have electrical and water turned back on. You can stay with me if you like while you get your place situated."

"Thanks, but I can camp out." Even without electricity, the place would feel luxurious compared to some of the places I'd lived over the last ten years.

My plan had been to break into the cottage, although my grandmother's lawyer said he could get me a key. I hadn't wanted to deal with him, or anyone else, longer than necessary. I'd arrived too late for her funeral, then learned she'd given my brother her Connecticut home, and me her beach cottage. Those were the only two items in the will my brother left out of the dispute.

A young teenager whizzed down the narrow black asphalt road in her two-seater cart, her long blonde strands flying in the wind. The low hum from a cranked-up radio overpowered the island lull. The surfboard strapped to the top of the golf cart delivered a wave of nostalgia. An intense longing for those carefree, sunny, warm days with a wide-open future struck hard. My grandmother's crackly voice rang through my mind. "How was the surf today?"

The golf cart reached the peak and tipped down out of sight as her golden strands whipped behind her. "Go along and meet a new friend, Tate. Enjoy the day." Nana's words wrapped around me as if her spirit were here, welcoming me back home.

Every summer I begged to spend here. My brother would ask to go away to camp or on sailing trips to the Caribbean. Not me. Every single summer, I asked to spend with Nana Pearl.

Cars weren't allowed on the island, so everyone got around on bikes or golf carts or skateboards. You could go anywhere, and none of the adults worried. The golden girl going by in a bikini and flip-flops reminded me of all the bikini-clad girls I used to hang out with every summer, on constant rotation as the renters came and went. The setting sun reflected in her sunglasses, and her blonde hair offset a perfect Coppertone tan, the smooth, even tan a summer in the waves delivered.

I closed my eyes, luxuriating in the sun's warmth. It had been over ten years since I'd stood here, since I'd seen Nana, and almost that long since I'd spoken to her. My last visit had been over Christmas break before graduation. "That water is too cold for me. I tell you what, I'll have some hot cider waiting for you when you get back."

Winter on the island held a unique appeal. In the offseason, the island pared down to the two or three hundred locals. The ache in my chest drilled home what I had already known before ever stepping off the ferry—I missed all the seasons.

"Come back with me. I'll get you your golf cart. Give you the numbers you'll need to get things turned on in your place. It's almost dinnertime. You can make an old woman's day by agreeing to have dinner with her." Nana's friend's voice broke my reverie, reminding me she stood nearby.

I lifted the brass key from her palm and slipped it into my pocket. I squelched the desire to roam through the cottage, to see what kind of disaster waited inside, and climbed into her golf cart. All my life's material possessions leaned against the front door of the place, but I knew they'd be safe. The people who came to Haven Island, well, they weren't the kind of people to steal. You could leave an umbrella or surfboard out on the beach all day— all night, even—and it would be waiting for you when you returned. I guessed that was why I expected so much when I set out on my own.

"I'm Alice. Do you remember me, Adrian?"

I smiled at her and bowed my head in reverence, for some reason I didn't understand. Just felt like the right way to address her. It felt natural she'd call me the same

4

name my grandmother used. Nana had been the only person I allowed to call me Adrian; everyone else called me by my nickname, Tate. I slipped my hand into my pants pocket, located the smooth sea glass, and flipped it between my fingers as she drove deep within the island. "Yes, I do, ma'am. But please, call me Tate. Everyone does."

Her withered, warm hand patted my thigh the way you'd pat a dog. "Just like your grandmother." She drove slowly and spent more time studying me than watching the road. "Tell me. Are you running? Or are you home?"

two

LUNA

Alice's dark green two-story home, nestled into a canopy of trees with a matching dark green picket fence, came into view as my golf cart bounced high, sending the little basket of leathery turtle shells into the grass.

"Luna, is everything all right?"

I scooped up the last piece of shell and rose. "Forgot to hold on to the basket—those blasted speed bumps."

"You mean you were going too fast on that cart of yours. Kids like you, that's why they had to install those speed bumps." Her words scolded, but she wore a teasing smile as she took the basket from me and fingered through the egg remnants. "Those tourists didn't take much, huh?"

"No. The group last night showed more interest in the constellations."

"If I know you, they left with a solid appreciation of

the sea turtle plight, and a healthy respect for the cages dotting our beach protecting those nests."

"Let's hope." Alice and I met on the night of my first turtle watch, back when I was a homesick intern questioning the path I'd chosen. She'd helped me build my first cage. Others saw her as the island eccentric, or the weird old lady, but her iconic beauty reminded me of Toni Morrison or Maya Angelou. Others found her collection of alligator teeth, feathers, animal skulls, and such to be freakish. Not me.

"Come inside and have some iced tea."

"I wish I could, but I'm running behind today. I'm supposed to meet Mr. Blaid. He has some extras he plans to toss."

"He keeps building those spec homes, and this island is going to lose its charm." She wasn't the first person to gripe about his success, nor would she be the last.

"Our business wouldn't be doing nearly as good without his referrals," I offered as a defense of the balding builder.

"I know. And I like what you and Laura do. You renovate. There's an art to making the old new. And that, I think, is good for Haven Island. Good for the world. But this constant tearing down of trees and destroying undeveloped land, it's gotta stop."

"It's a problem everywhere. They call it suburban sprawl."

"Well, Haven Island is not the suburbs." She propped both her hands on her hips, ready for a verbal duel.

"Right you are." Her white teeth flashed as she accepted my agreement. "I'm off to renovate. Maybe Mr. Baird has found some new owners who need someone to come in and freshen things up." He often passed on minor projects that weren't worth his time.

Savvy investors knew they could buy one of the island's weathered cottages and, with some extra updates, flip the house and make a nice return. REVO was really Laura's business, and I helped her out when I wasn't needed at the conservancy. Shiplap boards on the walls, a fresh coat of paint, updated waterproof flooring, and kitchen and bathroom facelifts meant a cottage would sell above market price within hours.

I slid back into my golf cart, and Alice came around to the driver's side and wrapped her weathered fingers around the stainless steel bar holding the plexiglass windshield. "There's a new man on the island," she teased with one dark eyebrow arched.

"I'm sure there are many. Every week we get ferry loads full of vacationers. Loads of married men and sometimes high school or college aged kids." She ignored my college age quip, even though, technically, I too was a college student. As a grad student, I considered myself above the undergrad set.

"But this one…" she reached out and tapped the tip of my nose, "this one, you should meet."

"Are you trying to play matchmaker?"

She grinned, and I shook my head at her. I slipped the lever over to the R, and the reverse warning blared over the low hum of crickets and frogs surrounding Alice's marsh side home. "If he comes out for a turtle watch, I'm sure I'll meet him. I'm working every night this week."

"He needs you." Her plea had me moving the lever back to N. The jarring reverse alarm ended, and the marsh once again filled the air with a shrill chorus.

"Moved here yesterday. Doesn't know anyone. Needs lots of repair work. Think you can help him out? His grandmother is a good soul."

"You're talking about Pearl, aren't you?" Alice's sad nod and gentle smile said it all.

"I'll stop by and offer my help." I had been sad to hear that Pearl had passed away. I'd spent more than one afternoon sipping iced tea with Alice and Pearl. And I loved seeing her carry her board out to the waves. There was something kick ass about watching an older woman with long gray hair climb on a surfboard. She'd also been an active volunteer at the conservancy where I worked. She spent most of her time helping with the fundraisers, but I'd seen her every Wednesday at the Turtle Trots, the 5Ks we ran through summer to raise money. Another intern told me she used to bring cut up oranges and bananas, but she'd pulled back on some of her involvement last summer—my first summer as an intern. Rumors swarmed that she wasn't feeling well, but she didn't show it. I thought of her every time I drove past her cottage and saw the peeling paint and rusted nails.

"How's that Poppy doing?" She nudged me, and her teasing smile brightened the space between us, and I barked out a laugh. Poppy used to be the bartender at Jules, the restaurant and bar at the marina. Then COVID hit. The pandemic was now behind us, and life had returned to normal with the help of the massive vaccination rollout, but Poppy never returned to bartending. Still, everyone on the close-knit island knew and loved her. She and I were among the few year-round residents our age, so we'd bonded pretty quickly when I moved onto the island at the beginning of summer for my one-year stint as a junior scientist.

"She's good." I wrapped my fingers around the lever, conscious of the time.

"What exactly is Poppy doing now?"

"I'm not sure anyone knows. She keeps changing the subject every time I ask."

"Well, can't be proud, can she?"

"I don't remember her bragging all too often back when she was bartending." *What in the world, Alice?*

"Bring her by sometime. I have an herb blend for you both."

"Is this in the tea or brownie variety?" She mixed her concoctions in soups, teas, and even gooey desserts. I didn't think she used marijuana, but her lot backed up to the marsh, and if she wanted to grow a few plants, no one would catch her. Potted herbs filled her home and all around her property.

"What would you two prefer?"

"Whatever you like. What about we try to make it by this weekend?"

"I'd love that. I'll be here. And you'll stop by and offer Pearl's grandson some help?"

"Absolutely." I waved goodbye, pressed the accelerator, and caught air over the remaining speed bumps on Currituck Way.

Mr. Blaid's spec house on Horsemint Trail came into view just as a text alerted me one of the turtle cages on Access 36 had been tampered with. My job at the conservancy took priority. I whipped the cart around and changed course to head up Long Wynd to meet the volunteer interns and oversee repairs. I cranked up the volume to a Jack Johnson tune and hummed along.

The road curved down, and Pearl's weathered cottage caught my attention. A tan, bare-chested man stood by one of the porch posts. Unruly light brown with sun bleached streaks hung below his ears, a mass of loose curls. He tucked the front pieces behind his ears. The rough, golden scruff along his jaw glinted in the sun. His longboard shorts hung low on his waist. He focused on the hammer in his hand as he pulled the screen taut.

The faded, worn shorts exposed hip bones that jutted out slightly, and a narrow band of pearly white skin hovered above the waistline, below his bronze tan. He looked like a typical surfer, with lean and fluid muscular lines.

My foot slipped on the pedal as I passed by, taking in every detail as if I'd never seen a shirtless man. Every part of his skin bore the sign of time spent under the sun. There were no tan lines, other than along the edge of the top of his low-slung shorts. A tattoo of a large compass accentuated the muscles of one bicep, and foreign lettering trailed up and down his rib cage on one side.

The cart almost rolled to a stop, and he turned. He wore sunglasses, and I couldn't see his eyes, but his stare burned with the same searing sensation of the sun's rays. My stomach fluttered and throat tightened. In the blazing sun, the temperature rose, and perspiration threatened. I lifted my foot and gunned the accelerator. The wind whipped around me and cooled my face.

Sweet Joseph, you'd think I'd never seen a good-looking guy before. Did Pearl's grandson hire someone to fix the place up? Or was that sun god Pearl's grandson? Would Pearl's grandson have tattoos? Pearl had seemed proper, even if she did surf. For crying out loud, she wore a sun hat out on the beach. But that could explain Alice's matchmaking attempt. Alice had commented more than once on the tattoo running along the inside of my forearm. And I could see her setting me up with a fellow surfer. If Mr. Tattoo turned out to be Pearl's grandson, helping him would be a pleasure, in the way working with eye candy is always enjoyable. But I learned my lesson with Brandon. Friends and family placed hope on relationships, and they got hurt needlessly when the end came.

My phone vibrated with a text from Dr. Wilton asking what time I'd be in the office today. I picked up the phone and used Siri to text back. "Fixing a tampered cage. Should be in by eleven."

A seagull glided overhead, and I flattened the accelerator on the back wall of the cart, racing along the coastline. I breathed in the salt air and soaked in the words inked on my arm, *One with the sea*.

three

TATE

"I don't care about the money, Mr. Williams." The phone burned against my ear. Lengthy conversations did that.

"It's not that simple, Adrian. Your brother is contesting the will. If you want to negotiate with your brother out of court, that is your choice. You can tell him what you want and see if he'll drop the suit. But I strongly recommend you get your own counsel before doing so. Let a lawyer negotiate for you. I shouldn't even say that much, but I've known you your whole life. Be smart about this." A fatherly tone colored his words. Truth be told, I couldn't even remember what Mr. Williams looked like. I knew he'd been at our house a few times growing up, but his face blended with all the other faces of my parents' friends who stopped by on random occasions.

"I thought the only thing Gregg cared about was the

business. He wants my business shares. I don't have a problem with that. We all know the only reason she left half to me is she was aiming to be fair. She wasn't thinking about the business." I pinched the bridge of my nose while watching the waves crash in the distance, a calming and focusing technique I learned in Asia.

"Adrian, when you find your own counsel, have them contact me. Please, son, obtain counsel."

I knew he was stepping on lines he shouldn't be, all out of some sense of obligation to look out for the kid he remembered. There was a good chance he remembered tousling my hair, teasing me about how much I'd grown, or maybe I looked like his son. Or maybe he felt an obligation to my parents. But I wished he'd let me settle and put this ugly fight behind me.

"I will. Thank you, Mr. Williams."

I let my grandmother's screen door slam behind me and headed to the beach. Once the sand filtered between my toes, I lifted my cell out of my pocket and called Gabe. I disconnected from this world over a decade ago. But Gabe was a childhood friend. The kind of friend you could go a decade without talking to and pick right back up where you left off.

"Goldman Sachs, Gabriel Chesterton's office." The words came out in rapid-fire, spoken like a no-nonsense New Yorker.

"Hi. This is Adrian Tate. Is he available?"

"He's in a meeting. I can let him know you called."

"Great. Thank you."

"What did you say your name is?"

The ocean water circled around my ankles, cooling my bare feet, as I finished giving my information to an assistant who sounded skeptical her boss would return my call. My tight, sore muscles cursed at me for declining Alice's guest room. This body of mine was getting too old for lumpy sofas. But until I got the AC working, the downstairs sofa had my name on it. Besides, the mildew smell on the upper floor approached unbearable.

I stretched my legs along the waking beach, passing families staking out umbrellas and all forms of contraptions designed to create shade as they settled in for a day in the sun. One older man held his dog's Frisbee, and the moment I walked past him, the black lab leaped over the incoming wave in hot pursuit of the flying plastic disc.

I slowed as I neared the peak where the Cape Fear and the Atlantic Ocean intermingled. A furor of crashing waves denoted the long sandbar formed by the swirling waters. Stories of families venturing out onto the sandbar and getting caught far out by a fast-rising tide served as island urban legends, and fuel for my grandmother's warnings to always be aware. Even close to shore, the almighty ocean claimed lives.

"There's a riptide warning today, boys. Be careful." Her words floated across the breeze, as crisp and clear as if she stood beside me.

I cast a glance back toward the Shoals Club. The Cape Cod inspired architecture sat majestically on the point, above wispy blades of grass blowing in the wind on the dunes. Back in my youth, the club didn't exist. Now it featured multiple pools overlooking the ocean, and my grandmother had told me in one of her emails the restaurants were worth the money.

Her mostly unanswered emails weighed heavily. I always meant to sit down and send her a long response. "Will you send me a letter telling me what your average day is like?" Only once did she ask. If I'd just done it when she asked, I could have told her about life on the seas tracking a ship, watching dots on radars. The fear one of those dots might be a modern-day pirate ship. I held back, not wanting to worry her. That was before my days became the stuff of nightmares.

A drumming beat pulled me out of my introspection, and I cast a glance up the beach. A young woman knelt in the sand near the point, pounding a white square contraption with orange plastic rectangles into the sand with a rubber hammer. She wore a yellow string bikini top and short denim cut-offs. Her long hair flowed down her back, but only the lighter blonde strands took flight in the wind. The bulk of her hair was wet, weighted down from her most recent dip in the ocean.

A younger man clambered across the boardwalk to her, shouting, "I heard. A new nest. Do you need help?" Within minutes, a swarm of college-aged kids, or possibly younger, gathered around her. A buzz of energy surrounded the group. These were the island conservationists, working to save the sea turtles.

I watched from a distance, admiring their energy and envious of their optimism. In a prior life, I would have marched up to them, introduced myself, and offered to volunteer. Offered to join their ranks and save as many baby turtle lives as possible.

In that other life, I'd ducked out on my doctoral program and joined Greenpeace, hell-bent on saving the ocean from overfishing. Those excited kids, chattering on the beach, I'd bet money they hadn't heard of land sickness. Had no concept that you could spend so much time at sea that when you stood on land, you vomited until your inner ear acclimated.

Those kids would make a difference, just like me. The kind of difference one made if you plugged one small hole in a ship that rammed an iceberg.

The bikini-clad girl stepped back, admiring her work. She had an even tan, svelte curves, and a scripted tattoo barely visible on the inside of her forearm. An open conversation starter for the right guy. A decade and a half ago, I would have been that guy. The guy asking her if she wanted to go surfing, if she wanted to catch some waves. Asking if she wanted company when she watched the turtle nests at night.

I stood there watching her, this young girl who was everything my former self would've been intrigued by. He would've followed her around, offering help and friend-ship while hoping for more. Enamored by her love of nature and her belief she could make a difference.

She twisted slowly, as if aware of a nearby gawker. She smiled a full smile, the smile of youthful innocence, and held up her long, lean arm and waved.

I gave a quick nod and moved on along the beach.

"Hey...are you Adrian Tate?" Her melodic tone rose above the crashing surf.

"Mm-hmm. And you are?" I asked, curious how she knew my name.

"Luna Fisher. I knew your grandmother."

Ah, Nana Pearl. Two hundred year-round residents on the island. No doubt everyone knew her.

"She said you work with Greenpeace."

"I did." Uneasy, I dug my toes into the sand and leaned

away from her, gazing down the beach in the direction I'd come from.

"Luna, do we need to photograph this?" one of the college kids shouted to her. Another guy stood, his straight hair falling into his face. He stepped forward, watching me with a possessiveness I recognized. I too had been in love before.

Luna held her hand over her brow, shading her eyes from the rising sun, as she nodded an affirmative answer to her friend. Then she addressed me, friendly and open.

"I'm with the island's Nature Conservancy group. We all are. We'd love to have you come down and talk with us."

I dug my foot deeper into the sand.

"How many turtles are nesting on the island these days?"

"We had eighty-six nests last year. Expecting more this year." Excitement punctuated her words. And pride.

"Sweet." I fingered the sea glass in my pocket while she talked to me about the coastal science program.

A strong wind gusted, portending the line of thunderstorms headed our way. Sand granules whirled about, stinging my skin. A gold choker with a starfish pendant glinted in the sun around Luna's neck. My gaze trailed down until I stared at the small triangles barely covering Luna's rounded, perky breasts. Her shorts fell low on her hips, and the thin line of matching bathing suit bottoms stuck out along the waistband. The tiny shorts curved around her ass, and thin strings from the denim cut-offs traced her lean tawny thighs.

She was still talking, telling me things I should care about, about the conservation program on the island and success rates. The college guy glaring our way, he knew what I'd been staring at, where my mind had gone. The old guy gawking at the college kid.

I looked to the guy, even though he stood a good fifteen feet away from us. "Sounds like a good program. Best of luck."

four

LUNA

I knocked hard on Poppy's door. Any patience evaporated with the third mosquito bite. I twisted the knob, discovered it was open, and let myself in. Poppy lived in one of my favorite marina side homes on a quaint street named Transom Row. A picket fence ran along the front of her tall, narrow cottage, and she had planted colorful flowers in front of the fence and in window boxes along her porch rail. The white and purple blooms spilling out below her windows complemented the bright pink roses along the fence.

I would've expected the rent to be astronomical, but she said she got a deal by signing a year lease. The owner couldn't make it here as often as she liked, and while she wasn't ready to sell, she liked having someone living in it so it didn't sit vacant. The front porch looked out onto Transom Row. Tall, narrow beach homes lined the street in a variety of hues, with white picket fences separating the sidewalk curb from the tiny, blossoming front yards. The center of the street featured a landscaped divider dotted with swaying palm trees.

The back porch of Poppy's place looked out onto the marina. Across the marina, you could see Jules, the restaurant she used to bartend before COVID hit. That was a while ago, though. Jules was now back in full swing, and Poppy had found a new career that clearly paid well.

"Poppy?" I called, stepping into her bright kitchen. The owner painted the cabinets lavender and added a bluish clear beach glass backsplash. Large windows lined the back wall. Thanks to the open downstairs floor plan, you could cook with a view of the marina, and just beyond the marina, the mouth of the Cape Fear. If you walked out onto her back porch, leaned over the railing, and looked to your far left, you could see the lighthouse that kept ships from running aground as they made their way to the mainland.

I slid my hand along the pine banister and stepped cautiously up the steps. The faint sound of music circulated as I climbed. When I reached the landing, bright white flashing lights forced me to protect my eyes. "Poppy?"

Her head appeared from behind the white sheet held up by a stainless steel contraption. "Hey? What time is it?"

"What are you doing?"

Her cheeks flaunted a full pink glaze. She stepped closer. Makeup caked her face, and heavy eyeliner and mascara decorated her large blue eyes. And she wore lacy white lingerie.

"What are you doing?" I repeated, my tone so high I risked sounding judgmental.

"Working. Give me a minute. I have a client I need to respond to, and then I'll be down. Help yourself to whatever you want from the refrigerator. Or wine. Do you want wine? I want wine. Open a bottle and bring me a glass. I need wine. Do you mind?" She rattled on as I scurried down the stairs.

I found a bottle I recognized with a duck on the label, uncorked it, poured two glasses, then drank half of one. Poppy hadn't really shared much about her career change. She'd been a master at changing the subject when asked. I'd more or less assumed she found a company doing something online, research or managing ads or doing something with spreadsheets. Nothing worth talking about. Never did it ever occur to me she'd find a revenue source that involved lingerie. And photos. Because that curtain and flashing lights, she had to be taking photos. There had been a couple of umbrella-looking things scattered around the room. I'd seen that kind of setup at photographers' studios.

I refilled my glass and made my way back up the stairs.

"Here you go."

She sat typing away on her laptop, clicking keys at a speed that showed she could be an award-winning typist if there were such a thing. A floral silk kimono hid her lingerie, and she'd removed the cat eyes. Without the caked-on makeup and the long, dark eyelashes, she looked more like my friend.

With a final loud click, she closed her laptop, lifted a

wine glass from my hand, chugged it, and said, "Okay. So, now you know."

"Know what?" *You do video sexting?*

"Do you think it's awful?" she asked with a grimace.

"What exactly are you doing?" I could make assumptions, but…

"Have you heard of OnlyFans?"

"No."

"Oh. Okay. Well, come downstairs."

I followed her down the stairs and onto her porch.

"I share photos of this gorgeous body," she waved her hand down her voluptuous frame, "and men who get off on seeing pics of fat chicks in lingerie pay me. Some of them I build relationships with, and yes, don't judge me. Some of them I have sexy conversations with. Well, really emails. Messages. But I make a ton of money. Like, so much money. I can show you how. You can totally do it. And I bet with a skinny body like yours, you'd make even more money than me."

"Ahem, wow."

"Do you want me to show you how? You can use my photo studio."

"Ah…that's okay."

"Oh, my god. You think I'm a perv. That I shouldn't be doing this. That I'm an awful person. You are going to slut-shame me." Her neck and face flamed pink.

"Slow down, there, girlfriend." I reached for her hand. "Calm it down. No judgment here. I'm just wrapping my head around it, that's all. Give me a minute."

She swallowed her wine with her enormous eyes trained on me, like a convicted person awaiting the sentencing from the judge.

"Stop it," I demanded, and she dropped her gaze to her lap. "If this is what you want to do, I'm for it. You know me, I go with the flow." I glanced to my wrist, *one with the sea*. "But you're not fat. You're sexy. I can see how there'd be lots of men paying for… Do you enjoy it? I mean, that's what matters."

She sank back into the cushion and exhaled loudly. "You know, I do? It's weird. It started on a whim one day when I was debating if I should pay rent or buy food. And at the right angle, these tatas look pretty good, right?"

"I'd imagine they look pretty good from almost any angle." Poppy might think of herself as fat, but I never had. She was what I'd call bigger boned, curvy but well-proportioned. I knew her weight bothered her because she'd always made comments and put herself down. Out on the beach, she hesitated to take off her cover up. And she never walked on the beach without something wrapped around her waist. But the 'tatas,' as she'd called them, were attention-getters. Whether we were out surfing or walking the beach or meeting up with friends at a bar, guys always noticed Poppy. Or, rather, they always noticed the tatas.

She pulled her robe tighter over her chest. "Thanks. It started as cleavage shots. You post pics, and people like them and pay you for more shots. Private shots. I set my camera on auto and take pics. I delete most, but there are some good ones with the right light and angle. A little Photoshopping. And, I mean, it's people I'll never meet in real life."

"If it makes you happy, who am I to judge?"

"Yeah. It makes me happy. I'm good at marketing. The first thing I do each day is check my numbers. I was never the pretty girl, you know? I've been the fun friend, the one everyone loved to hang around but didn't want to date. Now, I have these men from around the world paying to see my photos. It's sort of rocking."

"How do you know they're men?"

"Oh." She blinked several times as my question registered. "Well, it's the internet. I suppose it could be women too. Hell, it might be a boatload of fifteen-year-old horny boys. I suppose this is like a modern-day *Playboy*. But the point is, who would have thought I'd ever be the centerfold?"

"You've always sold yourself short. If you like doing it, that's all I care about."

"You are such a sweetie. I love you." She wrinkled her nose and reached out and tapped my arm. "How're you doing?"

"Good. I think we'll surpass one hundred nests this summer. Last night, we had two nests hatch. Of course, true to my luck, I was on the far end of South Beach, and both hatchings were on East Beach."

"Great." She sipped her wine and rocked her chair. "Any non-turtle news to report?"

"Actually, yes. There's a new guy on the island."

She snorted out her wine. "Honey, there are new men on the island every week. Married with children. Or still in college and living off mommy and daddy. Loads of new men to choose from each week." She smirked as she crossed her legs, taking care to keep her lingerie covered. "Those interns of yours are the best thing going. And those surf instructors." She clucked her tongue in mock appreciation.

Poppy didn't lie. But the thrill of sitting on the beach

with a lukewarm six-pack each night had waned. While I'd barely had a year of being legal, I preferred to hang with the twenty-one-and-over crowd.

I shifted to the edge of the rocking chair. "This new guy is better than any of the interns. Trust me. He's smoking hot. Not married. No children. He's a resident. And…he needs help renovating his beach house."

"He's an owner?" Poppy's chin dropped down.

"Do you remember Pearl? The nice older lady who was good friends with Alice?"

"Yeah. I liked her. Didn't she die?"

"Last winter." A vision of her weathered cottage came to mind, and I brushed it away. "Anyway, the hot guy? He's her grandson, and he inherited her beach cottage."

"Jake's Watch?"

"Yep." All the cottages on the island bore a name, similar to the way all boats did. Jake referred to a cherished family dog. Legend had it Jake had come back as a dolphin, and could still be glimpsed offshore, keeping an eye on his old family.

"And you like this guy?" Poppy tilted her head, her grin spreading wide.

"I do. I mean, you know, from afar. We spoke on the beach briefly. He didn't say much. Everything about him screams surfer. But he's also got the bad mood brooding thing going. It's like he needs to be wrapped up in a warm blanket and hugged. Does that make any sense at all? Definitely crush worthy."

"You got all that from seeing him on the beach?"

"Yep."

"Well, let me get dressed."

"What? Why?"

26

"It's Friday night. What else are we gonna do before you ditch me to watch sand? Besides, I've got to see this guy."

I waved my hand in the air, dismissing her. "Nope. Not tonight."

She ignored me and trounced up the stairs. Moments later, she returned in a loose, flowery sundress and flip-flops. "Let's go."

"No way. He's older. He wouldn't want to hang with us."

"How old?"

"I don't know. Not intern age. Maybe thirties? Like, he's distant crush material. Not spend time with the crush kind of material."

"Please. The thirties are not old. Trust me. I have clients who are way older, and guess what? They dig twenty-something girls."

"No. Let's just go for a bike ride." I should have never mentioned him to Poppy. I should have kept him as my safe secret crush, like a book boyfriend.

"Hey! You said he needs help refurbishing. Someone on the island needs help from Ms. Luna Rey. That means you've got to flip those golf cart sirens into the flaring red position and get to it." She snapped her fingers. "Let's go. Hop-hop. I wanna to see the new guy!"

"No. Absolutely not."

"Come on. We'll bring a bottle of red. Grab an extra glass and corkscrew in case he doesn't have."

five

TATE

The wood splintered and cracked as I ripped it up, board by board. Water damage had cast a gray sheen over the slim pine boards. This floor had probably been put in during the eighties when two-inch floorboards and high varnish reigned supreme. Over the years, sandy feet wore down the varnish, and the last hurricane had brought the tide high enough to coat the floor in seawater.

Sweat dripped down my forehead and drenched the inside of my heavy-duty work gloves. The old nails proved stubborn. Without lifting an arm, my body odors permeated the air. Something I didn't need to worry about, as I was doing the job alone. The stench brought me back to the ships.

"Diaz, I need a shower. Or a bath. Where do I go?"

"_Que?_"

Fish guts covered my chest and coated my shorts.

"Shower?" I made a note to learn the Spanish word later, but it should have been obvious what I needed.

He pointed to the back of the ship and called out to his shipmate. "Go," he told me with a glare.

An Asian man awaited me. Motioned for me to back up. I peered behind me, and a blast of cold water shot down over me. I screamed. Howled. The icy water burned. The wind froze the raw skin.

Men clustered around, laughing and pointing.

"*Mas*?" Diaz called from the front of the boat.

Three times, ice cold water poured over me before all traces of blood were gone. Shivering, I'd descended into the bowels of the ship, my fingers and toes frozen. Past the empty hammocks. My bag with all my clean clothes rested where I'd left it. Black, beady eyes startled me. The long, naked tail skittered away into the shadows. Bile rose in the back of my throat.

I wiped my forehead with my glove, staring out the back window, through the screened-in porch, searching for whitecaps through the blades of grass on the dunes. I homed in on my view out the window, seeking to forget the fishing boat and my fact gathering expedition for Greenpeace.

A knock sounded at the door. I might have ignored it, but I welcomed the reprieve. I flung the door open.

The dirty blonde from the beach stood before me in a navy halter top and short jean cut-offs and flip-flops. I recognized her instantly. A different pair of short jean cut-offs hugged her curves today.

A smattering of freckles below golden brown eyes captured my attention. Bright, full of life and spirit. She smiled, exposing straight, pearl white teeth, offset by tan, smooth skin. Her honeyed blonde highlights glinted in the sun.

I propped my foot against the door to keep it open and waited, half-expecting her to offer me Girl Scout cookies or to join the conservancy up the street.

"Hi." She rocked back on her heels and brushed the loose, golden strands out of her eyes. "I'm Luna. We met on the beach? Alice said you might need some help with renovations, and I came by to see if I could help. I stopped by with a friend of mine last night, but you weren't home. I left you a note. Did you get it?"

I shook my head.

"I told Poppy I didn't think it would stay. Not in the wind. I slipped it under your doormat. Oh, here it is. It did stay." She bent down, and her hair fell forward, the tips brushing the wood on my front porch. "So, here it is. My note." She held out the piece of paper.

I stared at the sandy, ripped piece of notebook paper, then at her.

"We wanted to see if you wanted to have a glass of wine. You know, to welcome you to the island."

"You're old enough to drink?"

She laughed. "Yeah. I'm almost twenty-three. I'm a junior scientist at the conservancy. I work for Dr. Wilton. He's the senior scientist at the center. I'm currently pursuing my master's in marine biology. I'll spend one year here overseeing the sea turtle program and assisting on coastal science research, then I'll return to university to complete my program."

"My undergrad degree is in marine biology." I leaned against the doorframe.

"Really? That's so cool." She bounced on her feet.

It registered that I was blocking the entrance to my cottage with my body and that it might be polite to invite her in. I closed the door behind me and stepped forward onto the front porch.

"Where'd you go to school?"

"Brown." Her light brown eyes widened. Emphasizing our fifteen-year age difference, I added, "A long time ago."

"Oh. I'm at the University of Florida. This is technically a one-year internship for me." She lifted her shoulders and slipped the tips of her long, tan fingers into her jean pockets.

"Good school," I offered. For marine biology, it was. Brown used to be the best, but they discontinued the program.

"So, do you currently do work with your degree? Or do you do something now that's totally unrelated?"

I wiped my palm over my mouth to cover the smirk I couldn't hold back. So many thoughts about that damn degree and my life choices rose in response to that question. "Ten years in Asia. Many roles. Not all related to marine biology. Now, I'm in between jobs." And that was all she'd get out of me. She didn't need to know more.

"That's so cool," she shrieked. She had the self-awareness to realize she'd been overly exuberant and bowed her head. She stepped back, closer to the porch step. "I volunteered for Greenpeace. All four years of undergrad. I'm currently torn between coastal biology or research on reefs."

"Are you on the PhD path?" I stared off across the swaying grasses on the dunes, cursing myself for engaging in conversation.

"I'm not sure. Undecided. Did you—"

"No."

"It's expensive. But I love the work. And the classes. Especially with professors who have worked in the field, you know?"

I nodded.

"I'd love to talk to you more about your experiences sometime. You might even have some ideas for the conservancy."

"I'm pretty busy these days. If I get some time later, maybe." I rested my hand on the porch rail, preparing to back into my grandmother's home.

"Oh, yes. Your renovations. What all are you doing? I've spent the last two summers on the island as an intern at the conservancy. This summer makes my third here. But now, I'll be living here the full year. What about you? Are you staying?"

"Unsure." I held the screen door handle, attempting to signal an end to the conversation.

"What do you mean?" she asked, upbeat and bright, oblivious to my brush off.

"I'm going to fix up the cottage. Then decide."

She pushed past me and walked into the foul-smelling unit, talking as she stepped inside. I stood there a moment, watching her shapely ass sway. Stunned.

"Oh, you're replacing the floorboards. That's such a smart thing to do. Do you know what you're going to replace them with?"

"Hadn't decided." I let the screen door slam closed behind me. "Figured I'd go with whatever they had at the hardware store." Last time I'd been here, there was one hardware store on the island. I didn't expect that had changed.

"Oh. You should do manufactured wood. It's water-proof. And environmentally friendly. Do you have a design planned? Because if not, we had a house that ordered flooring then changed their mind. They had to buy it, but I'd bet Mr. Baird would sell it to you at a huge discount. The people already had to pay for it. They're like those kinds of owners with crazy money who don't mind throwing away a bit here and there. She changed her mind, and it was like…" She snapped her fingers in the air to finish her sentence. She glided farther in, past the kitchen and into the demolished living area.

"If you redo this place correctly, you can literally increase the value so much. That's what Mr. Baird does. He buys the run-down places that are selling for the price of the land, then guts them. New floors, new cabinets, counters. We've been doing shiplap on the walls, which is super easy to do, and it adds so much. Paint. Sometimes we replace fixtures. Depends on how dated they are or if they're rusted." She looked up at the light in the center of the room. "You've got rust. It's a lot, but at the same time, it's not. Paint. That's the big piece on these cottages. Sometimes a new roof. Does this place need a new roof?"

She'd been scouting for nails as she checked the downstairs out, and I'd been focused on the way she filled out her cut-offs. My cock twitched, threatening to come to life. Christ, it had been too long since I'd been near a woman. She caught me staring, and I stepped past her to open the window further. The whole place felt too warm and stuffy. There wasn't enough ocean breeze coming through, and the mold smell remained trapped inside.

"Have you checked the roof yet?" she asked, skepticism leaking through her words. Like she was wondering if I knew what I was doing. Like maybe somehow she'd inspected my floorboard project and discerned I'm a renovation amateur.

"No."

"What all are you gonna do?"

"Don't have much of a plan." I'd started ripping up the boards because it needed to be done and it felt good. "Someone—I think Alice, maybe—had most of the furniture moved upstairs before the storm. So, I figured I'd start down here. Fix it up. Then move upstairs."

"Did you have damage upstairs?" The innocent girl did not understand what kind of loaded question she just asked.

"Only down here. Whole place needs a fresh coat of paint." The bathrooms could probably use a refresh too, but they were palatial compared to a plank with a hole in it.

Without asking, she charged up the stairs, and I followed along in her wake. Whereas downstairs was one sizeable room with a kitchen and living area, the second floor had a hallway with three doors, and the stairs continued up to the third floor. Two doors led to bedrooms, one door to a bathroom. A standard configuration for these cottages.

She opened the doors, glanced inside, then charged up to the third-floor bedroom.

I rolled my head back, stretching my shoulder muscles, and followed. By the time I caught up with her, she was running her fingers along the windows. The view of the ocean from up here was breathtaking, but you couldn't see it so well, as years of salt spray coated the glass panes.

"You need to replace these windows," she said with the air of a seasoned renovation expert.

"What?"

"Yes, you see how they're bowing in? And come here." She waved me closer.

I reluctantly stepped forward. She grabbed my hand, and shockwaves cycled up my arm. No one had touched me in...I couldn't remember.

Her fingers wrapped around several of mine, and she held them over a gap where the double-hung window joined, then along the perimeter.

"Feel that?" she asked, referencing the air flowing in freely from the outside. But I was still hung up on my physical reaction to another human being's skin. She was close to me, watching as she moved my hand, searching for a sign I felt the breeze as she directed my wrist around the window's perimeter. I breathed in her coconut sunblock. I envisioned coating her back with the white lotion, lifting her hair out of the way and stroking her smooth, flawless skin.

I snatched my hand back and moved to the center of the room.

"You replace these windows, and you'll see a huge improvement in your electric bill. Not to mention, look at all the corrosion."

My heartrate quickened, and I placed my hands on my hips.

"Look at all your fixtures." She pointed at the overhead light. "Rust." She stepped forward, into the small bathroom. "Yeah, come see. Everything here is rusted or corroded."

This room happened to be my favorite. The room I

stayed in as a kid when I spent summers here. Water dripped from the ceiling vents. One problem she hadn't yet identified. Troubling water stains marred the ceiling.

"I'll be happy to help you. I can make a list for you of what you need done. Laura and I have helped with the redesign on over a dozen island homes. I have references. I can get Mr. Baird to come by, too. He can tell you about the roof or any structural issues."

"Alice already had him come by and check it out."

"Did he mention if it needs a new roof?"

"No." If I recalled correctly, he only checked out the electrical after the hurricane. I ran my hand through my hair and found it hanging loose and wild. I pulled it back with the extra strap I'd worn on my wrist.

Luna paused, watching me. She swallowed, and I watched the movement in her throat and let my gaze wander farther down, to the tiny starfish perched over the dip in her clavicle, to her breasts bound today by her tummy baring halter top, and down those long, golden legs.

"I'll be happy to help you out," she said, more slowly this time, as if she knew where my thoughts had strayed. She sounded tempting. Willfully so.

I shook my head and led the way down the stairs, escaping the stuffy, too hot attic room and the mildew and rust. I heard her footsteps following me as she continued speaking.

"I can get you deals on materials through Laura and Mr. Baird. And, like I said, I think you can get a killer deal on the floorboards. I can bring over some paint samples and get an idea of what you like."

I spun around, and she held out her phone to me.

"Look at these photos of some work we've done. If you see something you like, we can go off that."

I took her phone and flipped through several shots of cottages. Clean lines, muted colors. Nice. Expensive. I handed her phone back.

"I can't afford you. I'm sorry."

"I'd be happy to help you for free."

"Free? You work for free?"

"Well, no, that's what Laura's done with her company. I help her out, and she pays me. But this is a chance for me to build up my own portfolio, so I can take on other projects of my own."

"I thought you have a job. As a scientist?"

"I do. But a lot of what I do is at night right now. And it's pretty flexible, anyway, so I have some extra time. Plus, Alice asked me to help you. And I'd do anything in the world for her. So, it's for Alice, really. Not you."

"At night? You watch the nests," I said, answering my own question, dazed.

She nodded with a smile. "I can't wait to get started. I can go home and get my notepad. Bring over some samples. Oh, and Adrian, I'll bring by a sample of that flooring," she said, acting as if it was a done deal. Like she'd waltz right in and take the lead.

"Tate."

"What?"

"I go by Tate." She stepped forward, close enough that her coconut scent overpowered the stench of my sweat. I allowed myself one deep inhale, then backed up before she regretted standing so close to me. "I think you need to focus on the turtles."

six

LUNA

The ocean waves rolled in, tranquil, low, and calm. The sun shone over the smooth waves, shimmering like stardust. I straddled my board, legs dangling in the warm Atlantic, lost in my thoughts, barely registering the families filling the beach as the sun rose higher in the sky. Without waves to catch, my mind wandered to our island newcomer.

Hooks for surfboards hung on the wall of his porch. It wasn't a stretch to think he surfed. After all, his grandmother did. There weren't many surfers out today. The surfing school that set up near Access 42 rescheduled morning lessons for later in the day, hoping for better waves. I scanned the beach, searching for him. Anyone who knew the island and wanted to surf would come here, to the east side.

Another surfer straddled his board, far off in the

distance. Too far for me to make out his facial features. He appeared out of nowhere, and I stared, snapped out of my reverie, thinking it might be him. My fingers tingled, tempted to paddle closer. Tate's attitude made it clear he had no interest in me, but that kind of made him more intriguing. The fallout from my last relationship made me a little gun-shy on relationships. But I had no problem crushing on a guy. Being on the lookout for a particular someone added a layer of excitement to the day.

A figure on the beach waved an arm back and forth while jumping up and down. I waved back and paddled in.

"No waves today, huh?" Poppy asked as I scooped to lift my board beneath my arm.

"Yeah. But we've had several good days in a row. It's the way it goes."

Poppy pointed at the unidentifiable surfer. "Is that the new guy?"

"I don't know. I can't tell."

"Do you want to go down and see?"

"No." How foolish would we look, gawking from the shore?

"But he might need your help on the house. He's a potential client."

I dropped my board onto the sand and wiped my face with the towel. I folded my towel and readied my beach bag. Once I had everything ready to go, I opened up, letting my excitement ooze out slowly in a controlled manner, like steam drifting from a teapot.

"He does need my help."

"You talked to him?" Poppy squeaked.

"Yes. I stopped by. I told him I'd be happy to help.

He doesn't seem to really want my help. Maybe he's one of those guys who doesn't like help from a woman or something? I'm not sure. But he needs my help. His cottage is a full project. And he has zero renovation expertise."

"So, wait, what's he like?"

"He worked for Greenpeace. And he's a marine biologist."

"Oh, my god! It's kismet."

"I don't know about that," I told her, even though I absolutely loved that Poppy had the same thoughts I had. Two marine biologists living on the same small island. What were the odds? "But I'm going to help him with his house if I can."

"Oh, I think you'll help him with his house, all right." She pushed on my side, and I shoved her back.

"He's cute. That's for sure. But he gave no signs of interest. Which is fine. It's not like I'm boyfriend shopping."

"Uh-huh. What thirty-five-year-old wouldn't want to go for a twenty-two-year-old surfer girl?"

"You think he's that old?" The tattoos and the longish hair had had me thinking younger.

"Yeah, I'd say so. I mean, he doesn't have a dad bod, and his hair gives him a younger vibe. But, as you know, I have experience with older men. It's the lines around the eyes. And the hairline that's a tad bit higher. Gives the age away."

"He's very serious." He could be older. Not that age was an issue, but I'd hoped he'd be more like me, maybe open to having fun. Nothing too serious. I didn't have any experience with older guys, so I didn't know how they worked. But the last thing I wanted was another Brandon situation.

"He's an older dude. He doesn't have the baby-smooth face of someone just out of college."

"You're an expert on judging age now?"

"Yes. I look at photos of men *all the time*. Admittedly, half the time I don't think the men are posting real pics of themselves, but you know, when they send something other than a dick pic, you kind of study the photo. I mean, I do. You're sitting there texting them…" She paused as I stared. "What?"

"Are you, like, doing sexting?"

"No. Well…maybe kind of. With some clients. You said you don't judge."

"I don't. I'm not." We reached my golf cart, and she helped me lift the board onto the top and strap it. "Hey, I love you no matter what. I'm only trying to better understand. As for Tate, no matter how old he is, he told me to focus on the turtles. At the time, I took it as a brush-off, but now I'm thinking maybe he just meant it as career guidance. I mean, the whole renovation side business is a big detour from my work at the conservancy. And, once school starts back up, it's going to be a lot."

"I don't like that kind of talk." Poppy wagged her index finger. "No, momma. You do you. If you want to renovate on the side, fix away. It's a killer business on this island."

"Yeah, that's what my parents say." My parents still lived in Sanibel. My mom's diner pretty much took up all her time twenty-four-seven, but as a roofer, my dad always had odd jobs on the side. With so much free time during the day, it felt completely natural to me to look for an additional income source. The conservancy job fell in the awesome category on my resume but barely paid the bills. If they didn't supply housing, I wouldn't have been able to accept the position here.

After waving goodbye to Poppy, I hopped on my golf cart and headed to Mr. Baird's inner island job site, hoping to catch him. When I pulled up, nails pounding into wood filled the air.

Tony, one of Mr. Baird's regular crew, sat on a piling, smoking a cigarette. He greeted me with his favorite smackdown. "Look-a-there, if it isn't my favorite do-gooder."

"Hey, Tony. Is Mr. Baird here?"

"He's already moved on to the custom job on East Beach. But he told me if you stopped by to say you can have the discarded wood. You got a Habitat for Humanity project or something?"

"No, just helping someone."

"Of course you are." He smiled, but it came off as more of a leer. He had a rough look and an attitude to go with it. Tony referred to me with words that by themselves weren't necessarily bad, but the way he said them made me feel like he felt the need to put me down. When I told him I was in grad school, he'd lifted his eyebrows and said, "Oh, you're a smart one."

I earned the name do-gooder when he learned I worked to save sea turtles, and he'd gone on about how I was probably one of those who fought oil projects that would lower our price of gas and raise the GDP.

Tony reminded me of my dad. He also chose a life in construction, which gave him a lot of flexibility. If he wanted to take a day and surf, he could. But the similarities ended with lifestyle choices. My dad grew up in California and had a different world view than Tony. To my dad, working to help the planet was admirable. To Tony, environmentalists threatened the economy with their nonsense.

"Right this way, little do-gooder."

"What do you mean?"

"Mr. Baird had me load up the wood for you. You can take the contractor truck to deliver it. We'll need it back by noon."

"What? How much is he going to charge for it?"

"Sounded to me like it was free. That's something you liberals love, right?"

I gritted my teeth as I followed Tony around the lot to the alley. The beat-up pickup truck was loaded down with boards, still packed in cardboard boxes. It could be enough for Tate's whole downstairs. It seemed too good to be true, so I pulled out my phone.

"Mr. Baird, this is Luna. Tony said you're giving me this wood? It's still in the packaging."

"Yeah, take it. The client already paid for it, and I don't have a good place to store it. We're booked solid with custom jobs for the next year. Besides, you're always helping me and not charging enough hours." He was right. I hated charging for a partial hour here and there.

Buzzing with the excitement of delivering an awesome gift, I pounded on Tate's door until my knuckles throbbed. The door cracked open, and Tate stood before me, damp hair tucked behind his ears, wearing only board shorts. I focused on the cerulean blue of his irises to avoid gawking at his ripped tan chest. His gaze cascaded from my face and down. I felt it, the sensation tickling across my skin like water droplets drying in the sun. At that moment, it registered that I still wore my bikini. Living on the beach, wearing a bikini became as natural as flip-flops, and I thought nothing of it. But Tate's gaze brought on a new level of self-consciousness.

I swallowed and wrapped my arms around my waist. "I have a surprise for you."

He blinked rapidly a few times.

I pointed behind me at the dilapidated pickup. "Mr. Baird gave you the wood I was telling you about. If you want it. I need to unload it, though, so they can have the truck." The island forbade automobiles, but contractors could have them and use them when needed.

I skipped back to the truck, eager to show him the boards. The color ordered would be perfect for his cottage, if he liked the gray flat sheen. The heat of his gaze on my back had me self-consciously tugging on my bikini bottoms. They had gathered up, possibly giving me a wedgie. Of course, my mom, beach baby hippy woman, used to always tell me we should never be ashamed of our bodies. She went to nudist beaches, and when I was a kid, she hardly ever put me in a bikini top. I pleaded for a top the summer after my fourth-grade year. It was a bathing suit at the beach. No big deal, I reminded myself, as my fingers tugged on the fabric.

I opened a box for him, and his gaze slowly transitioned from my ass to the box. His facial muscles didn't move, making him difficult to read. He reached out and ran a finger over one of the boards.

"He's giving them to me? Why?"

I explained.

"I can pay him. I don't need a handout."

"I know. I really think it's just a good timing kind of thing. He doesn't have ample storage and shipping them back to Southport is a hassle. And he's a good man. He's not looking to double charge for the same item."

He tugged on his chin, and those piercing blue eyes waffled between the boards and the cottage. He exhaled. "Thank you. Much appreciated."

He picked up one of the long, heavy boxes, and I rushed to get the end to help him. Within ten minutes, we'd emptied the flatbed and stacked the wood in his golf cart house without sharing a word.

"I was thinking I could bring dinner by tonight, if you like. I could share those plans I've done. Talk about colors. I could come up with a project outline for you. I can also give you the lowdown on the island contractors."

"Over dinner?" he asked as his gaze traveled over my top. The fabric was still damp from my morning swim, and the way the thin material stretched over my breast highlighted the outline of my nipple, something I hadn't realized until that exact moment. My face heated, and I curled my toes in my flip-flops.

"Do you eat meat?" I asked, as much to direct the conversation as anything else.

The summer heat ticked up, and I lifted my damp hair off my back, seeking a breeze.

The corners of his lips shifted upward ever so slightly. "How old do you think I am?"

"Ahem, I don't know. Early thirties, maybe? Why?"

"I'm thirty-five. And you said you're twenty-two?"

"Almost twenty-three."

"You're too young for me. You get that, right?"

"I wasn't asking you on a date," I blurted, my cheeks

flaming as mortification rose. But I also didn't quite understand. "Why does age matter?"

"It's not a chronological age thing. It's a life age thing. And trust me, you never want to be as old as I am." His gaze wandered briefly down my body once more, and he shook his head before responding. "You need to be hanging with the college crowd, Luna. If you want to help me with the renovation, I'd appreciate the help, and I'd be happy to let you put it in a portfolio. I get that you're building a business. But dinner implies something. And showing up at a man's door in what you're wearing, asking about dinner, that's inadvisable."

I felt an overwhelming urge to respond with a *yes, sir*, but I held it inside and swallowed it down. "We're casual on the island, Tate. If that's a problem for you, I'll keep it in mind. When would you like to get together to discuss your project?"

"Any time after you're dressed works for me. I'll be here."

"After...got it. I'll be by later." I spun around so he wouldn't see my grin as the implications of him being uncomfortable in my bikini-clad body set in. He did find me attractive. My interpretation of his gaze had been spot-on. I called out before climbing in the truck, "Hey, do you surf?"

"Yeah."

"Where?"

"East Beach." His serious look returned, and I took it to mean he was trying to figure out where I was going with my questions.

"I'll keep an eye out for you. And I'll wear a surf top." I actually always wore a surf top to protect my shoulders from the sun, but I'd taken it off once I reached my golf cart.

"Luna." He said my name the way my father did when I'd done something wrong. He said it in a way that if he knew my middle or last name, I was sure he would have tacked them onto my name too.

"See ya soon, Tate," I called, waving through the rolled-down window, the flow of air lending a temporary reprieve from the summer heat.

As I pulled away, my phone rang. One glance told me it was my sister. "Nova, what's up?"

She sighed heavily into the phone, a sure sign drama would follow.

"I didn't want you to see this somewhere on social."

Oh, jeez. "What?"

"Brandon is dating Tory."

"That sounds like it could be a reality TV show."

"Are you upset?"

"Jesus, Nova. No. Brandon and I broke up two years ago. He can date whoever he wants."

"Even your best friend?"

"Tory wasn't my best friend."

"She wasn't?"

"No, she was one of my friends. And I haven't seen her in ages either."

"They looked like they could be serious."

"Good. Good for them. Brandon wanted to get married and have kids. It was only a matter of time before someone scooped him up." I almost drowned in guilt when I broke up with him. Him being happy would be a good thing. If only my family could accept our break-up. If I didn't have a strong relationship with them, I'd suspect they loved him more than me.

"I guess it's good if he's happy. But I always wanted it to be you," she whined.

"You like him that much? You marry him. I have no interest in spending the rest of my life in South Florida pumping out kids."

"He's a good guy. You know he still comes by and visits Dad each week. I don't think he's over you."

"You just told me he's dating someone else. We're young. We get over things quickly. Remember Wally?"

"Wally who?"

"Exactly. Three months ago, you told me you'd met the guy you were going to marry."

"Well, I was a little off on that one. But you and Brandon dated for ten years."

"I'm not entirely sure you count elementary school. Anyway, where is this all coming from?"

Right then, a revving engine overpowered her response —a familiar engine sporting a tampered exhaust pipe.

"Oh, my god. Are you with him right now?"

"No. Don't be silly. When are you coming home to visit?"

"Nova. I love you. Tell Brandon I said hey and tell Mom to call me when she gets a chance."

seven

TATE

Tropical Storm Rita neared the Carolina coastline, and a dark horizon signaled heavy rain would soon arrive. The waves had amped up, and a few fearless surfers on East Beach hung tight to their boards, enjoying the accompanying adrenaline rush from the bombs mixed in with the chop. Once upon a time, I'd been like those guys. Fearless. The concept of death or injury was a vague notion of something that happened to others, to unlucky bastards or the old.

The plastic flaps to my golf cart flapped loudly in the wind as I coasted away, then down Wynd Road, on my way to pick up my friend. A lone surfer caught my eye, coming into view briefly between the houses. The guy was way too far out. On South Beach, where the waves crashed fast and hard. Not ideal surf conditions on a good day. I slowed down and watched, looking to see if I saw anyone else out there with him. I caught a glimpse of someone standing on the beach and pressed the accelerator.

The loud, billowing horn sounded, and I sped up. I parked in a spot at the same time the ferry glided into the harbor. Within minutes, my clean-cut friend meandered down the stainless steel plank in a pressed button down oxford, khaki shorts and leather loafers, chatting up one of the other passengers. He saw me, waved, and headed my way.

"Hey, man, so good to see you."

"You too. It's been a while."

He slapped me on my back and shook his head, right as large, chilly water droplets rained down on us from above. We slid into the front seat as the sky opened up. Rain splashed our legs and covered the seat as we struggled with the zippers for the side flaps. We laughed with relief once we had it all zipped up.

Once again, I pressed the accelerator, but with more caution, as the windshield wipers on my grandmother's decades-old golf cart barely functioned. It wasn't like we were in danger out here on the roads of the island, but I didn't want to ram someone in the ferry parking lot or on the way back home.

"I brought the good weather," Gabe joked.

"Only for today. Rest of the weekend should be nice. Tomorrow morning's surf should be good."

Lightning cast a shot of light across the horizon, and I searched the waves heading back, hoping the lone surfer had found his way home.

Gabe hit the side of my arm. "What's up? Ten years. It's good to see you."

I glanced at the ocean one last time, then focused

straight ahead on the road, which now had several inches of rain over the black asphalt in places, sending sprays of water out both sides of the cart.

"Keep an eye out on the waves as we pass by, okay? I saw one nut job out there by himself."

"On this side? I thought all the surfers were on the other side." Gabe had spent plenty of time here, too. I'd spend my entire summer here, but he'd always come down for a week to visit.

"Yeah, that's where the surfers who know what they're doing go."

Gabe got it and dutifully twisted so he could watch out on his right side as the angry, white-capped ocean came into view between the houses and dunes. Not exactly Coast Guard protection, but it made me feel better knowing we were keeping an eye out.

As we drove up Killegray Ridge, all the cottages went dark. "Shit. We lost electricity."

"You got beer? We can sit on the porch and watch the storm."

I thought about the dark, musky smelling cottage and the slim pickings I had for food. My plan had been to take him out to dinner, anyway. "How do you feel about going to Jules for a few beers and dinner? My treat. They should be on a generator."

"Works for me. Let's at least stop by the cottage to drop off my bag. I need to change shoes too." He kicked up a leg to show me his rain-splattered leather loafers. "This is flip-flop land," he added with a grin.

So much about Gabe made him an unlikely friend. Everything about him said preppy, conservative, financial business guy. He even had a framed photo of Ronald

Reagan in his bedroom growing up. And then there was me, tattoos, faded tees, Greenpeace activist, and, while I tried to avoid the haze of U.S. politics, I sure as shit didn't think much of any Republican. Yet we'd been friends since we were four. The kind of friendship that acknowledged differences and appreciated our shared history.

We parked as close to Jules' entrance as I could manage and ran up the wooden steps to the marina side restaurant. Rain gushed down on the vast, open deck overlooking the marina. The single glass door tinkled as I pulled it open. I nodded at the hostess and led the way past the small indoor dining area, down a long narrow hall, to the lacquered L-shaped bar in the back.

The seafood restaurant had two different menus to select from. One with seafood, a lot of it fried, and the other a sushi menu. If you ordered from both menus, your food almost never came out at the same time. The drink menu catered to the tourists, with a wide variety of sweet concoctions with Jimmy Buffett inspired names. They also offered a decent selection of drafts. In peak season, waits here often exceeded an hour. Fortunately, in September, the crowds had thinned, and we easily found two barstools.

The bartender slid our beverages of choice over to us, and before we had a chance to discuss food, Gabe lit into me.

"So, dude. I don't get it. Why no contact?"

"It wasn't a choice. Believe it or not, there are places on this planet without signal." A mirror hung on the wall behind all the shelved liquor bottles, and I attempted to avoid my reflection.

"Is that why you missed the funeral?"

A dull throb intensified, and I rubbed my forehead, attempting to ease the ache. I'd hoped Gabe wouldn't dive right into everything the moment he arrived. No such luck.

"For the thousandth time, I was on a ship in the Bering Sea when Dad died. You don't just book a flight and make it back in forty-eight hours. It's not physically possible. And I've explained this to Gregg. Over and over. I didn't think I'd need to explain it to you too."

"Gregg didn't seem to have an explanation. He's pissed."

The bubbles in my beer rose, and I rubbed a finger along the condensation so I could better see the pattern.

"So, what? You were out on these ships for ten years? Don't you have to dock at some point?"

"Sometimes. You can get gas from ships that come out to you." I closed my eyes, not wanting to think about all the years spent on the vast ocean. "Even when you dock, the places we docked, they were third world."

"Like what? Where? If you needed money, I would have sent you money. Your grandmother would have, too."

"I know. And I appreciate it. But the issue wasn't money. When we docked, it wasn't for long. And it's not like I was twiddling my thumbs. Or we were around people I could ask to plug my phone in for a charge." I thought of the tamped down red dirt floors, the filthy fabric hanging from slim dried bamboo, the men, women, and kids in tattered clothes, many barefoot. How did I communicate any of that to someone like Gabe?

"What'd you end up doing?" He tapped my shoulder with a lighthearted smirk plastered on. "CIA? Were you

53

kidnapped? Like we had a million theories. Personally, I think the CIA option is the best one." I chugged my beer, doing my best to ignore him. He put on his serious face. "But, for all Gregg's anger, he was worried about you. He'd stop by the house, talk to my dad about his options for trying to track you down."

I scratched my head, letting that sink in. My conversations home had been brief and short by necessity. But it wasn't like there'd been tears. The lawyer my brother hired to contest the will certainly told a different story. A text informed me of Dad's heart attack. A text alerted me to Nana Pearl's passing. She'd been in hospice, and no one contacted me.

Gabe tapped my arm. "Hey, you don't have to tell me anything that you'll have to kill me over. Just give me the highlights."

"I don't even know where to begin." I'd seen so much, done so much. On the other hand, so much of what I'd seen was all the same, and I hadn't done nearly enough. "I started out on the *Panglossian*. That, you know, right?"

"Yeah. And we all got it, at first, that you didn't have a way to call home. And your goal was to track boats that were violating international fishing law? Did you catch any bad guys?"

"It wasn't exactly like that." I chewed on my lip, thinking about the results from four years of my life following ships around, tracking their activities. "We stopped two of the big offenders."

"So, you saved lots of fish?" He leaned his side against the bar with a smirk.

I sighed, ignoring his slight. "These fishing ships nowadays. Did you know they have nets that can trail two miles back? Freezers that let them haul catch for months? They're depleting the oceans." Something of the old emotion I used to feel stirred at his amused expression. He'd always seen me as the crazy one, the one who cared about fish.

"It doesn't matter. You stop one boat, another three set sail. Until governments care, and someone tries to police the ocean, it's...even if they care, it's not something that can be solved easily."

"You giving up on our planet?" I side-eyed him, and he still wore that blasted smirk, but there may have been a shadow of concern.

"No. Not giving up. I don't know. Aside from the fish, which I know you don't care about—"

"Hey, I care about the environment. Just because I didn't join Greenpeace doesn't mean I'm an ass."

"Aside from the planet, it's the living conditions. The humans." I stretched my fingers out before me, struggling with how to explain. "The men on those fishing ships. Most of it's modern-day slave labor. You dock in ports that, let's just say, tourists don't visit. Kids—like, kids, Gabe—are in brothels, if you can call them that. You can walk down alleys and step inside a room and have your choice of a ten-year-old girl or boy, to do whatever the fuck you want for a dollar American. It's..." I closed my eyes, aiming to prevent those images from resurfacing.

"What'd you do after Greenpeace?"

"Helped an organization get women out to sea so they could have abortions. It's a women's organization that helps women in countries with no rights."

"Damn. I guess I can see why you didn't want to tell your grandmother about that."

I knew what he was assuming, but he'd be wrong. My grandmother was pro-choice. I'd taken the job sometime after my dad died. He would have wanted me to pursue a more lucrative career, but I didn't expect he'd have more of an issue with my helping desperate women than helping the planet. And Nana Pearl, she was supportive, period.

"But I guess a phone was still hard to come by on those missions?" he prodded.

"I worked for that group for less than a year." The group had been tiny, but it wasn't the kind of thing you could do long term. Not only was it dangerous, but it was emotionally grueling. I saw battered women, women who looked like girls, too young to even get pregnant. I swallowed, trying to shake the eyes. It was the eyes, the dark pupils set on white, that haunted me. An ever-present reminder of the other human beings with the misfortune of being born into squalor.

"And then? Ten years," Gabe prompted.

"I started working for a man based out of Mississippi."

"Let me guess. Saving whales?"

I slung back the rest of my beer and slid it forward for a refill.

"Hardly. Stealing boats behind on payments."

"No way. A repo man."

"Yep. Paid good. That's about it." Yes, I'd set out to change the world for good. And all I'd really done is ended up joining the capitalists.

"Did you ever get kidnapped? Was there a reason you went a year without calling home? Gregg considered trying to hire contract help to find you, but they weren't even sure where to start. Said the GPS tracker your dad bought you stopped working your first year."

The tracker had gotten crushed sometime early on. Didn't matter, as I hardly ever charged it. I'd forgotten about that thing. Gabe wanted answers. Sounded like there'd been more worry and concern than I realized. But, at a certain point, I'd evolved into more of a drifter. My past felt distant, another universe away.

eight

LUNA

Poppy and I ran up the wooden ramp, laughing, completely soaked from the torrential downpour by the time we tugged open the heavy door. A slim awning hung over the door, providing zero shelter from the deluge. Even the hostess had abandoned her outdoor stand and stood just inside the door, holding a clipboard. Her apologetic smile told me a lengthy wait existed for one of the indoor dining room tables.

They designed Jules with the beach crowd season in mind. It had a wide deck sitting over part of the marina, and an upstairs deck for overflow, but inside, there weren't nearly as many tables. Indoor tables weren't often needed during the busier, warm season, as everyone wanted to sit outside and enjoy the harbor view. That made getting a seat in inclement weather difficult, even in the fall shoulder season.

"Any seats at the bar?" I asked.

"Probably. You can check."

Poppy led the way back through the front seating area, past the narrow hall and kitchen, into the barroom. The bar took up about half the space, and there were a few more tables set back along the windows.

My breath caught, and I stopped short in the doorway. Poppy, ever oblivious, moved on, pulling out a barstool and sitting on it before searching for me.

"What's wrong?" She might as well have shouted across the bar.

Tate nodded an acknowledgment. I shouldn't have been surprised to find him here, but I felt shellshocked. I searched for him every day when I surfed, and we never crossed paths.

"Hey." The guy he was sitting with turned my way and flashed all of his teeth in a grin so big it stood as a direct counterpoint to Tate's furrowed brow.

"Well, hello there," Tate's friend said.

Poppy had chosen bar stools a couple down from the guys. I held my hand up and wiggled my fingers in a silly girl half-wave as I made my way to the stool Poppy had commandeered.

Poppy pushed a cocktail menu my way, and as I read through the specials, my skin tingled and warmth radiated off my rain-drenched skin. I lifted the wet strands off my back and looped them to twist into a bun, and only then did I dare to glance his way. Our eyes met, and I felt him, all of him. I breathed deeply, opening my core to the energy flowing between us, taking him in, accepting. *One with the sea.*

He blinked and twisted on his stool, showing me his

back. His friend leaned around him, smiling. "You ladies want to join us?"

"We'd love to." I picked up my menu and took the stool beside Tate.

Poppy walked around to stand in front of the guys.

"Hi. I'm Poppy. Are you guys vacationing here?"

I doubted Tate would speak up, so I did. "Tate lives here now. He's the guy I told you about." I raised an eyebrow and gave her a tight smile, hoping she'd connect the dots.

"Oh! We went by your house one night. That's right. You weren't home," Poppy said with a snap of her fingers.

Tate gave me a questioning look, squinting, no doubt wondering when I stopped by and why. He'd probably forgotten my showing him the note we left when we missed him.

Poppy ignored us and centered her focus on Tate's friend. "So, are you visiting?"

His clean cut, dark-haired friend smiled, and his posture and smooth grace reminded me of a politician. "Tate and I go way back. I'm Gabe." He shook Poppy's hand and held on to it for a beat before letting her hand go and setting his gaze on me. "And you are?"

"She's no one." Tate's voice broke through. I gasped, and he added, "Not no one. I mean, she's a young girl who lives on the island." His voice was stern, and embarrassment lit my skin at his emphasis on the word *girl*. He glared at Gabe as he spoke, as if warning him.

"I'm a coastal scientist at the Haven Island Nature Conservancy. And I'm assisting Tate with the redesign of his cottage."

Gabe looked back and forth between us and covered his mouth with his hand. Even with his mouth covered, you could tell he wore a big grin. His eyes gave him away. Then he looked to Poppy. "And what about you?"

Poppy had a good base tan and wore her everyday level of blush, but I could swear I saw tints of color expand along the sides of her face and down her neck. I jumped in. "Poppy owns an internet business."

"Oh, what kind of business?"

"Photography," I blurted.

Poppy asked Gabe, "What do you do?"

"I'm a hedge fund manager," he answered.

Poppy slid onto the stool on his other side. As they continued their conversation, I asked Tate, "How long is he in town for?"

"Just the weekend."

"Where's he from?"

"New York."

"Wow, that's quite the trip for one weekend." It wasn't that North Carolina was far from New York, at least by plane, but there weren't many direct flights from New York to Wilmington, which meant he probably had a connection in Raleigh then a drive to the beach and then a ferry. Even with a direct flight, it was still a hassle getting to the island.

Tate grunted then offered, "We hadn't seen each other in a long while."

Tate frowned at his friend's back. Gabe and Poppy sat engrossed in conversation, their heads noticeably close together for two individuals who just met in a bar. Tate held up the menu.

"What's good here?"

"Oh, I normally order the salad with quinoa." The menu didn't offer an abundance of options for a vegetarian. "But they offer several farm-raised fish options if you're interested. You can ask Julie, too. Sometimes there are some options not on the menu. And she can tell you where she sourced the fish."

My subtle reminder that I too was aware of the dangers befalling our Earth's ocean seemed to elevate me in his eyes. He sipped his beer while gazing at me.

Gabe leaned over. "We're ordering sushi rolls. You two want in?"

Tate kept his eyes on me when he answered, "Nah, we're good."

"What're you getting?" Gabe asked.

"We're getting the salads." If Brandon had ever ordered for me, or even answered for me, I would've become irate. But instead of anger, a thrill vibrated through me. Tate and I bonded, and even if it was over something as benign as ordering food, it felt good.

Poppy expanded on Tate's statement with, "Luna's a vegetarian."

"Do you not eat fish?" Gabe asked, thunderstruck.

Tate looked down at the bar, but his lips spread into a smile.

"On a blue moon I'll eat farm-raised fish. It's just not something I'm in the mood for right now."

"They have chicken," Gabe prodded.

"Vegetarians don't eat chicken," Tate said, more amused than annoyed. "We'll be fine with the salads."

"Why'd you bring me to a seafood place if you don't eat fish?" He leaned back on his stool, so he could include Poppy and us in the conversation. "He picked the place," he told Poppy while shooting Tate an accusatory glare.

"Well, in all fairness, there's a limited number of restaurant options. Jules has the best bar. The clubs each have restaurants, and then there's Delphina's, and then there's another seafood restaurant on the inner island, Provisions, but half the time we just go to the market. You can get takeout Chinese and Italian over there."

"Huh, yeah, that all sounds familiar. So, I guess as animal saving marine biologists, you both feel the need to not eat meat?"

Tate gave him an annoyed look, and Gabe pushed on his arm.

"What? The Tate I knew loved a good burger, could inhale shrimp, and ate sushi every other day of the week."

Tate grimaced. "Let's just say I'm more aware now."

"Whatever floats your boat, man. Not aiming to give you hell. I certainly don't care what you eat as long as you don't care what I eat."

"What're you guys ordering?"

He rattled off the names of a few rolls, and I read today's menu. Tate's jaw muscles flexed, and I rushed to calm him down. "Jules only offers sustainably farmed fish." Suzette, the owner, committed to sustainable practices, and her menu fluctuated based on what she could get fresh each day. Today she offered tilapia and wahoo, both responsible choices in North Carolina. I loved that she insisted on carrying lionfish and included a note for customers that ordering lionfish helped the environment, as the population needed to be controlled.

Tate grumbled, "It's okay. I learned a long time ago that

it doesn't matter. We're not going to make a dent in the problems by what we order at a restaurant."

"That's a rather skeptical view," I argued. "Suzette only orders farmed shrimp and oysters. It might be one restaurant, but if most restaurants move to this, it could have an enormous impact. When people shop in the grocery store, just looking for a sustainable tag, it can make a difference."

"Trust me." He grimaced. "If you went to Asia and saw the hauls those boats bring in. The demand for fish in the Asia market alone. Sharks. You know about them, right?"

I did. Horrible, some of the things going on. Asians loved shark soup, sometimes paying astronomical sums for one bowl. To feed the supply, a fisherman would cut off the fins, the only part needed for the soup, then dump the live shark down in the ocean. The shark couldn't swim and would fall to the bottom, only to be eaten alive by other sea animals.

Tate swallowed. "I've seen hundreds dumped to the bottom of the ocean. That's one haul." He held up his index finger for emphasis.

"But it's being regulated now, right? Finning is illegal almost everywhere. There's been a ton of press about the issue."

He looked at me like I was a naïve child. "No one regulates the ocean. Not really. Countries have been banning the practice for over twenty years, yet restaurants still carry fins. And regardless of a sustainable tag, there's a damn good chance the source is shady. Fishermen make too much money from it. It's worth breaking the law. Besides, no one is policing it."

I was ready to argue, to point out the victories we'd had, and all the current environmentalist initiatives. I knew the statistics weren't positive. A huge percentage of shark species were at risk of extinction. Yes, I heard him and understood where he was coming from, but I had to believe we were making headway. Before I could formulate my argument in a way that sounded knowledgeable and not youthfully optimistic, I overheard Gabe.

"No way. I have an account. What's your, ah, stage name?" He held up his phone, tapping away on the screen. His back was to us, but I couldn't help but wonder why in the world Poppy would tell him.

"Stage name? What's he talking about?" Tate asked.

"Nothing," I said.

Our salads arrived well before the sushi, and the meal turned into us being paired off at the bar. I peppered Tate with questions about various Greenpeace initiatives. If I kept the conversation on overarching programs, and not his specific experiences, he'd talk. He didn't hold out much hope for environmental efforts, at least without a global initiative and policing of the seas.

Tate stood to go to the restroom, but something on Gabe's phone laid out on the bar caught his attention. He leaned over Gabe's shoulder for a better view. He looked between the two of them, then back at me with disgust painted across his face. Judgment.

"What're you doing?" he asked Gabe.

"Discussing business with Poppy. That's all."

He pulled out his wallet and dropped two twenties on the bar.

"Later."

Gabe called out, "Man, our food isn't even here yet."

He pounded the few steps back to us and dropped a golf cart key onto the bar. "I'll leave you the cart."

"Man, just wait. We'll be done in twenty."

"I need to get out of here," he grunted. "Walk will do me good."

The lightning had abated, but the rain still poured down.

"What did he see that got him upset?" I asked as we all watched him disappear down the hallway.

Poppy's entire face, neck, and chest flamed magenta.

"Poppy?" I asked.

"He saw my OnlyFans account. But why would that upset him? Is he religious?" she asked Gabe.

Gabe scratched his head, flummoxed. "Nah. I mean, he wasn't. But who knows now? He's a different guy, like night and day. The old Tate, he'd know everyone's name, be laughing with everyone. He was everyone's friend. Laidback. Loose. Now, he's, like, I guess…he's aged. We are older now," he rambled to himself.

I leaned over to see his screen. It had gone into screen-saver mode. It didn't matter, anyway.

I pulled out my credit card and handed it to Poppy. "Here, use this to pay for me. I'll get it back from you later. I'm going to go give him a lift home."

Gabe's hand engulfed mine. "Nah. I got it. Don't worry about it. Tell him I'll be home later."

It didn't take me long to catch up with Tate on Wynd Road. His lone, dark figure trudging down the right side of the asphalt wasn't hard to pick out, given he was the only one walking in the downpour.

I pulled up beside him and shouted, "Get in. I'll take you home."

He waved his arm and shook his head.

"It's pouring. Get in," I repeated.

"I need the walk. Go home."

He took the steps to an access point to the beach two at a time, then disappeared down the boardwalk into the darkness, as the rain hammered down and the pampas grass whipped in the wind.

I drove back to my tiny cottage, flustered. It wasn't like Tate would melt in the rain. He wasn't in danger walking home along the beach. But his reaction to whatever was on Poppy's phone confused me. I picked up my phone to research OnlyFans, and it rang in my hand. The photo of Brandon and me lit the screen. I hesitated but answered. I promised him we'd still be friends.

"Hey, there. How goes it?"

"Good. Well, not good."

"What's wrong?" I propped a pillow up on the headboard of my bed and settled in, pulling a blanket around my legs.

"Tory's pushing for us to move in together."

"Wow. That's fast."

"Tell me about it."

"But if you're happy, why not? Isn't that what you want?"

"I thought so. But I wanted it with the right girl."

Heavy guilt weighed down on my chest. My mom had told me the feeling was similar to grieving, and maybe she'd been right. I did mourn the loss of the relationship Brandon and I had. But I suspected guilt played a much bigger part of this crushing sensation. I fell out of love. The silence across the line threatened to strangle me.

"You don't think Tory is right for you? Nova said you were happy."

"And hearing about me dating someone, that didn't bother you at all?"

"Brandon…did—"

"You really are over me, aren't you?"

"Brandon, I still love you—"

"But you're not in love with me. I know. You've told me. Maybe one day I'll fall in love with Tory. She's definitely way more into sex than you ever were."

"So, are you dating Tory?" I rubbed my forehead, confused. These weird games were part of the reason I didn't always pick up when he called.

"Yes, I am. Does it bother you?"

"No! I told you, I want you to be happy."

"Are you dating anyone?" A vision of Tate working on the loose screen came to mind, and my annoyance at Brandon evaporated.

"No."

"You hesitated."

"I'm not dating anyone. There is a guy that I kind of—"

"I don't want to hear about it."

I breathed in and exhaled loudly. Brandon and I had been around and around and around. But he still needed more time. Life would have been so much easier if I'd been happy with him. Regardless, he deserved someone who would make him happy. It occurred to me sitting in my dark room, listening to him breathe, that maybe my picking up the phone when he called wasn't a kind thing to do. Not when he still hurt.

"Maybe I should let you go."

"You already did that."

"I mean—"

"I know what you mean. I'll always love you, Luna

Rey, you know that, right? Always." His words faltered, and the guilt pressed down around my chest so hard it hurt to breathe.

"Bye, Brandon." A better person could have come up with a better way to say goodbye. God knew I'd tried over the last two years. I curled up in my bed and traced my inked skin. *One with the sea.*

nine

TATE

As I was pouring my second cup of coffee, the door to the cottage creaked open. Gabe tiptoed in, head down, in stealth mode, until he saw me and straightened. He kicked off his flip-flops by the door and stepped around me for a mug with a conceited smirk plastered on his face.

"Have a good night?" I asked. Although I really didn't need to. The answer was written all over his face.

"It was good." He exhaled relief as he sipped his steaming black coffee.

"Awesome." I tapped the counter with my fist then headed back out to the porch to drink my cup of joe and read more of the news. I had no desire to pry into his prior night's experience. Back in college, sure, I would've been all over him, goading him on to tell all. Things changed.

He followed me out and sank into the matching dirty Adirondack chair.

"Poppy is something else."

"Stop." I held up my hand as I scrolled through the Apple News, my coffee perched on the wide armrest. "Don't want to hear about it."

"Why'd you tear out of there last night?"

I dropped my phone in my lap and looked over at him. "What is she? A porn star?"

Coffee sprayed across the porch. "Shit. That's what you thought you saw? No, she's not… she doesn't do porn."

He looked ahead, shaking his head like I'd said the craziest thing. But I knew what I'd seen on his phone. A revealing photo, on some site or app, and payment options. For all I knew, she picked up clients by showing them her phone and arriving at an arrangement.

After I'd calmed down, I realized that even in the worst-case scenario, she was in a better arrangement than the kids I'd seen. She had a choice. She had options. It wasn't for me to judge her choices. It was just that I left all that behind me. I didn't expect to see it here.

"That's what you thought she was? A porn star? That's funny."

"No. It's not."

"Have you ever heard of OnlyFans?"

"No." I went so many years without internet, or really slow speeds if I had it, that I disconnected. Apps, social media, all those things fell into an abyss. I'd only found Apple News because it was a prompt when I purchased an iPhone after returning to the States.

"It's like, you can see nudie pics and stuff like that. You can also do sexting. It kind of took off during the pandemic, when bars shut down and everybody had to isolate."

71

"And she does that?"

"Yep. I'd actually seen her photos. Never clicked. She's kind of, you know, more of a plus size model. But I might be her biggest client moving forward. I should ask her how much she'd charge for me to be exclusive."

"What?"

"Yeah, I mean, I don't really like the idea of other pervs looking at her photos."

"Are you going to date her?"

"Date? Like, girlfriend? Nah. I live in New York. She's here. But I like her. She's…" He trailed off, resting his head on the back of the chair and closing his eyes, a look of near ecstasy crossing over his face.

"Man, if you are gonna sit there and replay last night, go in another room."

He opened his eyes and smiled. "Last night was fantastic. We didn't do what you're thinking. But…I'm not gonna forget her."

"Do you expect me to believe the two of you didn't do the deed?" I asked in disbelief. "You know what? I don't care."

"She said she doesn't do one-night stands. Unbelievable, right? A girl who makes a living selling nudies." He shook his head like he couldn't believe it. "And nope."

"But it was still fantastic?"

"Oh, yeah. Fanfuckingtastic. I'll be back to visit you again." He grinned.

"She's young. You know that, right?"

"She's out of college. She's not a porn star or anything. When did you become such a prude?"

"I'm not a prude. I'm just saying, we're older now."

"She's the same age as a lot of the girls I date in New York."

"Seriously?" Dating was one of those things I hadn't focused on much. I'd spent a lot of time on boats with mostly men. But surely men in their mid-thirties like us typically dated women closer to our age.

"Yeah. I mean, I don't target the younger women, but I suppose the places I go often—"

"You mean strip clubs?" I interrupted.

He barked out a laugh and nodded.

"So, does Luna do that, too? That app thing?" I'd been wondering that all night.

"It's not an app. It's a website."

I stared him down. I didn't give a shit about the logistics.

"I don't think so. Pretty positive, no. I thought about asking Poppy, but I didn't want to sound like I was into her friend."

"Considerate of you." He completely missed my dig.

"Yep. But here, we can look for her." He whipped out his phone from his back pocket. "Wait. She wouldn't use her real name. We'd need to know her screen name to find her. Or just look through a shitload of—"

"That's okay."

"I doubt she does it." He put his phone down. "Poppy stumbled into it when she lost her bartending job. She makes a lot of money, though. She's, like, celeb status. Over one hundred thousand subscribers." His eyebrow raised. "Her dream is to own a cafe or a bar. I offered to be an investor, but she turned me down. Probably a good thing. I'm not sold investing in a restaurant on this island

73

would be smart. I'd need to see the numbers. I'd imagine there's a pretty stiff drop-off in the winter."

He looked questioningly at me, as if I had market numbers to share.

"Don't look to me. I'm about to spend my first winter here. Right now is considered shoulder, and from what I've heard, weekends stay pretty full through Thanksgiving with island weddings, then it goes dead. Only locals around until the spring wedding season kicks in, maybe around March."

He tugged on his chin thoughtfully.

I stood and stretched. "You wanna catch some waves?"

We strapped two boards to the top of my cart. The storm had passed last night, which meant a rather flat sea could greet us, or it could still be wicked rough, possibly even rip currents. Didn't matter to me. I needed to meditate.

My reaction last night had been extreme. Something about a woman, or any human being, selling herself. It made my insides curl. Memories I tried to suppress hit full force. Smells, groans and grunts, the dusty grit on my sweaty, grimy skin, all of it swirled around me. The whites of the eyes.

"A dollar? You got a dollar, sir?" Their voices rained around me. Innocent expressions as they offered their mouths. Some girls dropped their hands inside their panties as temptation.

The idea of Luna ever doing anything like that didn't occur to me until much later that night, after I'd made it back to the cottage. Luna, to me, she was light. Youthful energy, full of hope and positivity. I didn't want to think of her shedding her clothes for any guy, but especially for payment.

Hell, when I'd suggested she wear more than a bikini, I'd done so because I didn't like every guy gawking at her all day. And I knew they'd gawk, because I did. If I closed my eyes, I could imagine every curve, the barely there line between her ass and her thigh, the gentle slope of her breasts, the curve of her waistline, and her flat, smooth stomach and the deep, circular bellybutton. Yeah, that made me a dirty old perv. No matter what age Gabe preferred his women, twenty-two was too young for me. I had no business looking at her the way I did, or thinking about pulling on those strings and seeing that scrap of material fall to the ground. No business at all.

Of course, if she happened to be making extra money from selling nude photos...I'd be supporting a friend if I paid for those photos. Right?

Wrong. I knew the answer. It'd been too long since I'd been near a woman. Too many years at sea. Gabe needed to get the fuck back to New York, so I'd stop thinking these inappropriate thoughts.

ten

LUNA

Sunday morning, I treated myself with avocado toast from Sand Piper, the little coffee and ice cream shop near the marina. After the storm passed, I'd headed out and watched the nests on the beach by myself. Alice must have known the weather would cancel the session with the tourists, so she found me on the beach, alone, sitting between a few cages on south beach.

"I had a premonition," she told me.

"Yeah?" I'd asked. I loved Alice. She once told me she was a Santeria, and I'd looked it up, halfway hoping to discover it was another word for witch.

"This is what I want you to do." She tapped my knee and didn't proceed until I gave her my undivided attention. "You fill a bucket with water. Any kind of water. Understand? From the spigot, from the sea, doesn't matter the source. Then take that bucket full of water and leave it hidden in his home."

"And what will this do?" I'd asked.

"Evil spirits are lurking. It'll send them on their way."

Yeah, if a foul mood equated to lurking spirits, I could see where Alice was coming from. But somehow I didn't expect an open bucket of water would transform Tate. Poppy told me that all he'd seen on her phone was one of her boudoir shoots. Now, why she was showing those shots to Gabe, a guy she'd just met, I had no idea. That was as odd to me as the bucket of water.

To each his own. It was a phrase my mom repeated all the time in her diner. She said it got her through the day when a customer would spout off about something she completely disagreed with. Or when someone came in and spent an hour getting regular refills and left a twenty-five-cent tip. I always took it as her way of accepting the things she couldn't change.

Thinking about home had me pulling out my phone. The diner would be packed, and Dad would either be there helping Mom or out surfing or fishing. So, I pressed Nova Fisher.

"Good morning," Nova chirped.

"Morning. Catching you at a good time?"

"Sure. I stepped outside to thaw. I don't know why they crank the AC so high in hospitals. This time I remembered, and even in my hoodie, my nose is like an ice cube."

"Why are you in the hospital?"

"Oh, I thought that's why you were calling. Dad fell off a roof yesterday. He had to stay overnight. He's supposed to be released this morning, but they don't want to release him until the doctor comes by and sees him."

"What? Did he break something? A concussion?" I ran through the injuries roofers sometimes incurred. Death, of course, being the worst, but he was getting released, so we bypassed that one.

"Concussion. And a broken arm. We thought he might have broken his back. He fractured his pelvis. Could have been worse."

My sister's statement qualified as an understatement.

"Why didn't Mom call me?"

"I thought she did. But everything's okay. She probably just didn't want to worry you."

"Is she there now?"

"No, she's at the diner. He's okay, Luna. I wouldn't have even mentioned it if I thought it would get you worked up. He really is okay."

"I wish I was there."

"Why? He's going to be a total grouch."

"Any chance he's considering a different line of work?"

"We haven't broached that subject. Not yet, anyway." There was a smile to her tone, and I understood. Dad wasn't exactly amenable to the idea of growing too old for roofing. Amenable or not, it was the truth. Stubborn man. "How's school going?"

"Fine. The nice thing about online classes is I go at my own pace. I have one class that's live, but the rest post each week, and we have assignments. I like it." As a graduate student, I had no issues being virtual.

"Don't tell Mom and Dad that. Next thing you know, they'll be pushing for me to go virtual, only they'll make me stay here to help them."

"Did you come home because of Dad's accident?" I

winced. She lived close enough to come home easily. I did not.

"Yeah. Mom called when she was driving to the hospital. She wasn't sure how bad it was."

"And no one thought to call me?"

"What could you have done? Worry. That's all. There's no point."

"But I still want to know," I whined.

The person behind the counter called out, "Luna."

I tucked my phone between my ear and shoulder to free both hands, and before I could pick my food order up, two large hands reached around me and slipped the food onto a tray. My phone clattered to the floor as I stepped back, surprised.

Tate bent down and blew onto the phone, cleaning remnants of sand from the surface, and handed it back to me. Then he picked up the tray and exited onto the deck.

"Luna? Luna? Are you there?" Nova's voice echoed.

I put the phone to my ear while looking into Tate's probing aqua eyes. "Yeah. Sorry, I dropped the phone. Can I call you back?"

"Everything okay?" Tate asked after I ended the call with my sister. His eyebrows angled in on each other, forming a deep crease.

"My dad had an accident, but he's going to be okay."

He nodded and picked up his coffee cup from the tray.

"You want to join me?" I asked. He'd set the tray down on one of the small tables out on the deck. It seemed he planned on picking his breakfast up and sitting somewhere else.

I couldn't tell from his sober expression if he was

79

concerned or if he might be debating how to escape eating breakfast with me.

"Sit down." I pushed the seat at the table out for him with my leg. *I won't bite.*

He pulled the chair out farther and sat down. One other couple sat at a table about ten feet away on the deck, but otherwise, we were alone.

"Where's Gabe?" I asked.

"Just dropped him off at the ferry. He's on his way back to New York."

"He seemed like a nice guy."

"He liked your friend."

"Yeah, they seemed to hit it off." I unraveled the paper wrapped around my plastic fork and knife.

"Yes." He nodded a few times. His steaming cup of grits, cheese, tomatoes, and chives looked good, better than the avocado toast I'd ordered. He dipped his fork in and stirred it around, his gaze flicking between his breakfast and me. A low pulse of energy surged between us.

"I overheard some of your conversation." He sounded guilty. I'd kind of forgotten where I was standing when talking to Nova, but it didn't matter to me if anyone overheard.

"So, you heard my dad fell off a roof?"

"Everything okay?"

"It will be. I wish I could be there to help, that's all."

"Where's there?"

"Florida. It's not easy to be far away. But, then again, I guess you of all people know that."

He paused for a moment, mid-chew, then swallowed.

"I have some ideas sketched out for you, and some

paint colors that we've used in other cottages. If you want me to bring them over later, I can."

"I'd appreciate it. The floors are done. I'm thinking I might do what you suggested, put some shiplap on one wall downstairs, then it'll be ready for painting. Unless I tackle the kitchen."

"Did you do the floors by yourself?"

"No. This guy Tony helped. Do you know him?"

"He works for Mr. Baird's construction company."

"Yeah. He had a couple of days off. I think there was a delay in some materials being delivered or something, so the job was on hold. He stopped by and asked if I needed help installing."

"Are you happy with the floors?"

"Oh, yeah. They look great. Pretty easy to install, too, snap 'em in place." He sipped his coffee while I chewed on my avocado toast. A seagull landed on the deck railing, eyeing our food. Tate raised his arm, waving it, and the seagull flew away.

"How close are you and Poppy?" he asked as he crossed his leg, resting one ankle on his knee. With his t-shirt and board shorts and hair pulled back, he bore the laidback look of a surfer. But his somber vibe aged him.

"Pretty close. She's my best friend on the island, by far." I waited, wondering where he was going with this line of questioning. If he aimed to judge, I'd defend.

"Do you guys...do you work together?" he asked.

I laughed out loud. "Oh, my god. Is that what's bugging you? You're wondering if I'm an OnlyFans girl, too?" He shrugged and lifted his eyebrows, prompting me to say more. "That really bothers you, huh? That she sells photos?"

"She does more than sell photos." I raised my eyebrows at both his tone and his words. "But no," he added, sulking. "Well, yes and no. I wish we lived in a world that no one had to sell their body for money. But if she chooses to do so, and she wants to do it, then I guess I don't have an issue with it."

"That's right," I added forcefully. "To each his own. No judgment." I studied him, thinking about him tearing off in the rain, refusing a ride home.

His teeth scraped slowly over his bottom lip. "So, you didn't answer. Do you do that, too?"

"Would it bother you if I did?" I kind of liked the idea that he might care.

Those blue eyes lifted to mine, and I thought he was going to open up, but he balled up his napkin, scooped up his trash, and tossed it in the nearby trash can on the corner of the deck.

"Tate?" I asked.

"Like you said. To each his own. Come by anytime. We haven't discussed your rates yet. Prepare a proposal. And an hourly or project rate. Okay?"

"I'll come by this morning." My pulse quickened as he stood before me, close enough that if I raised my arm, I could touch his worn t-shirt, or graze my fingers over the rough, unshaven auburn growth along his jaw. I breathed in the faint familiar scent of lemongrass. It reminded me of the Citronella Campsuds body soap my father insisted on using at home. He always said it served a double-duty by being good for the sea and keeping the insects away.

Tate gazed down, introspective, oblivious I'd been breathing him in. He swallowed, and I watched the movement in his throat. I had the craziest urge to lean forward and trace kisses from the underside of his jaw and down his neck. He turned his back on me as he called out, "Later."

eleven

TATE

After leaving Luna, I didn't return to the cottage. I couldn't handle being caged in by walls. The long stretch of beach welcomed me, the mammoth ocean calming my frayed psyche.

I stood, staring out across the horizon, seeing faces. A heavy chain around a fisherman's neck. His dark, pleading eyes. Rain splattered his bare chest up on deck. The putrid odor emanated from below deck as I descended the stairs into the lower levels. My sneaker tripped over the coil of a rope on the floor. A rat squeaked.

Grunts. Skin slapping skin. My feet followed the dull noise. To the side of the stacked barrels, the captain stood, his pants down around his knees, his bare ass clenched, hammering into the dark backside. The man bent over a barrel, his head hanging down. The fisherman tilted his head, and the whites of his eyes glowed in the shadows.

Bile rose in my throat as the sound echoed above the crashing waves, as the rancid smell of the bowels of the ship rose, replacing the fresh, salt air of the present. No matter how far I traveled, I couldn't forget.

My phone vibrated. It took a moment for the active phone to register. I pulled it out of my pocket as the ocean tide circled my ankles. *Greggory Tate. Fuck.*

"How'd you get my number?"

"Mr. Williams. You know, my lawyer?"

"What do you want, Gregg?"

"What do I…? You know, you are unbelievable." A feminine voice crossed over the line with a "Greggory" and a faint "calm down." Growing up, the scolding voice would have belonged to our mother. I hadn't met his wife, but I assumed she'd taken on the controlling Gregg role.

Silence filled the phone, long enough for me to hold it away from my face to see if I'd lost connection.

"Adrian?" my brother asked.

"Yeah, still here."

"Gabe said you're back. Here in the States."

"Yes." I was sure Mr. Williams informed him of all of this, but I felt a stab of betrayal that he'd talked to Gabe. Unjustified emotion, as I never asked Gabe to not talk to my family.

"And you're on Haven Island. Staying at Nana Pearl's place?"

I exhaled. "Are you calling to talk about the lawsuit?"

"No. I don't want to talk about the lawsuit. I'd like to talk to my brother. If you're back here for money, we'll work it out. I don't want you to be destitute. I don't want you to be a freeloader either. Nana Pearl completely ignored Dad's wishes by leaving you in the will." I gritted my teeth. Despite the asshat's opinion, Dad and I hadn't had any issues before he died. "I have a responsibility to my children. If I could've reached you, it probably wouldn't have come to this."

"I don't care about money. You fucking know that. I've told Williams. If he hasn't communicated that to you, then that's on him."

"Then we need confirmation you are of sound mind, so it can't be contested later. Can you come home?"

"You think I'm crazy?"

"I think you need to grow up. And when you do, you'll realize what you're giving up. And for what? Why? Did you save the whales? Some aquatic species no one's ever heard of?"

"You can be a real dick, you know that?"

"Me? Do you have any idea what you put Dad through? And for what?"

My thumb hovered over the red circle. I pulled it together and put the phone back to my ear. "Email me whatever you want me to agree to. I want Nana's cottage. I don't give a damn about anything else."

I hung up and threw my phone into the air, hurling it back toward the dunes, and roared out all the frustration bottled up inside. A seagull squawked overhead. The phone landed in the sand near a white plastic cage nestled near the base of a dune, protecting a turtle nest. *And for what?*

twelve

LUNA

Tate's cottage felt empty. I knocked and held my iPad and a paint chip book close to my chest. A golf cart buzzed by, speeding down Wynd Road, and I waved. Whoever drove the cart waved back.

A well-worn path from the front door, along the side of the cottage, to the back, lay just beyond the picket fence. The narrow path measured a few inches, barely wide enough for a single foot, but the white sand showed through the tangled briars and weeds. I climbed over the short fence and followed it to the screened-in porch facing the ocean.

He told me to come, so I didn't expect he'd be surprised to find me here. His golf cart was parked out front, so he had to be nearby. A surfboard hung on the porch wall.

I sat back in the Adirondack chair, setting the things I'd

brought on the side table, and waited. The wind blew, casting a cool breeze. The sound of the waves crashing carried over the dunes, and I closed my eyes, resting.

The screen door creaked, then banged against the door frame. I slowly opened my eyes, reluctant to stir from the relaxing lull. Tate's windblown hair curled around his face, and his aqua irises swept over me. Water stains darkened his board shorts along the hem, a sign he'd waded out into the ocean while on his walk.

I licked the salt off my parched lips. "Hi," I offered to his silence.

He blinked several times then ran his fingers through his hair and pulled the loose curls on one side behind his ear. "You bring stuff for me to look at?"

"Yeah." I reached around for my iPad and brought it to life. "What's the Wi-Fi password?"

"Connection's spotty out here on the porch. Come inside." We weren't far from the mainland, but we were far enough away to have spotty and often unreliable internet.

I followed him. His bronzed, broad shoulders tapered down to a trim waist. His board shorts draped over perfectly rounded buttocks. He could model for Billabong or any surfing brand. He might be mid-thirties, but between his loose curls, salt blown hair, and his athletic physique, modeling could bring him some extra dough.

"You want anything to drink?"

"No, thanks, I'm good." I stared down at my feet and took in the smooth, well laid flooring. "Wow. The floors came out great." I breathed in the air and noticed a distinct fresh smell.

"Tony helped me knock it out in one day. He's good. Efficient."

"He's helpful." The wide wood panels gave the cottage an updated feel. "You're gonna love these floors. The synthetic boards stand up to water and sand well."

He had an old leather sofa on one wall and two chairs with slipcovers tugged over them, and one coffee table. The place felt like a rental cottage. "Didn't your grandmother live here?"

"She did. But Alice had her personal stuff packed up after the damage from the last hurricane. It's somewhere in storage."

"I was gonna say that it doesn't feel like an older person's home."

"Well, Nana wasn't typical. She surfed right up until they made her leave. And this was always a vacation home for her. She and my grandfather have a home in Connecticut. Or...had." He sat down on one end of the sofa, then popped back up and charged toward the kitchen bar and sat on one of the four stools.

"Let's see what you brought."

I joined him at the bar. The bar portion stood higher than the counter on the other side, serving as the division between the kitchen and the dining and living area. I tapped my iPad to life and handed it to him when the prompt for the Wi-Fi password appeared. A stack of mail sat a few inches away. An envelope with the return address to World's Children and a logo with a modern take on children holding hands rested on the top of the stack. The mail lined up square and orderly against the edge of a notepad with the Tate Financial Services logo at the top.

He handed my iPad back to me, drawing my attention back to our meeting. I brought him through my presentation and the ideas I prepared. My knee brushed his. The hairs along his leg brushed mine. He leaned closer, our heads inches apart. The faint scent of his soap filled the air. He breathed in deeply and shifted, and he wrapped his arm behind my back, his attention rapt on the computer screen.

The tips of his fingers grazed my wrist. A surge of energy lit along my skin and ignited in my chest. I snapped my arm back as if shocked. The iPad clattered on the counter. Neither of us made a move to pick it up.

"Any interest in surfing?" he asked.

"Sure." His fingers picked at my top, a long sleeve, loose, cover-up. I had my bathing suit on underneath it, as my plan had been to stop by here and then hit the beach. Now that we were in the offseason, I had little to do on Sundays, as it was the kind of day most people were coming or going.

His fingers toyed with the loose cotton, and I glanced down to see what he was holding on to. The cotton pulled tight across my chest. He stood close, close enough I could hear his shallow breathing and pick up his outdoor, wild ocean scent. A scent of the sea, mixed with man.

"Do you always wear see-through tops when you go to visit clients?"

"It's a swim cover-up. It's not that see-through." He chewed on his lip, and his gaze fell to my breasts, covered by a bandeau top. When I surfed, I'd throw on a tight-fitting Lycra surf top to protect from chafing and sun, so it worked.

He'd told me twenty-two was too young, but it didn't

feel like he thought that was a problem anymore. To test my theory, I raised off the stool, setting my feet on the new wooden floor, closer to him. His chest rose and fell with increasing speed, as if enduring exertion, comparable to a slow jog.

I lifted my lips to him and inched closer.

"What are you doing?" I paused at his gruff tone, but the lust in his gaze gave me courage.

"This." I lifted on my toes and placed my lips against his. A soft press. His hand dropped from my arm to my ass and he pulled me closer, so my hips rested against his.

"What do you want?"

"You."

His breathing deepened. He maintained a possessive grip on my ass and held me up against him, tight enough his hard erection pressed against me.

"You're too young." Skepticism laced his words.

"Twenty-two is legal. Years past legal."

I pressed closer, so my loose top brushed against his tee. I lifted his tee and fingered the bare skin below it. He shuddered. With closed eyes, he looked to the ceiling, as if seeking guidance. His obvious desire emboldened me.

With both hands, I explored the lines on his stomach, up to his chest, pushing his t-shirt higher. My thumb glided across one nipple, and he pressed me harder against his groin. I flexed my hips against the unmistakable pressure of his erection through his thin board shorts.

He opened his eyes and traced my bottom lip with his thumb. My teeth grazed the tip of his finger, then I sucked on the tip. His hungry gaze sent my heartbeat through the roof.

He lifted the bottom of my cover-up. I raised my arms.

In one smooth move, the top flew off my body and onto the floor. He walked me backward, his gaze locked on mine. The moment my back hit the wall, his mouth fell to mine, and I opened, a thrill coursing through me.

His tongue lashed against mine, his kiss hungry and needy. This was not the kiss of a college boy. His unshaven bristles scraped my skin, and I reached up to tug on his hair, frantic for more, to feel him everywhere. His shirt hit the back of a chair.

I lifted one leg and wrapped it around him to bring him closer and harder against my core. He tugged on my bikini top, and it fell to my waist.

He paused, his breathing rapid, loud, his gaze on my breasts. "You are so fucking sweet."

The tips of my fingers skimmed along the waistband of his board shorts, to the tip of his erection, peeking out from the top, and my thumb rubbed over the soft flesh, circling the pre-cum, and he tilted his head back to the ceiling. "Fuck."

When he lowered his head, his gaze found mine, and my skin lit under his inspection. His palms slammed against the wall on either side of my head, and his biceps bulged as he pushed against the immovable object.

He groaned, a twisted sound of agony and frustration, and moved away so quickly it took seconds to register why cool air surrounded my nipples. My back was pressed against the wall for support, my top around my waist, my legs shaky beneath me.

"You are too fucking young," he shouted, his bare back to me.

"I'm twenty-two. We aren't doing anything wrong here," I argued to his back, matching his tenor, defiant.

Somehow, deep down, I knew he needed this, more than I wanted it. He'd been ripped into somehow along the way. He needed to not be so alone. Even if all I could give him was a physical connection, it would be good for him. I didn't pose a risk to him; I wouldn't break his heart. No, I could make his world better. "What are you afraid of? It's just sex."

"And you're okay with that?"

"Sex is natural." I said the words my mom had used when she'd first handed over a box of condoms.

"What do you want?" he asked, his back to me.

"I'm not looking for forever, if that's what you're worried about." I could only guess at what his issues were, his fears. Maybe he figured a young girl like me would aim for marriage. But he didn't know me, or what I'd been through. I definitely knew some girls in college with sights on marriage. But I'd say most of the girls my age, they might want a boyfriend, but they weren't thinking about marriage. Hell, for a relationship averse guy, a twenty-something girl should be a dream.

He dropped his hands to the back of a nearby kitchen chair. He gripped the wood so hard the skin on his fingers whitened. I watched him and waited. I pulled my top up over my breasts as he deliberated. I awaited the verdict.

Finally, his words slower, calmer, measured, he asked, "Shouldn't I take you out on a date? I don't want to treat you like..." His words trailed off.

I cautiously approached with silent steps, the way you would approach a wild animal, expecting it to flee or possibly attack at any moment. The pads of my fingers lightly touched his back, and he dropped his head forward. With measured strokes, I kneaded the muscles along his back and across his sinewy shoulders.

"It doesn't have to be anything. Or it can be something. We're simply doing what feels good."

"And you're okay with that? I could be gone next month."

"I have zero expectations." And I didn't. Sensation, experience, sexual release, these were the things I wanted. There were no reasons to fixate on what anything meant or where it would go. Tate was the most gorgeous guy I'd ever come across. He was older, worldly, and experienced, traits that made him even sexier.

"Luna, it's been a long time for me. Once we start, I don't know if I'll be able to stop. Are you sure about this?"

"I've wanted you since I first saw you. I like sex. I don't understand your hesitation. I like that you're older. Experienced."

His back lengthened as he stood straight. My arms dropped to my side as he twisted around. His striking aqua blues met mine with a frisson of anticipation.

"Upstairs."

thirteen

TATE

I followed her up, determined. Agitated. Needy. Angry. She flounced around, barely dressed. In front of a man who'd spent far too long in the bowels of a ship.

About mid-flight, guilt caught up to my libido. My gaze remained glued to the sway of her hips as she stepped up each narrow, high wooden stair. She seemed like the type of girl who believed in fairy tales. The type who would want the fairy tale.

She was too young, too naïve, too optimistic. No matter what she said, she probably believed something good could come out of this. I told myself all these things, but when she led me to my bedroom, with the sunlight pouring through the open windows unencumbered, I let my need win out.

"Clothes. Off," I commanded.

Without ever breaking her gaze, she unsnapped the

back of her bikini bra and let it fall to the floor, revealing youthful, perky breasts, snow-white skin, and dusty pink nipples. Acting the part of a seductress, her fingers unsnapped the buttons on her short shorts. She wiggled her hips ever so slightly. The denim fell to the floor, cascading down her shapely, lean thighs, in a heap by her ankles. Her thumbs hooked the sides of her bikini bottoms, and she ran her tongue over her bottom lip as she leaned forward, wiggled, and let her bikini join her shorts in a pool at her feet. Her tan skin contrasted with the velvety whiteness of her unblemished triangle, leading to a small, closely trimmed patch of dark blonde hair.

She stood before me, stunning, open, and asking for me to take her any way I wanted. My cock pressed against the waistband of my board shorts, painfully erect, eager. It had been years, years since I'd felt desire, much less acted on it. I considered having her drop to her knees and take me in her mouth. But the desire to explore her exquisite, smooth, unblemished skin won out.

"Lie down on the bed."

Like a good, obedient girl, she did as I commanded, never breaking her gaze from mine. She lay back on the bed, situating herself in the middle, her back against the pillows I'd tossed against the headboard. She raised one leg demurely, partially covering the triangle I had every intention of exploring thoroughly.

I tugged on the drawstring and let my shorts join the remnants of her clothing, releasing the pressure and freeing my needy cock. I crawled up the bed, ever so slowly, until I hovered over her, one arm on each side of her. I bent to press a light kiss on the outside of her thigh.

She let out a little moan. I paused, filled with indecision over what part of her mouth-watering body to taste first.

I trailed kisses along her hip bone, along her flat belly, to those firm, small, natural breasts. The curves that had been teasing me since I first met her flaunting her youthful, perfect figure in a wet string bikini. She tasted of sea salt with a hint of coconut. Her breathing quickened, and she rocked her hips, and I settled my body down over hers. The crown of my cock rested at her core, and I lifted my hips, feeling her warmth. She spread her legs wide, welcoming me. Fuck. I wanted to slide in, to take her raw, to feel her pulse around me.

The sight of my cock, lying in her wet heat, dipping the tip inside and pulling out, playing, begging for more, to dive in, was enough to make me growl in frustration. I pulled off her and crashed onto my side. "Fuck. I want to. But I don't have a condom. We can't do that today." I croaked out the words for my benefit, to remind myself I needed to get my body under control.

Her fingers trailed my chest, along my jawline, and found their way into my hair, winding through the strands. Light sensations scurried down my spine as her fingers continued weaving their spell and her lips found mine. I pressed my body against hers, skin on skin. And just like that, my cock returned to her core, pressed against her as her hips ground against me.

"It's okay. I'm clean. I have an IUD."

This young, innocent girl having an IUD gave me pause at the same moment her wet folds slid along my erection, enveloping it in warmth, tempting me, begging me.

"Fuck," I moaned. Determined, I gripped her arms and

pressed her flat on the bed, then kissed, sucked, and nipped my way down her body. I spread her thighs wide and tasted her velvety, delicate skin. So fucking sweet. She mewled as my tongue went to work, licking her to a frenzy, as her hands gripped my hair, tugging and pushing as if she couldn't decide if she wanted me deeper or if I was about to break her. I didn't let up and found the pearl and sucked, working her with my tongue and fingers until she shrieked, her body half rising off the bed.

I pressed my mouth against her thigh as her hands loosened their vise on my head, and I kissed my way back up her body, allowing myself time to fondle those perfect, tempting globes while her rapid breathing calmed.

"You know what you're doing. I knew you would." She sounded so eager I chuckled. Pre-cum dripped from the tip of my engorged shaft, and she noticed. She circled her thumb around the head, and I hissed. It felt so good that if she kept it up, I'd be coming all over her hand from her light touch alone.

She pressed me against the bed, taking her turn exploring my body, kissing my chest, grazing her teeth against my nipples, much the way I had done to her. She fingered the tattoo that trailed my rib cage, Mandarin lettering. She looked up, inquisitive. "Roughly speaking, it means be here now. Live in the moment." She kissed the smooth points of the lettering, and goose bumps rose across my arms.

She worked her way down my body until she reached my stiff erection. She lowered her head, watching me. Her tongue circled the crown, then she licked up the shaft, treating my cock like a dessert. I looked on, fascinated. When she took me fully into her mouth, the sensation, combined with her fingers massaging my testicles, had me on the verge of release. Too fast. I lifted my hips as familiar sensations rocked my body, the tensing of muscles, the tightness at the base of my spine. Her lips popped off my cock, and I snapped to attention, watching as one hand maintained a firm grip, stroking up and down, while she sucked on an index finger, sexy as hell, unlike anything I'd ever seen. Her wet lips lifted into a brief smile as she gave me a tantalizing wink, her hair tousled and wild, and took me back in her mouth as the coated finger circled. I registered where her finger was. And what she was doing. Dirty girl. She pushed inside, and I gasped. Without warning, I exploded into her mouth. She pulled back, my thick cum leaking from the corner of her mouth as I continued to pulse, spurting along my stomach and into strands of her hair.

"Fuck," I exhaled. "That was insane. Holy shit. Where did you learn to do that?"

She sat back on her legs, wiped the cum dripping down with her finger, then licked it off. My cock twinged, threatening to come back to life right the fuck now. I dropped back onto the pillow, spent. I had thought of her as this young, innocent thing. No more.

She fell down against my chest, aligning her body with mine, and I pulled her head back and kissed her. A deep, thorough kiss, so deep the flavors from our mutual exploration mingled, and my cock, for years forgotten, surged back into full form. Her fingers grazed the tip, eliciting moans.

"I still want this."

I swallowed hard. Fuck, I wanted it, too. Jesus, I wanted her. Fucking twenty-two, and I wanted to claim her in every way imaginable. Keeping her in my bed for the rest of the day was only the start.

"Why do you have an IUD?" It didn't really matter, but some part of my brain grasped for maturity, responsibility, and wanted to understand why she was making herself so available, so willing, why she was so free. Nothing added up or made sense.

She wrapped her fingers around me and stroked while answering my question. "My mom encouraged me to get one. Said they are far more reliable than any other form of birth control." I moaned once more as her grip tightened. "I haven't had a boyfriend in two years. And they tested me at my most recent annual check-up. What about you?"

My head fell back on the pillow, lost in the wonders of those fingers. Me? God. "Longer than two years. Fuck." Her thumb pressed around my crown, then she kissed and licked it. I groaned, lifting my head to watch her. "It's been a really long time. And I always used a condom."

My answer must have been all she needed. She positioned herself over my cock and slid down, ever so slowly, groaning as she claimed me, inch by inch. Fuck. She felt so good, so tight, absolute perfection. She moved up and down, rocking her hips at times. I reached forward to fondle her breasts and tease her taut nipples. She placed her thumb on her mound and pressed, closing her eyes and moaning as she used me and her own hand simultaneously to bring herself to the edge.

"Fuck, Luna."

Her lips lifted into a sexy little smile. She tilted her head to her shoulder, and those lips formed an "oh" as she stilled, quivering over me as her body milked my cock.

I flipped her on her back and drove in, taking over, unleashed, skin on skin.

I used her body all afternoon. I took her from behind, against the wall, on her side. My finger found her pearl and experimented with rubbing and pinching and pounding, learning her body and what would make her scream, elicit a moan, or send her body into quivers.

She unleashed a part of me I'd locked down and barricaded away. As the sun set, I pulled her into the shower to clean off the sweat and the stench of sex. My stomach growled, reminding me we hadn't eaten lunch.

The water from the walk-in shower sprayed cold. She squealed, and I captured her against the white tile, using my body to shield her until the water warmed. I kissed her, slowly and deeply. Sated. A relaxed calm fell over my muscles. The water warmed, and I soaped her up, washing every inch with care. We took turns. I massaged her scalp and worked conditioner through her tangles, and she returned the favor. I discovered the three tiny sea turtles gliding up the back of her neck, in full color, seemingly swimming into her hair.

"Nice art. Where'd you get it?"

"Miami. Scheduled the artist, like, months in advance. What about you? Where'd you get yours?"

"Rhode Island. College on a dare." I tapped the shark on my right bicep, then tapped the left bicep, the compass and the globe. "Bangkok. I saw it on a wall, and it spoke to me. I thought it would remind me…"

"Of what?" She kissed the curve of my bicep on the bottom of the globe through the warm shower stream.

"Direction. Of what I wanted." The temperature of the

water cooled, no doubt a sign the water heater ran low. I lifted her arm and fingered the script. "I like this. I get it."

"I'd imagine you do." She smiled and stepped out of the shower, passed me a towel, then wrapped one around her dripping wet body.

She picked her clothes up off the floor and dressed in front of me. Not once did she try to hide her body in shame. I found a clean pair of board shorts and covered myself. I stepped up behind her and helped her with the double-wide clasp on her bikini top, then moved her hair out of the way and traced kisses along her shoulder and up her neck, following the turtles etched on her skin.

She spun around and beamed up at me. "That was fun."

She practically skipped downstairs, and I followed at a lumbering pace, my mind blown.

She fixed us sandwiches from the limited options in my fridge, and when we finished eating and she announced she needed to go check the cages, she wiggled her fingers to wave goodbye.

Dazed, I watched the door close. *What the hell just happened?*

fourteen

LUNA

"Tell me about Greenpeace."

The moonlight lit the way along the beach, reflecting on the dark, swirling ocean. We were only a few days away from a full moon.

"What do you want to know? You're a marine biologist. Surely they've already canvassed the University of Florida with information."

"Obviously. I know about the organization. But you worked for them. And you went abroad. What was it like?" I squeezed his fingers, and he lifted our linked hands. He ran a thumb along a vein on the back of my hand, then flipped my hand over and traced the long lines. I thought he might tell me something about my lifeline.

"Greenpeace is a mammoth, worldwide organization. There's so much going on, so many projects, sometimes from the lower levels, it can feel a bit like there's a shotgun approach, so many issues and not enough resources to do anything effectively. So, that can be frustrating. But it's filled with people who genuinely want to make the world a better place. Many volunteer, work for free."

"Were you one of those people who stood outside on the street with clipboards?" My question earned a grin.

"I did that in college. Those are usually volunteers."

He stopped walking and pulled me to him. He took a loose strand of hair, flying sideways in the ocean breeze, and tucked it behind my ear. His fingers traced my neckline and curved around my chin, tilting my head up to his.

"You're beautiful, you know that?"

In the night sky, his eyes were dark. I stroked along the strong outline of his jaw. I never thought of myself as beautiful, but hearing him say the words warmed me on the inside. College boys didn't use words like that, or at least, none had ever with me. Brandon and I had started dating in second grade, so it hadn't been a word in our relationship vocabulary. I inched closer, wanting a kiss.

"You're too beautiful for me. Too full of hope. You'd be one of the people standing on the street all day with a smile on her face, even when someone cursed at you or shouted for you to stop vandalizing property."

"Did people shout at you?" His lips met mine in answer, my question no longer important. He drew back and dropped a kiss on my nose then tugged my hand to continue our walk.

"I didn't encounter many haters in Rhode Island."

"But in other parts of the world?"

"I wasn't looking for donations. We were tracking ships that were egregious violators."

"Was it dangerous?" His thumb caressed my knuckles

as we walked, the sensation a buoy in the dark, but there was something about the movement that made me think it comforted him more.

"It could be. But mostly it felt futile. We'd spend a year tracking one boat. Meanwhile, a hundred new boats launched doing the exact same thing. Without government interference, it's not going to end. And it's not really in the government's interest to interfere. I mean, sure, in the long term, many countries will be hit hard by a depleted ocean. Hell, the entire planet will be. But governments tend to be short-term thinkers. It's all about today's money." He stopped and pointed at one of the cages nestled against a dune and pointed. "That's one of yours, right?"

I nodded. The nest had hatched two nights ago. I'd planned to come along on Monday and pack up the materials, clean them, and store them for next summer. "The last nest is down the beach this way."

"So, all these questions about Greenpeace. Is that your goal? Do you want to work for them?"

"No. I've been researching opportunities in Central America. Potentially researching coral reefs. Maybe pursue my doctorate later on. I'd like to find a program that couples research with advocacy. You know, maybe something with a camp element that strives to get the community, or at least kids, as enthused about environmentalism and science as I am. And work on programs to save the manatee. I'm partial to manatee. Keeping the marshes clean. Initiatives along those lines."

"Sounds like a good plan. Do you think you need your PhD?"

I smiled. He sounded like my parents asking that question. "No. But maybe I'll teach. I don't know. It feels like a natural next step. It's a lot of time and money, and if I don't need it…" I kicked at a shell as I trailed off. "We'll see."

We arrived at the last remaining nest, and I pulled him down with me. In truth, we didn't have to watch the nest. But in case any of the turtles were misguided by some of the lights onshore, I liked to be here. During the season, I'd have people paying to come out and watch the nest, hoping to witness tiny baby turtles clawing through the top layer of sand and scurrying toward the ocean, guided by instinct.

He situated me between his legs, my back to his chest, and his arms wrapped around me. He looped my hair and twisted it, presumably to keep it from whipping his face. He cupped my breast and ran his thumb across my nipple as if it was the most natural thing in the world. The intimate gesture felt warm and uninhibited as I leaned back against him. Any intimidation I felt from his being older had drifted away.

"Tell me, Luna. What does a young, beautiful girl with a bright future saving the world want with an old washout like me?" He nipped at my earlobe, and tingles traveled down my spine.

"A washout? Who called you a washout?" To me, he was anything but a washout. He'd gone out into the world and made a difference.

The sound that escaped from his chest wasn't quite a groan but rather a garbled noise, as if he couldn't bring himself to mumble the words or complete the thought.

I twisted around and climbed on his lap, one leg on each side of him, my crotch settled on his groin, so I could better see him. I fingered the scruff along his jaw, loving the prickling sensation across the pads of my fingers.

"Don't call yourself a washout. For one, you're way too young."

"Feels old as fuck to me."

"But you're not. You're still young. You have so much left to live and to do. I feel like maybe you came here to recover from whatever happened."

"What makes you think something happened?" His brow creased, and his tone deepened.

"You have that look. And you don't need to tell me. If you want, you can. But it doesn't matter. What matters is that you heal. And I think this island is good for that."

"See, an optimist. Always seeing the possibility. Determined we're on a course for improvement. For things to get better." He nibbled on my neck, and goosebumps rose all along my arms.

"If we each do our part. That's all it takes," I said, angling my head to expose my neck.

He leaned back on his arms, creating space between us, and chuckled.

"What?"

He turned his head to the right and left while sucking on his lower lip. "I used to be so much like you. God. It's like looking in a mirror from ten years ago."

"Is that bad?"

"No, it's just…don't change. And you should probably stay the hell away from me to make sure I don't rub off on you."

"But I like you rubbing on me," I teased, ready to let the serious conversation go and do fun things in the sand.

"Why? What're you looking for, beautiful girl?"

"Looking for? I'm twenty-two. Why do I have to be looking for anything? Can't it just be about experiencing life? Living?" Jesus, that was what I tried to tell my parents when they were devastated about my breakup. Dating Brandon didn't equate to a lifelong commitment. Life was too short.

"I wish I'd met you when I was twenty-two." He brushed a kiss across my forehead and along my cheek, and my insides melted around him. If he'd been in my grad program, we could've been inseparable.

I tugged on the neck of his t-shirt, exposing the top portion of his chest, and I dipped to place a kiss. The fresh soap smell from our recent shower lingered, but he tasted faintly of salt.

"Did you have a girlfriend then?" The question popped into my mind as I tried to envision a younger Tate, the guy Gabe described as irreverent and carefree.

"I did."

"What happened? Did she break your heart?"

"No. When I set sail, she broke up with me. Lots of couples broke up around graduation, headed down different paths." He sounded wistful.

"Oh, I don't know. Some relationships might not last forever, but that doesn't mean they are any less important. Relationships come in all shapes and sizes, and all levels of magnitude." I no longer loved Brandon, but our relationship shaped me. If anything, it scared me, because I fell out of love, and I didn't understand why. And maybe that wouldn't have been such a big deal, but it hurt my parents, my sister, and Brandon.

He pulled me down for a deep kiss, and our tongues

tangled. I ground my hips against him, and he groaned. He broke the kiss and cradled my face.

"All shapes and sizes, huh? Is that the voice of experience?"

"Sort of?" I asked.

"Lots of boyfriends, Luna?" He pulled back, putting more room between our chests. I prepared to explain, but his next question derailed me. "Do you work with Poppy?"

I grinned, instantly understanding his question, since I avoided answering the last time he asked it. "No. I don't work for the site she works for."

"Good."

"That would bother you? If I made some extra money on the side?"

He pushed me back, and sand spilled down the top of my t-shirt and into the waistband of my shorts, but I ignored the scratchy sensation and focused on the warm weight above me. He kissed me again, and when he pulled away, I repeated my question.

He raised up on his forearms, his chest hovering above me.

"I don't like the idea of any human being using their body for income."

"But it's her right."

"Yes, and I know that. And I don't have any rights over you. I can't tell you no. But you asked. I wouldn't like it if you did it."

"I kind of like that you wouldn't like it." And I did. His possessiveness, or protectiveness, it infused a warmth around me. I lifted the bottom of his t-shirt, but his hand wrapped around mine, stopping it.

"We can go back to my cottage."

"But why not out here? Under the moonlight and the stars, with the ocean breeze blowing? It's a fantasy of mine."

"Hmmm," he hummed as he kissed my chin. "Fantasy. I like the sound of that. But sex on the beach is one fantasy I've tried, and I can tell you it's definitely better as fantasy than reality."

"No one's going to come around. Even if they did, we're so far up toward the dunes no one would see." I reached for his crotch, hoping to convince him. "My name is Luna. Making love under the moon feels natural. Like it's meant to be."

"Sand gets everywhere. We don't even have a blanket."

"Now you sound old," I complained. Then I had an idea. I positioned him on the sand on his knees. He had no idea what I was doing, but when I lowered his shorts and his erection jutted out into the night air, he quickly got the picture.

I took him in my mouth, working him with my tongue and every now and then grazing his silky crown with my teeth, listening intently for his moans and groans as his hand gripped my hair, both holding it away from my mouth and guiding me up and down

"Fuck, Luna. You have no idea how good that feels. So tight. So fucking good." His cock widened in my mouth, and his hips flexed several times with increasing urgency.

Voices carried over in the wind, and I snapped up, looking up and down the beach. A bright yellow flashlight shone, and the shadows of two bodies could be seen in the distance. Locals would use a red light, so as not to confuse any hatching turtles. I considered going to explain why their flashlight was a bad idea, but Tate's groan brought me back to the moment and the sand digging into my knees.

Tate's abandoned dick stood out like a flagpole, and I pulled his shorts back up, giggling at his frustrated expression.

"Are you kidding me?" he growled.

"Wait. I've got to go talk to them." I ran down the beach to the couple. I explained there might be a hatching, and we'd appreciate it so much if they didn't use the yellow light, which might confuse the hatchlings. The older couple was gracious and turned off the enormous flashlight they'd been carrying. The whole thing took less than two minutes, and I scurried back to Tate as quickly as I could.

"Let's go back to your place."

He pointedly looked down at his tented board shorts.

"You can do it," I teased.

"Fuck, Luna," he whined while I giggled like a school-girl the entire way back to his cottage.

He rushed me down the boardwalk, pinching my ass or my nipple as I squealed while we made our way home.

I stopped to pick up the hose to spray the sand off our feet, and he scooped me up and carried me inside.

"But the sand."

Before the screen door slammed shut, his shorts hit the floor, and then his fingers tugged on mine, delivering them the same fate. Within seconds, he had me against the wall, my legs wrapped around him, his hard, needy cock fill-ing me.

"Fuck, you feel so good."

"This what you needed?" I gasped as he stroked up and down.

"Yes. This. It's exactly where I fucking. Need. To. Be."

fifteen

TATE

In the morning, I woke as the sun seeped into the bedroom. Luna's long, tangled hair fanned out across the bed, as did her arms and legs. Somehow, the girl laid claim to the entire bed. I took up my one portion on the right side. Her head lay below the crook of my arm, one arm draped over my stomach. Her naked body flailed out wildly, unencumbered and unashamed.

My college self would have fallen madly in love with her. Not necessarily because she was the epitome of a free spirit, because there were plenty of those in college. Not even because we shared a major and the same passions and causes. The marine biology department was a niche, but not that niche. And we were all environmentalists. All of us were idealists, yet to be burned by life's reality. But no, Luna had that heart of gold that Neil Young endlessly searched for. An idealistic dreamer, yes, but an energy and a zest for life and a willingness to risk and go for what she wanted that appealed to me...or back then, when I was younger, I would have been a shark to blood.

At thirty-five, oddly enough, I still couldn't stay away from her. At twenty-two, I knew what I wanted from life. I wanted to make a difference in the world. As a teacher, she made a difference in our community, in individual lives. I thought I could be like her, only do more. I thought I could take up a cause and right wrongs.

At thirty-five, I knew nothing. I lay in bed with Luna, clueless. She didn't seem to have any expectations, not for us. I had forgotten how free it felt to be twenty-two. Your entire life in front of you. Why would she be worried about tomorrow? Or where the relationship was going? She just wanted experience. She had a steadfast optimism that everything would work out, that she'd achieve her dreams. At her age, I had been the same.

I should have been okay with that. Happy to have this gorgeous young woman sprawled out naked in my bed, for me to do as I pleased. But my older brain worked differently. Now that I'd allowed myself a taste, I didn't want to let her go. But go, she would. And my thoughts circled reality nonstop.

She'd finish her assignment here and move on to Belize or to the Galapagos. Somewhere tropical and exotic. And then after that, she'd accept a new gig. Maybe she'd end up in a doctoral program, or maybe she wouldn't. But she'd go years bouncing from one exciting opportunity to another. Doing field research in safe locations. Exactly as she should.

For my part, I had a commitment on the horizon. One I

wouldn't back away from. My opportunity to make a real, indisputable difference.

She rolled over onto her back and spread out like a starfish. Her nipples peaked, exposed to the breeze of the overhead fan. I considered taking one in my mouth, but instead positioned myself between her legs and dipped my tongue, tasting her, while watching for her to awaken. She wanted experiences. I aimed to give her many.

She moaned, and her thighs tightened around my head and her hips gyrated ever so slightly against my mouth. As she squirmed, she mewled. Undecipherable sounds of pleasure. "Tate." She whimpered my name. And my cock grew painfully hard at the thought of being in her dreams. I found her pearl and circled my tongue, then grazed my teeth over it just the way I knew she liked. Her eyelids fluttered, and her head snapped up as her body quivered.

"Good morning." I smiled from between her thighs.

"Yes. It is." She pushed her hair out of her face. "Now, I want you." Damn this girl. A dream.

After a rather fantastic wake-up routine, I stumbled downstairs and searched the refrigerator for breakfast options. The coffee pot dripped, and the faint sound of the upstairs shower mixed in with the hazy sound of waves. A strong paint odor replaced the mildew stench. Covering the drywall and ceiling water stains had done wonders for brightening the place. Day by day, I replaced rusted vents and fixtures. One of Luna's recommended contractors replaced the windows and the shingles on the roof.

I leaned against the counter and contemplated shower design options that could better accommodate us both. Five loud knocks shook the kitchen wall. I closed the refrigerator door, confused. The knocking continued, demanding and urgent.

I swung the front door open. A burly man pushed inside. I focused on the pistol hanging off his belt. I didn't know the man, but his heavy work boots, dusty jeans, and angry, forceful persona all added up. I'd been expecting someone like him.

The shower turned off overhead, a reminder we weren't alone.

"I didn't invite you in." I balled my hands into fists.

"Don't need an invitation." He twisted his head and glared down at me. Then he scanned the room, pausing on the coffee pot. "I'll take some of that. Black is fine."

"Who sent you?"

"I'll give you three guesses."

"What does he want?" I had known my last repo gig would haunt me. I just hadn't known when the ghost would show.

"There's another ship. He says it's the motherlode. Sent me to find you."

"No." I shook my head, emphatic. "I told Zane I'm done."

"This gig—it's a million-dollar contract. Zane says he'll split with you." His hand rested on the handle of his gun as steps on the wood upstairs creaked. "You gonna get me some coffee?"

I poured him the coffee, then took down a to-go mug from the back of the cabinet.

"Let me get my guest out of here. Then we'll talk."

His leer lit a visceral reaction in my gut. When he asked if I had someone special, bile rose.

"Not special."

I climbed the stairs two at a time and met Luna on the landing.

"Is someone here?" Her youthful complexion glowed, and her freshly showered hair lay flat against her back. She wore the same clothes she'd had on last night, and I felt a rush of gratitude she wouldn't be walking by the skank downstairs in a bikini.

"Yeah. Do me a favor. Don't talk to him. Just walk out without saying a word." Confusion crossed her face as I placed the to-go cup of coffee in her hand. "He's not a friend," I added in the same hushed, low tone, hoping the man couldn't hear.

Her brown eyes questioned me, but like a good, obedient girl, she did exactly as I said. As soon as the door closed behind her, I turned on the goon in my kitchen.

"I'm sorry you came all this way, but I'm not taking on another project."

"Hey, that's between you and Zane. I get paid for dropping off this." He slid off his backpack as I watched his every move, on edge, braced for the worst. He unzipped the black bag, and with a twitch of his wrist, a disposable phone clattered across the tile kitchen counter. He shrugged. "Zane doesn't like not being able to get in touch with you. If I were you, though, I'd take the gig."

Once again, his fingers circled the butt of his Magnum.

"How'd you find me?"

"So, you were hiding?" He chugged on the coffee, all the while keeping his gaze locked on me.

The answer was obvious. I wouldn't have gone to live in a cottage I'd inherited if I'd been hiding. At the same time, it couldn't have been that easy for anyone to find a guy named Tate in the United States. It wasn't like I filled out a W-9.

We stared at each other until he broke our stare-off with a grin.

"I'll admit. Tracking your ass to an island with golf carts isn't my normal. Did you know I had to walk two miles from the marina? The cart rental place doesn't open until ten."

I didn't bother telling him that in the off-season on a Monday, regardless of what the sign said, it probably wouldn't open at all.

"Finish your coffee, and I'll drive you back."

"Nah. There's a golf cart parked outside that I can take back on my own. If needed." He gave me a pointed look. "Zane's preference is that you take this gig. It should be an easy repo."

"Yeah, so easy he hired a tracker to locate me."

"The ship's veering too close to Iranian waters."

"Sounds easy. Definitely a job for an American." He smirked, entertained. The Iranian Navy didn't have a strong humanitarian history with boats that ventured into their waters, even though the nationality of a boat in that part of the world was only a matter of paperwork. With Iran, Americans on board could be valuable pawns.

I sipped my coffee, monitoring the shark, knowing he could bare teeth, even if unprovoked.

"Zane says he can't force you to take a gig you don't want. Your call."

"I no longer work for Zane. You don't need to leave a phone."

"Keep it. He'll give you a month. Said something about

he thinks you'll change your mind if that inheritance you took off for doesn't come through."

I bounced his words around and deciphered them. Fucking small-town local newspapers. I bet someone got wind of the Tate inheritance being contested and it got written up.

I weighed my options as I gripped the handle on my coffee mug. Zane must have decided I quit on him because of the inheritance. My father's death might have been responsible for the events that led up to me unraveling, but the money had nothing to do with it. All these men thought everything centered on money.

With Zane Gianelli, the repo man of the seas, money was god. I'd worked for the man for a couple of years. I'd seen him as the solution when no government could come into play. I'd thought I was teaming up with someone who would get things done. I'd been so wrong. Only one thing made him worse than the governments who bowed to the same god. The repo man could go incognito, often untraceable. As the saying went, there were no skid marks on the ocean.

If he ever discovered what I'd done to his last ship, I'd be dumped overboard somewhere in international waters. But so far, his tracker had given no sign he suspected I had a role.

"So, now that you've dropped off the phone, that's it? That's your whole job?"

"Yep." He smacked his lips and set the empty coffee cup on the counter. "That's my end of the bargain. He calls you, you pick up. He's a good man. He wants to work with you." The man had a straight face when he said it, which meant either he didn't know Zane, or he knew how to lie. Either way, I wanted him gone.

"He'll be in touch." With a sinister leer, his right hand returned to his holster. I hated guns, and this guy couldn't quit touching his. "The good news is Zane likes you. And now we know you got a girl. That'll make Zane happy."

"She's not my girl. She's someone I fucked. That's it."

"Nice young thing. You doing good. I'll tell Zane. Now, drive me back to that marina. Who the fuck moves to America and lives without automobiles?"

I opened my door and waited. With the tough act over, now he wanted to shoot the shit. I left this life behind. All the repo men had the same schtick. Tough talk. Would swear up and down they did nothing illegal. They were merely negotiators on the sea. Clever negotiators.

Tattooed, weathered hands pointed at the phone he'd delivered.

"You keep that. Zane doesn't like not being able to reach you. He would've come himself, you know, but he's tied up."

I cast a backward glance at the object before pulling the door closed. I would have locked it, but I wasn't sure where I'd stashed my key. I drove the guy back to the marina, ignoring his feedback on the houses we passed. His commentary on island life competed with the distant crash of waves and the occasional seagull cry.

The moment the ferry he boarded departed, I pulled out my phone, the new one I got when I returned home. And I called Gabe.

sixteen

LUNA

"Poppy!" I yelled into her apartment as her screen door slammed shut with a loud bang behind me.

"What?" Tired, swollen eyes looked up from her over-sized ceramic coffee mug.

"I need you to come with me. Get dressed. Hurry."

"Come where?" she asked as she held her coffee mid-air.

"To Tate's. There's a guy at his house. I have a bad feeling about this. Come on." I stepped up to her chair and grabbed her wrist, tugging on her so she'd get moving.

"What guy?" she asked as she stood slowly, like someone who was injured.

"What's wrong with you?"

"I drank too much last night."

"Where'd you go?"

"Here."

"You drank too much alone?" That didn't seem like Poppy. Something told me I needed to dig deeper, but my nerves prevented me from doing so. Poppy didn't answer my question, anyway. She merely tightened the silk kimono around her breasts and lumbered around the table toward the stairs.

"What exactly are we stopping by to see?" she asked.

"A scary-looking guy stopped by Tate's this morning. Made me leave. Told me he wasn't a friend. Something isn't right. I just want to make sure he's okay."

"And why do you need me?"

"Because if something bad is happening, you can go get help. Safety in numbers." She looked at me like I was a cracked shell. "Come on. Get dressed."

"I'll come, but I'm still waking up. And I fail to see how my presence will make things safer. Did the guy look like he was going to beat him up?"

"Maybe. I don't know. There was all kinds of bad juju."

She dropped a sundress over her head. "Juju? You mean bad vibes?"

"Yes. Come on."

She didn't speak again until she planted her butt on my golf cart seat. "Tell me about this guy. Is he like a Gabe?"

"No. Nothing like Gabe," I answered, my foot flattened on the accelerator. "Definitely not someone from the island. Scary looking guy. Lots of scars, piercings, and a mean look. It could be nothing, but I'd just feel better if we stopped by and checked."

"If you're really nervous, should we get someone else to come with us? Like the police? Or a guy?"

"I thought about the police, but that would just be weird. I mean, if we went there and I told them I had bad vibes, they probably wouldn't take me seriously. It's not like he's broken any laws." My gut tightened and roiled, and my knee bounced like I'd had a double espresso.

"Yeah, bad things don't happen here. The highlight of their day is stopping people on golf carts who don't stop for stop signs. They probably wouldn't take you seriously."

An awkward pause followed. It didn't matter if she didn't take this seriously. At least I had someone with me. *Tate said the guy was not a friend—I am not overreacting.*

"What are we doing, exactly? Peering in windows or knocking on the door?"

"I think peering in the windows to start. Then maybe saying we stopped by to see if he wanted to go surfing?"

"Neither of us are in bathing suits."

"You're right. That doesn't work."

A group of men stood in front of one of the new homes under construction, and as we grew closer, I recognized Tony.

"Do you really think we should get additional help?" I asked Poppy. I jerked my head in the direction of the men. "I can ask Tony to join us."

"This is your parade. I'm along for the ride."

Tony saw us and waved. I took it as my opportunity and stopped. He squashed a cigarette into the ground.

"Hey, Luna. Poppy."

"Tony, can I ask you a quick favor?"

"Sure. What's up?"

"A stranger stopped by Tate's this morning, and I don't trust him. I want to make sure everything's okay."

A skeevy smile spread across Tony's face as he checked

the time on his wrist. "What were you doing over there so early? You two a thing?"

"Hey, I didn't even think to ask about that," Poppy said as she rubbed her face.

"Yes. We're seeing each other. But, Tony, this guy who stopped by. He was glaring at Tate. Tate told me he wasn't a friend and to leave without speaking to him."

"What'd the guy look like?"

"Black, shiny, almost oily hair. Dark skin. Beady black eyes. Scars on his arms, fingers. He's definitely not from around here."

"Black guy?" Tony asked.

"No. Straight hair."

"Some of them straighten their hair, you know."

"His skin was more olive-toned, just dark."

"Like Chinese?"

"I don't know. Asian of some sort. What does his heritage matter, anyway?" Stopping to ask Tony had *bad idea* written all over it, but before I could tell him to never mind, he climbed into the back row and tapped the back of my seat.

"Let's go. I got about twenty minutes before I'm supposed to clock in."

When I arrived at Tate's cottage, I aimed for quiet, but the wheels grinding rocks and pebbles announced our arrival to anyone listening. I flipped the key to off and set the brake on park.

No sounds came from the cottage. No lights were visible.

I put my finger to my lips for the universal hush, and Tony smirked. Exasperated, I looked to Poppy, only to find she too looked like she was about to break out laughing.

"Stay here," I hissed. At least I had back up.

I tiptoed around to the side of the cottage and discovered I couldn't see in the windows. I couldn't hear any shouting. The calming sound of the waves and the gentle breeze combined with the clear blue sky overhead made me feel foolish. Maybe I had dramatized the whole scene in my head. Maybe Tate simply didn't want to introduce me, so told me the guy wasn't a friend.

The back screen door slammed shut, and Poppy exited the porch. "He's not home."

I dropped Tony off at the construction site and delivered Poppy to her cottage. Poppy tried to drill me with questions about Tate. On a different day, I might have filled her in and told her that yes, I'd convinced him to give us a go. I might have told her it was the best sex of my life, and I'd developed the kind of crush that creates emotional waves. Maybe I would have enjoyed dissecting with her my highs. But I couldn't squish my unease, and visions of Tate getting beaten to a pulp kept circling, so I dropped her off with a terse, "I'll tell you all about it later."

"You promise?" she'd asked, hand on her hip, empty coffee mug flailing in the air.

"I promise." I'd tell her plenty, when I could focus.

I circled the island and couldn't find any sign of Tate other than his golf cart parked by the ferry landing. The only logical explanation was that he boarded the ferry with his non-friend and left the island.

An unease settled into my gut. I would have texted him, but I didn't have his number. Half the time texts didn't go through, and service was so splotchy phones didn't feel necessary.

Back at the conservancy, I sat down at my desk and performed some of the mindless tasks. Read through updates from conservation groups, answered an email from someone seeking to arrange a private group educational visit, and updated the website with offseason information. Then I pulled out some of the readings due for one of my classes.

I read the same paragraph over and over, then gave up and called home.

"Hello." The familiarity of the gruff timber settled my unease.

"Hi, Dad. It's Luna. How's recovery going?"

"It sucks. But you know how it goes."

Yeah, I did. This wasn't his first injury. "Have you started physical therapy yet?"

"No. I need to heal a bit more before they torture me. How're things out there?"

"They're okay."

"When are you coming back home?"

"I'm not sure yet. We'll see what makes sense."

"What's going on, Lil Ariel?"

Ugh. I should've known he'd pick up that something was off.

"Nothing."

"You met someone?"

"Why would you ask that?"

"Because you're at that age."

"And what age is that?"

"The age when I met your mother."

"Dad," I droned.

"What? I'm not happy about it. If I had my choice, you'd still be five years old and excited to go to kindergarten. I miss my little girl. Doesn't mean I can't recognize it when my adult daughter has something weighing her down."

"Dad."

"What? If he doesn't see you for the amazing woman you are, then he doesn't deserve you. You just remember that."

"Dad."

"What, baby girl?"

"I love you."

"Ditto. You know, your ex keeps coming by. Brings me sports updates. Snuck me some beer. Always asks about you."

"How's he doing?" I hated to even ask at the risk of getting my dad's hopes up for a reunion.

"He's getting along. He's been home every weekend since I fell. He's a good boy."

"He always liked you. How're his parents doing?"

"You know they got divorced, right?" I had known that. A year ago. "Well, his dad moved away. Montana, I think. His mom is dating. I don't think he's crazy about seeing that. Probably why he spends so much time here."

"Yeah, that's probably it. It's good he has you."

"Doesn't bother you any?"

"No. Why would it?" If anything, given my mom was never home, it was good Dad had someone coming by. Also probably took some strain off my sister. Did it stir up more guilt? Yeah, but I would never ask my family not to see him.

"Just checking."

"Why?"

"Because sometimes when emotions are raw, we can

tend to be a little irrational. And maybe your ex hanging out with your old man would, you know, rub you the wrong way."

"There's no rubbing."

"Huh. Then you're really over him."

I'd been over Brandon for years. If I had been honest with myself, I probably would have broken up with him in high school. Brandon gave me a promise ring our senior year in high school. Asked me for forever. As if I'd ever tie myself down at such a young age. Just went to prove he never really knew me. It struck me Dad might be probing, holding out hope for a reunion, because my Dad loved him like a son. "I am over him. But I love that the two of you are friends."

"So, tell me about this new boy."

I considered what to tell my father about Tate. "He traveled around the world. Used to work for Greenpeace." Dad would like that bit.

"So, there is someone. I knew it. I know my little girl. Greenpeace, huh? Is he a scientist?"

"A marine biologist. But now he's more of an activist. Or he was. Now I think he's trying to figure out what he wants to do next."

"Nothing wrong with that. Is he working at that conservation center with you?"

"No. He's fixing up his grandmother's place. She passed away, and he inherited it."

"Huh."

"I think it's good for him. He spent, like, over ten years in Asia. He doesn't talk about it much. Remember how Tim used to not talk much about his ex, and we never knew exactly what went down, but we knew it was bad?"

"Uh-huh."

"Well, he's that way."

"Is that right. Now, how old did you say he is?"

"Oh, I don't know. Mid-thirties."

My dad coughed into the phone.

"What?"

"You realize he's closer to my age than to yours."

"Yeah, but since when does that matter? You and Mom raised me to look beyond race and age."

"Hhmm. I remember raising you to be colorblind. I don't remember saying anything about age."

"Well, you should've. And in a way, you did. You always told us to have an open mind. To go with the flow. You'd say we have the sun and the sea, and that's enough."

"Your mom always told me that one was gonna come back and bite me in the ass."

The man could groan all he wanted, but in his soul, he was a free spirit. He'd like Tate as much as I did if he met him.

"I'm not sure I like this guy." He sounded stern. Unnatural. Even though he couldn't see me, I rolled my eyes.

"Because of his age?"

"Maybe I need to come visit you."

"Dad, you can't even leave the house. Tell me what shows you're watching."

A commotion carried on in the background. I stepped out onto my back porch and sat down on the step, staring out over the dunes. Whitecaps sprinkled the dark landscape, luminous for seconds before disappearing.

"Luna, is that you?"

"Mom? What're you doing home?" It was midmorning, time to clean up from the breakfast crowd and prep for lunch.

"Came home to check on your dad. Did I overhear correctly? You're dating someone?"

"Yes."

"Why is your dad shaking his head? What did I miss?"

"He's a little older." I grinned, mainly because I had a crystal clear vision of Dad tugging on the strands at the top of his head. He'd be bald sooner than nature planned if he didn't drop that habit.

"Tell me a bit about him."

"I already told Dad."

"But now I'm on the phone."

"Fine." I huffed but still smiled. "You guys are gonna love him. Really. His values are aligned with ours. He's dedicated his life to environmental causes. And he surfs. You always told me—"

"They're mellow and thoughtful. You remembered?"

"You said it all the time when we'd go out on the beach. 'Pick a surfer, Luna. Surfers are the best.'"

She chuckled. "Oh. My. Goodness. Luna has fallen in love."

"I never said the L word."

"You sound it."

"Mom, I'm twenty-two. I promise you, this guy isn't my lobster. I know where you're going in your head, and he's not the lobster."

"Oh, I don't know. Your voice didn't get all sing-songy when you talked about Brandon."

"I'm gonna hang up now."

"I told you. You're more like me than you care to admit. Your heart was bound to fall young."

"You read too many romance novels."

"I know my girl."

"Love you, Mom." I loved the woman, but she was dead wrong about me being anything at all like her. No way, no how would I get tied down and remain in one sleepy town for the rest of my life.

seventeen

TATE

The low hum of crickets, toads, seagulls, blue herons, and an unidentifiable mixture of sea life coming in on the high tide merged, lifting into a chorus. The sun cast a golden glow over the acres of marshland.

One of the nature groups built a long wooden path through a section of the estuary, connecting the island to a raised strip of uninhabited land. As a kid, I'd ride my bike out here and look for alligators. Spotting two lumps above the murky water had been a favorite pastime.

Not many island visitors explored the marsh. Most wanted to head to the beach. A few bird watching enthusiasts were known to canoe or even paddle board through the winding creek during high tide. But those trespassers were rare enough the marsh remained one place you could go and find solitude.

I sat out on the extended dock, swinging my flip-flopped feet, watching the shifting colors of the horizon, and listening for the popping of snapping shrimp.

"There you are." She found me.

"Hey."

Luna sat down beside me and caressed the back of my neck like it was the most natural thing in the world, and I leaned into her touch.

"I couldn't find you all day. I've been worried."

"Because of this morning?"

"Yeah, because of this morning. Who was that guy?"

I scratched the scruff on my jaw and stared at the distant setting sun. "No one you need to worry about." The words stung as I said them.

"Why are you doing that?" Her hand dropped from my neck.

Her shimmering brown eyes hinted at hurt. Wind-blown hair lay tangled down her back, and her well-lotioned skin glistened, smooth, fresh. In comparison, my skin bore a weathered appearance, like the wood we sat on, worn down from too many seasons exposed to the elements.

She reached for my hand and intertwined her fingers with mine. *A better man would push her away.*

"Where have you been all day?" she asked, tackling the gap between us from a different angle.

"Spent most of the morning in the business center behind the coffee shop. I needed to use a computer and have reliable Wi-Fi and phone service."

"Did you get a lot done?"

"Some. Got some balls rolling."

"Tate, who was that guy this morning?" A mosquito sting stabbed my calf, and I slapped at it, the sound barely registering against the backdrop of the evening marsh symphony.

"I'm turning into lunch meat. Want to go back to my place? We can stop at the market and pick up something for dinner."

She twirled one long blonde strand around a finger and considered my offer.

"If I come over, will you tell me what's going on?"

"Yeah, I'll tell you." She deserved that much.

She decided to swing by her place for a shower since she'd been in the ocean earlier in the day, and I picked up a frozen vegetarian casserole from the market, some cheese and crackers, and two bottles of wine. All the fixings for a date night. Something that probably wouldn't have been a strange event for most men my age, but the last time I dated, I'd been in college. When I returned to the States, I supposed I expected to transition back to a normal life.

The struggle to return to normal reminded me of what they called land legs. People always thought of seasickness when they thought of side effects of the sailing life. All sorts of pills and pressurized wraps around pulse points existed to help with it. Land legs equaled the flip side of sea sickness. With enough time on a ship, your body evolved to need the roll of the waves. Your physical being melded to the rhythm of the sea. When you found yourself back on land, your feet thudded against the ungiving earth. It wasn't unusual to see a seaman vomiting into bushes the first few days after landing.

My days of vomiting into bushes were over, but there were other ongoing adjustments. Almost thirty-six years old, and I had no career, no passion, no sense of what I wanted to do with my life. Day by day, working on my grandmother's cottage and surfing were the only two activities keeping me going. And when winter came and I'd fixed the beach place up, what then?

The screen door snapped open then slammed against the frame. She wore a sundress with thin straps, and a small black cardigan that fell off one shoulder, leaving it bare. The top of the dress sloped down into a V between her breasts and draped around her soft, slender curves.

In two steps, I captured her lips and pressed her body against the door. A fresh floral scent wafted around us, so different from the coconut. She gasped as I explored her body, massaging her perfect breasts, tweaking her nipples into eager peaks, and working lower as I lifted the hem of her short dress. My fingers led the expedition through her slick folds, and she spread her legs further, making room as she writhed against my body and fumbled with my shorts. As I pumped my fingers in and out, she gripped my cock. I wrapped my hand around the base and lifted her dress higher and pulled her panties to the side, out of the way. I drug my swollen head through her slick folds, and my whole body tensed, completely turned on, on edge, ready to erupt.

Her hips edged forward, welcoming me inside as we both watched my tip, entering, in and out.

She tugged on my hair, and I tore my gaze away, my hand still gripped around my base.

"Not against the screen door."

"There's something I saw once that I've been wanting to try. You game?"

She whimpered, and it sounded like *yes*.

"I'm going to lift you, and when I do, wrap your legs around me."

I lifted her body, every muscle in my chest and back flexing, and I slid her down onto my ready and waiting cock. Her warmth tightened around me.

"Fuck, you feel good."

She gripped my hair and tugged as I held her and moved her up and down my shaft. Soon, all my muscles burned ever so slightly from the strain of standing and lifting and owning her body, using it exactly as I needed. I pivoted, seeking the reprieve of a wall, and my shorts fell around my ankles. I stepped out of them as her muscles squeezed and pulsed around my cock.

I slammed her back against the wall and pounded into her. The sound of skin slapping against skin filled the room until I spiraled out of control, pulsing my release deep within her. Panting, I kissed her forehead then found her lips again, still inside her, at peace.

She slid her feet to the floor, and I held her tight, tasting along her neck and below her ear.

Finally, I backed away, picked up my shorts from the floor, and found my way to the bathroom. When I came out, an undeniable red dusting remained on her cheeks.

"Is that how you greet all your dates?" She handed me a glass of wine and didn't wait for my answer. "I checked, and we've still got at least forty-five minutes before that casserole is ready. Why don't we go outside and talk?"

The tips of her fingers found mine, and she led me onto the back porch. She went to sit in the far Adirondack chair, and I tugged her back to me.

"Uh-uh. Sit in my lap." I needed to feel her skin. I wanted her close. Even if I should've been pushing her away.

It took us a minute of adjusting to find a comfortable position, but we ended up with her legs draped over one side and her relaxing against my arm, the top of her head just below my chin. The hum of the waves crashing beyond the dunes filled the air, and the warm breeze spread goose-bumps across Luna's arms. I wrapped mine around her, holding her tight, recognizing the reverberations of her beating heart. I closed my eyes, reveling in the perfection and the easy way my body responded to her, falling into her rhythm, letting tension go, breathing easier, freer and deeper, as if she herself were the oxygen I needed.

She broke the peaceful silence. "Now would be a good time to tell me."

I kissed her forehead. "It's a long story, Luna. I don't even know where to start."

"Who was the guy?"

"I don't know him. He works for the same guy I used to work for. A repo guy. You see, at sea, fisherman don't always own their boats. Fishing companies don't always own their boats."

"They fall behind on payments. I know what a repo man is. I was in second grade when the repo man came and took my dad's Trans Am."

"Really?" I asked, amused for some inappropriate reason. "Were you guys...did that happen a lot?" It occurred to me I really didn't know much about Luna. She was in graduate school, so I'd assumed her background was like mine.

"Only time the repo man came. My mom refused to pay that bill with her money. She'd been mad when Dad bought it. He said it was a splurge and didn't seem too upset when they hauled it off. But we're not changing the subject. Tell me about the repo man of the sea."

I sighed, not really wanting to admit what I had evolved to, going from man on a mission to save the planet to man getting paid by an industry without regard for life.

"Well, I worked for him. At first, I saw him as being an effective arbiter of the ocean. The governments can only monitor two hundred miles from the coastline. That leaves a lot of open waters for all kinds of…crap." My fingers combed her hair, snagging on a tangle every now and then. "Some of the fishing boats he was going in and reclaiming were some of the worst offenders. Breaking all kinds of laws or agreements. Some of the captains had some of the worst working conditions for the crew. For years, we'd follow boats, trying to put an end to some of it, and I mean years. When I was with Greenpeace, we once followed one single offender for almost two years. Then this guy comes along. There's no following. He's like his own military operation. Smooth by night. Board the boat, take over. Drive the boat back to a country where new owners can take over, often a new fishing company. Only took me a few times to see that new didn't mean better. Different fishing company, same practices. Slave labor, dangerous, inhuman living conditions, two-mile nets. Catching anything, throwing back what won't sell."

"Slaves?" she asked, her tone incredulous.

"Slaves. Maybe not on paper, but it's indentured servitude. Some men literally bound in chains when not working. They sleep in the bowels of the ship with the rats and sludge. Ocean water for bathing and a plank over a hole for a toilet, sometimes. Some captains rape the men." I balled a hand into a fist. "I can still hear the sounds. It was…bad."

Her fingers scratched along my days old growth, and I caught her hand and kissed her open palm.

"I went too long cashing in, closing my eyes. It felt like it was a battle we couldn't win, so why try, you know?"

"What happened to make you leave?"

"One day, after we delivered a ship to Somalia, I watched the crew. Gave them some money, hoping they could get out of that circle. Most of them, when they come to work on the ships, they don't know what they're signing up for. They've only heard stories of good money. But a lot of them need to borrow money to get to the gig, or maybe to send back home until they're earning money. It's a trap. Captain makes up additional charges. Some countries are getting smarter, half-assing an attempt at checking that they are staying of their own volition, that they're getting paid. But it's corrupt, and like I said, it's half-assed. Ships change paperwork to belong to a different country all the time. Fishing is an important industry to most governments. Regulation might harm the business, make it less profitable. Can't have that. Money over lives, every damn time."

I rambled on. She listened, then pushed. "Something must have gone wrong?"

"*The Rising Tide*. I delivered it to Haiti like I was supposed to. And the captain acted like the men were a possession. Directed them to another rig. The new captain, and the new company, hadn't arrived yet. The captain was one who raped the smaller of the men, almost daily. I couldn't handle it. The cycle. That night, I took the boat out of the marina, way offshore, jumped into a dinghy, and set explosions to it. Sank it out in the middle of the Atlantic."

"Good for you."

"One boat out of commission. We didn't get paid for that mission. Zane, the guy I worked for, has no idea I'm responsible. Now, he does believe I should've stayed with the ship until the new crew arrived. But he has no idea I'm the one who sank the ship. I quit. Thought I'd never hear from him again. But that guy, he came to let me know Zane wants me to come back and work for him."

"Will you?"

"No. Absolutely not. There's not enough money in the world."

"So…that's when you came home? Back to the States?"

"Well, yeah. My grandmother died. It felt like it was time." Truth of the matter, it had been time for a long time.

"That guy looked scary. Do you think he'd hurt you?"

"Nah. The repo guys, they carry guns, talk a big talk. Intimidation is definitely a negotiation tactic. But I don't think Zane would ever break the law. Especially in the States."

"Why's he so desperate for you to come back and work for him?"

"That's a good question. There aren't many who are in this line of work. He trained me. Probably thinks I owe him. For the training, and for the last boggled project. It's that whole indentured servitude mentality. He's been on the ocean too long."

"So, what are you going to do?"

"I've told him no. Not much more to do. But Zane's henchman's visit has inspired me. I'm pulling together my experiences, and I'm going to submit it to the *Times*.

There's a reporter there who has been covering the ocean. It might help him paint a clearer picture of what's going on out there. Gabe is helping me with connections. Contingency plans. You know, it's like surfing. Always be prepared for the rogue wave."

"My mom says that, too. Always be prepared." Her lips brushed my cheek, and she ran her fingers through my hair. I closed my eyes as tingling sensations filtered down my back. She gently tugged on a strand, and after I opened my eyes, asked, "Have you ever considered finding an advocacy role? There are lobbyists and environmental groups who would love to have your experience."

I nodded, familiar with the roles out there. Something like that would give me a chance to continue making a difference, but Stateside.

She lurched forward and slapped a palm against my chest. "Alice told me to fill an empty bucket of water and place it in your cottage."

"Huh?"

"Yes. Something about it gets rid of bad spirits. She knew this guy was coming. We need to fill a bucket."

She jumped off my lap and scanned the perimeter of the porch. "Do you have a plastic bucket? Like one of those you use to collect shells?"

"Ahm, maybe there are some underneath here? I think I saw some of the buckets we used as kids."

She snaps her fingers. "Perfect."

"And what exactly are you going to do with those buckets of water?" I asked as she stood by the outside spigot, filling up a yellow bucket with a white plastic handle she'd commandeered from below the porch.

"You'd probably rather not know. But I trust Alice. We

should do this. And then, after dinner, I want to show you the paint chips. We can go across to the mainland this weekend and pick up the paint. Knock out the upstairs."

Her movement felt like a whirlwind through the house. I checked on the casserole and tossed a salad. After dinner, we went for a walk along the beach. One thing about this island, no matter how crazy the day might get, or how strong the swell, when evening rolled around, life fell into a gentle lull.

eighteen

LUNA

"Alice?" I knocked once more on the door. Chances were great the door, like all the others on the island, was unlocked, but I didn't feel right walking into Alice's home. Her golf cart sat in the adjacent shed, so she wasn't far.

I wandered down the path beside her cedar planked cottage, crunching dried leaves, sand, and sticks with each step to her back yard. Her place boasted some of the best marsh views. A blue heron stood watch on long, spindly legs. At my approach, his wide white wings expanded, and he glided off into the air.

"Ms. Luna. Did you come to help me pickle?"

"I can help if you need it."

"Come here and chop some of this cauliflower."

Alice had a large plank table in her back yard with mason jars lined along it, plus more stacked in boxes on the ground. Heads of cauliflower, celery, radishes, and onions filled several boxes on the ground.

"You pickle cauliflower?"

"Tastes amazing. I pickle it and sell it to some of the restaurants on the mainland."

Several cats meandered through her back yard, and one wrapped its tail around my leg, purring loudly like an engine. I picked up a knife from the counter and cut the good stuff away from the stalk.

"Why, look at that. Shelby likes you. She's been so sad, and here she is…you'd never know she has a lost baby right now."

"She lost her baby?"

Alice's knife moved with the rhythm of a practiced chef as she spoke, and I watched in awe.

"Yes, one of her kittens went missing. Doesn't mean good things."

"I can go looking for it. What does it look like?"

"Looks just like her momma. Slate. Magic blue eyes. A few shades darker than Adrian's."

"I'll go out and look. Couldn't have strayed far, right?"

"You're a good soul, Luna. I wish Pearl had been able to spend more time with you. She would've liked to know her grandson's girl."

"Girl? No, I'm sorry. He doesn't…we're not. It's not like that." My face warmed under her gaze, and I set my focus on the razor-sharp blade. There was no good reason to get Alice's hopes up. She cared for Tate.

"Not like that, huh? I see. Well, you think he'd help you search for Shelby's baby?"

I set the chef's knife down on the carving board, not because I was tired, but because I felt inadequate and unnerved by Alice as she expertly shredded vegetables beside me. The silver strands woven through her thick black braids leant a splendor to her countenance and a veil of wisdom.

"I'll ask." My words came out in a whisper.

"Oh, good. Go, now, child. Thank you. Shelby thanks you."

When I left Alice's home, I called out along the way, hoping to locate the cat before finding my way to Tate's. No such luck struck.

I found Tate outside, blowing away some debris with his electric blower. His faded t-shirt pulled tight across his chest, and his muscles flexed from holding the machine. *Sweet Joseph, lord, he is hot.* He smiled as I approached, and the loud whir of the blower ceased. "Hi." His slow grin tossed my insides with the force of a powerful wave.

"Hey. Alice sent me. One of her kittens is lost, and she wondered if you might be willing to help me search for it. I've been calling out to it, but I'm beginning to think it's not going to come out on its own."

"A kitten? How old?"

"I'm not sure. Judging from the others, I'd guess around twelve weeks."

He grimaced. "She lives close to the marsh. That's not cat friendly territory."

"Her other cats seem to do well there. She has a lot of them."

He hung the blower up on a peg in the small garage then stepped back out and squinted into the sun. "We've got several more hours of daylight. The biggest risk is the marsh and woods. Let's go back toward Alice's and search from there. Chances are the kitten is hiding nearby, scared."

"I thought I read that when a cat gets scared the flight response kicks in."

"Definitely can. But there's a good chance he's still close by. Did you walk here?"

"Yeah."

"I'll drive us back over. Then we'll comb the woods. What's the cat look like?"

"Dark gray, blue eyes. Do you know Alice's cats?"

"Can't say that I do."

"Well, he looks like his mom, Shelby. According to Alice."

I called out, "Here, kitty, kitty," as we cut across the middle of the island. After calling a few times, I stopped, and we rode along in silence. We both kept our sight trained on the passing woods. The deeper into the island we drove, the louder the world under the tree canopy grew.

Tate broke the silence. "Is Alice out looking for it?"

I laughed. "No. She's busy pickling. All these random veggies. To be honest, I'd think she's trying to play matchmaker, except that her kitten really is missing."

"You think she'd play matchmaker with us? Even with our age difference?"

I slid closer to him and touched his thigh. That got his attention.

"When are you going to get over the age difference? It's not that big of a deal. Jacques Cousteau was thirty-six years older than his second wife."

"No shit?"

"Yep. And they had two kids."

"Thirty-six-year difference? Wow."

"When you studied him, you don't remember that?"

"You know, I didn't really pay attention to his personal life. That's not my thing."

"No? You're not the kind of guy to pick up the magazine to find out if maybe this time Jen and Brad really are getting back together?"

He smirked. "No."

"Not once?"

"Nope. Although, I will say, I was surprised to see that line on the covers of rags, leave for ten years, then return home and see it still pops up. Some things don't change. Or, well, the Kardashians. I'd say that's a new one. For me."

The wheels scrunched over dried leaves as he turned and parked off the road near Alice's home. He surveyed the area.

"Let's start with the back of her yard, where it backs up to the marsh."

"What do you think Cousteau's biggest contribution was?"

He pointed at the ground where I walked. "Be careful. Look out for sandy mounds. Those fire ants are vicious."

I stepped gingerly around the leaf strewn area. We both wore flip flops. He might fear ants, but snakes were my bugaboo. Once he was satisfied I'd skirted the ant mound, he answered my question. "The moratorium on whaling. If he hadn't gotten involved, I'd bet whales might be extinct."

"Do you think?"

"Yeah, I do. You know he has a son who has been instrumental in fighting long lines."

"I did know that. I follow him on Twitter. Technology is a double-edged sword when it comes to the ocean. Better freezers, nets that go on for miles, efficient engines that can allow ships to go farther with heavier loads, on the outset, they all sound like good things, until you consider the long-term environmental impact. And the fact that so much of the ocean has no governing body, no one to oversee it."

"Exactly. Trying to get people to care, it's hard."

We stepped up to the tall grass on the water's edge. He held an arm out, blocking me from moving forward. He signaled silence with a single finger over his lips then pointed.

At first, I didn't see anything. The dark, murky water shone black through the reeds. Then I saw it. Unrestrained, I bounced on my heels. Tate's arm snapped across my chest, protective.

"An alligator." I pointed to prove I saw it. "Right there." Skimming the surface of the water, a dark orb protruded. Only its eyes could be seen, the rest of the gator completely hidden. He'd have to come up to breathe, but they could stay underwater for as long as twenty-four hours.

He reached for my hand. Turned it left ninety degrees and lowered my pointed index finger. Another set of eyes. Then he pointed farther along the shore. A small gator rested in the sun on the shoreline.

"We've got to find that cat," I said. He nodded.

We both carefully inspected the shoreline, searching along every fallen tree, separating clumps of grass, searching for a hiding kitten.

The sun traveled to the west, and the shade in the

woods deepened. At one point, Alice brought us out freshly squeezed lemonade. We returned the empty glasses to her house then headed back off into the woods. Alice decided to come out and join in the search as the sun waned. The three of us separated, combing through the woods, searching for a mound of fur.

Sun reflected off a stick, partially covered by coppery pine remnants. Tate crouched up ahead, peering into a hollowed-out tree.

"Did you find him?"

I stepped forward, and the stick moved. I leaped back, screaming like a banshee. In a flash, Tate was at my side.

"Snake!" I shrieked.

He searched the ground while holding me back with his arm, protective.

"Sweet Joseph, that scared the bejeezus out of me."

"Where?" he asked.

"Over there. Somewhere."

"Probably a copperhead." He pulled me into his side and rubbed my shoulder, calming me down. "It's getting dark. Harder to see the ground in the woods."

He didn't say it, but I recognized the somber tone.

"There you are, you little wild one." Alice stood, hands on her hips, about fifteen feet away, completely unperturbed by my snake sighting.

"You found him?" I called.

"Here the little troublemaker is." She scooped down and picked up a fuzz ball.

I stayed close to Tate. Leaves crunched below Alice's feet as she approached us, holding out a scrawny gray kitten by the hair on his neck.

"Such the brave boy. Do you want yourself a cat?"

"Me? Oh, no. I can't even keep plants alive."

"Tate, what about you? You need a kitten, don't you?"

He shook his head with a grin as he placed pressure on my lower back, forcing me forward, in the opposite direction of the snake, so I obliged.

"Wouldn't Shelby be sad if you gave away one of her kittens?"

"I suppose so, but I'm currently at about fourteen cats. I could stand to find a few new homes for them."

"Fourteen?"

"That's why I keep most of them outside."

Tate muttered under his breath, "Won't be fourteen for long."

After saying goodnight to Alice, Tate drove us to the market, and we picked out dinner, and he drove me back to my place to get some fresh clothes for the night.

He leaned back against the doorframe and watched as I threw together a few things to change into. "Why don't you pack more? Keep some stuff at my place? You've been staying over all the time, anyway."

"You mean you want to give me a drawer?"

"Don't go mental. Just pack a few extra things." The grin plastered across his face made him look young. Happiness looked good on him. He pulled a phone out of his pocket and read the text. He stopped. His jaw flexed. All signs of carefree Tate vanished.

nineteen

TATE

"What're you doing here?"

"Is that any way to greet your brother? Who you haven't seen in years?" Gregg held both arms out to his side, palms splayed open. A defensive stance I knew well.

"Something wrong with the phone? You have the right to stop by and stay without a heads up?"

"I'm not staying here, you ass. I booked a room at the Inn. Heard through the grapevine you're doing a massive renovation." He held both hands on his hips and looked down on me, the way he always did, as if I was the wayward piece of shit he had to constantly look after.

Mother fucker.

"What? You think Gabe wouldn't make new friends? Is that what you expected? He'd be the same loyal friend following your lead after you diss him for ten years?"

Anger poured out of every single crevice. If I was a

ship, I'd be submerged in anger, on the verge of capsizing and cascading down to the sandy bottom below. The brushes I'd been cleaning lay dripping off the front porch, and I snapped one up and held it at him like it was a weapon to be feared. The anger had simmered since receiving his text yesterday, and in his presence, it surged, threatening to breach flimsy barriers.

He cracked a smile. "You going to beat me with a brush? You want a brush fight? Do I get one, too?" He leaned against the short picket fence and cocked his head with that familiar half-smile. "Remember when we used to fight with sticks? I beat your ass every time."

My right hand clenched the brush handle. And as quickly as the blades of grass over the dunes stilled in the absence of breeze, all that anger subsided.

"You always got the better stick."

"Bullshit."

"No. You had a knack for picking out the thicker stick."

"Well, you know." He wiggled his eyebrows, and even though he had trimmed hair and looked the part of an uptight businessman, I saw a bit of the brother who'd been my friend and the best fort builder I'd ever known.

I set the brush back down on the plank and wiped my brow and gestured inside the cottage with my head.

"Want a beer?"

"Sure."

A large eggplant and squash rested on the counter. I handed him a beer as I considered serving size. "We were going to grill eggplant and squash for dinner tonight and mix it in with a salad. You want—"

"As tempting as that sounds, I was hoping I could convince you to go to Delphina's tonight. I was pretty stoked to see it's still open. Their chips and salsa are calling my name."

"Sure. Works for me. What we have for dinner will keep."

"We?"

I smiled. Busted. But, yeah, for now, a "we." At least until she moved on. I closed the refrigerator door and pointed the green glass neck of my bottle toward the back deck. "Want to sit?"

Within five strides, he set foot on the deck. Those long legs of his had always made him faster. We were brothers, but he'd always been taller, smarter, more obedient, always looking to please our parents. Greggory, the first-born good kid and Adrian, the family misfit.

I slid back into the chair, facing forward, watching the dunes.

"So, who is the *we*?"

"A girl I met on the island. She's a scientist at the conservancy center."

"Ah, should have known you'd find another bleeding heart."

I tipped my beer back, swallowing the *fuck you* on the tip of my tongue.

As if on cue, the screen door cracked open.

"Tate, oh, hi." She stepped out on the porch. "I didn't know you had a guest."

My brother, ever the gentleman, leaped to his feet and held out his hand. "Greggory. Adrian's brother."

"Adrian?" she asked, her lips spreading into a wide smile.

Gregg didn't skip a beat. He smiled down at me, amused. "You still introduce yourself as Tate?"

"Yes, I do." I reached for Luna's hand and pulled her down onto my lap. Since we only had two chairs on the porch, it felt like the right thing to do. "This is Luna."

Gregg sat back down in his chair. His ring finger clinked with his beer bottle when he picked it back up.

"So, your wife is Laura, right? How long have you been married?"

He grimaced. "Yes, Laura. Seven years now. You're an uncle." He tilted his beer back, and I knew there were accusations he wanted to shout my way. I deserved every one of them, too. *What kind of brother misses his brother's wedding?*

I held Luna's thigh tight, pulling her against me like a shield. "We're thinking we might go to Delphina's tonight for dinner. You up for that?"

She wove her fingers through my hair, sending rivulets down my back. Her freshly showered hair smelled of strawberries instead of the coconut scent I'd grown to love. She watched my brother as I slipped a few fingers beneath her shirt to touch her soft skin.

"You know, I think I'm going to let you two catch up. Poppy wants to go to Jules tonight, and I've been ignoring her. Maybe you two can stop by Jules after dinner?"

"Luna, don't feel like you can't come out with us. I don't mean to derail your plans for the night." Greggory addressed her in a cordial, professional manner.

"Please, it's the beach. No plans can't be changed."

"Where are you from?" he asked her.

"Prepare yourself. This is the start of the inquisition," I warned.

"Ignore him," Gregg said. "Apparently, he's been away

from civilization for so long he's forgotten this is how the rest of the world functions."

I didn't appreciate the dig. Luna pressed her lips to my cheek, and the tension eased.

With a casual smile, she answered Gregg. "I'm from Florida. How old are your children? Do you have pictures?"

Gregg set his beer on the table and half rose to pull a phone out of his back pocket. "See, Adrian? This is how it's done." He swiped on his phone then handed it over to Luna. A photo of a toddler holding a baby shone.

"Aw. How cute," Luna gushed. I found it hard to swallow.

"The oldest one is Lucy. She's three. The baby is Lena. She's maybe two months in that photo, but she's six months now. They grow so fast. It's a whirlwind. Life-changing."

"All with an L, huh?" Luna asked as she flipped through photos on his phone with a warm smile plastered on.

"It's a tradition in Laura's family. All the women's names begin with L."

"No son? You going to keep trying for one?" she asked as she flipped through photos.

I wouldn't put it past Gregg to be that guy, desperate for a boy to carry on the name or some bullshit like that.

"No. I love having daughters. Didn't matter to me at first, but after we had Lucy, and we were spending time on playgrounds and with other families with kids, it didn't take me long to see little girls have some advantages. I felt relief when we found out our second would be a girl. The more time I spend around kids, the more appreciation I have for our mom raising two boys."

"That's what my dad used to say, too. He loves that he has two daughters. I don't think he would've minded having more kids, but Mom said no way."

"Yeah, two is enough. I see those families now with three or four kids and…no, two works. Are you the youngest or the oldest?"

"Oldest."

"Me too." Gregg sent an accusatory glare my way. My tight throat and the heat from Luna in my lap had me pushing on the ground, rocking the chair back and forth.

"My sister's my best friend. She's still in Sanibel with my parents. Or, well, she's in school at the University of Florida, but she spends a lot of time at home."

"Yeah, that's what they say about daughters. They're more likely to stay close."

A heavy weight sank onto my chest, and I lifted Luna off my lap.

"You ready for those chips?" I asked Gregg.

He checked the time with a quick flex of his wrist and shrugged. "Sure. I eat early these days."

I held the screen door open for my brother to pass through, and Luna stood by my side. My right hand drifted lower and cupped the curve of her bottom, giving it a gentle, clandestine squeeze.

"I'll see you later?" I asked her.

Gregg glanced back but moved forward into the house, giving us some privacy.

"Come by Jules if you want. Or text me later, and I'll come over. If you decide you want to catch up with your brother, that's cool. I can see you tomorrow."

I nodded. She stepped forward, and I pulled her back, leaning down to whisper in her ear. "I want to see you later tonight." I said the word *want*, but *need* was more accurate. I couldn't explain it, but my brother's surprise visit had me off-kilter, like one side of the ship was weighted too heavily, and I needed Luna to anchor for the night.

No sooner had she pulled away in her golf cart than Gregg turned to me and asked, "So, how old is she?"

I chuckled. "I'm surprised you didn't ask her yourself."

"Man, I don't give a damn how old she is. Stop acting like everything I say is a judgement."

"Well, isn't it?"

"No."

"Bullshit."

Gregg let out an exasperated sigh. "Look. She's clearly legal, she's in college—"

"Grad school." I glared at the sand lining his dress shoes.

"Fine. Whatever. Great. As long as she's eighteen and you're not at risk of being charged with statutory rape, I'm good with it. Really. She seems nice. I have nothing against her." He flipped open the trash compactor and dropped his bottle into it with a clang, then turned around. "I have nothing against you. I came down because I think you're in trouble. I'm worried about you. I don't know what you've gotten yourself into, but I'm your family. And I'm going to be there for you. I don't know if you've been running drugs, or if you've got some cartel after you, or what. But if you need guns for protection, I'll drive 'em down here. If you need lawyers, I'll hire them. If you need security, we'll get that for you. Gabe knows people. We'll do whatever is needed. You're my brother. No matter how pissed off I am at you, that doesn't change. You can always come to me. Got it?"

My eyes fucking burned, and I rubbed them, then inhaled deeply and forced a grin. "Guns? You'll bring me guns?"

"Whatever you need. I'm here."

"You've got quite an imagination."

"That's what happens when you go missing for ten years. It's a lot of time to dream up shit."

"I never ran drugs or met up with a cartel." I chewed on my lip, amused at his ideas.

"What'd you do?"

"I blew up a ship."

His entire hand covered his mouth, but based on the wrinkled corners of his eyes, my guess was his palm covered a fat ass smile. When he finally dropped his hand, his lips rested in a flat line, and he dipped his head as he moved to the cart.

"All right, then. Gabe said something was up. Let's talk about what we need to do over chips and salsa."

We took off towards Delphina's, both of us driving a cart since the Inn was down by the marina. We started off at a normal clip, but of course, by the time we approached the marina, we were full-on racing, our pedals flattened against the black of the cart, swerving around each other and attempting to run the other one off the road. It felt good. Like old times.

We found a seat against the back wall inside. Most everyone else was seated outside on the deck, but the temperature was dropping and the wind picking up, and I had a feeling we were going to be sitting down talking for a long time.

Gregg had me telling him my story before we'd been served our beers. Had me filling him in on where I'd been, what I'd done, and how I ended up blowing up a boat I was supposed to deliver. I didn't share as much with him as I did with Luna. Just told him I'd had it. I couldn't be a part of fostering those living conditions or…slavery. I couldn't do it.

"So, are you here hiding? Is that why you came back?"

"I'm not hiding." He gave me a look that told me he didn't believe me. Whatever. He'd always think the worst. "No one knows what I did. But that's what Gabe was getting at, I guess. I came back because Nana Pearl died."

"You missed Dad's funeral. But you came back for hers?" The accusation colored his expression and pissed me off.

"You know, I don't know if it's ever occurred to you, but it's not that easy to get back to Connecticut when you're near Antarctica. And it's not like I was on a cruise ship that had a plan for getting a passenger off it if needed. Your text that he died came through three days before the funeral. Two days, when you consider the time change. I was on the other side of the world. You get that, right?"

He balled up a napkin and gritted his teeth.

"I know it pissed you off. But there. Was. Nothing. I. Could. Do." I'd called him as soon as possible. I'd tried to explain. He wouldn't listen. Didn't matter if he listened or not. He never heard me.

"But when there's money to be passed around, you find a way back."

"Your logic is bullshit. You know that? I'm the one in

this family who has never been hung on possessions and bank accounts."

"Yeah, you want handouts. No way would you do something boring like get a job and work."

"How do you figure I haven't been working?"

"You had Nana Pearl sending you money, right?"

"No. Why would you think that?"

He leaned back in his chair, judging me. A younger version of myself would have crashed a chair against the wall, or maybe taken a fist to his head. But my older, beaten-down self took it. He'd believe what he wanted to believe. He'd go away, and we'd go another few years without speaking.

"Dad said he wired you money."

"He did. A few times. My ATM card didn't work in every country. For the first few years, my bank account was in the US, and my salary was on direct deposit. Sometimes I'd have him wire me money so I could have cash. Credit cards work in some places, but not all. You can't count on them. I wasn't borrowing money from him. He was just helping me out."

"And once he died, you had Nana functioning as your bank?"

"No, she never sent me money."

"She specifically told me she sent a package to you."

I shook my head, no idea of what he could be talking about. Then I remembered she'd asked me once about a package I never received. She'd sent candy, and I'd told her not to bother. The chances of a package making it to me were too slim.

"I think she tried to send me something once. I never got it. One of her care packages. So, you've been assuming

I've been off gallivanting, living in resorts, maybe, off their money?"

"You do surf."

"Nice, Gregg."

"Well, I came down here to tell you that you've got some money waiting for you. Your inheritance."

"That's currently in dispute." I raised my eyebrows.

"Not really. Not if we can come to an agreement. I've been growing the company, putting everything into it. It doesn't seem fair to me that you'd show up ten years later and take half of what I've worked for." He twisted the napkin in his hand, glancing back and forth between me and the table.

"You know damn well I don't want anything to do with selling insurance. I don't want to take half of Tate Insurance from you."

"It's Tate Financial Services now."

"Whatever it's called, I don't want it."

"I owe you some money for it. I'd like to buy your portion from you, gradually, as I can afford to without taking on debt."

"You don't need to. You know money has never been a driving factor for me." If anything, I almost hated currency and what it made human beings do to each other and the planet.

"Yeah. For years, I figured you'd come back with your hand out, like a typical liberal. Wanting to go off and play and then expecting a handout. For someone else to work and then you get the—"

"I get it. But no, you can keep it." I half-laughed and emptied my beer bottle, then set it aside so the waitress would see I needed another one.

"I was so pissed that Nana watched me work my ass off but yet didn't change her will. When I heard you'd come back to the States, figured you...But it's not like that with you, is it? And all these years, I assumed..." He assumed the worst. He didn't need to say more. "But why throw your family away?"

I balled my hand into a fist, then hid the aggressive reflex beneath the table. "I didn't. You think there's phone service out there? And besides, when I did call, it was always contentious. Someone stole my phone, and I never bothered buying another one." I thought back, trying to remember the why. "When I left, it wasn't a good conversation with Dad. He wasn't happy with my choice."

"He's not a fan of Greenpeace."

"Yeah, he acted like I was joining an extremist group and headed to prison. I didn't have a strong urge to keep in touch. And then, all that time on the ship. That kind of became my world. Everything back here felt like another planet. And time went by, and a call felt like a big deal, something I needed time for and not something to do on a borrowed phone. And then I just decided when I got back home I'd talk face to face. Email and a phone didn't feel... adequate."

"Why'd you turn off your GPS?"

"I didn't turn it off. It got crushed when our ship hit a storm." That had been one of many times I thought I'd die on monster waves.

"You didn't think about what that would do to us? We had no idea if you were alive or dead. If we should have a memorial service or round up a search party. We had no idea where to search. The last we heard from you, you were somewhere in the Indian Ocean. Did you ever think about Dad? Or Nana?"

A wave of guilt crashed over me. I didn't think. Not about them. I felt indestructible, and any concern by anyone felt silly. As the years went by, I didn't feel so indestructible, but I had detached.

"You showed up maybe a month after the reading of the will. No word for so long, and then, out of nowhere."

"You assumed the worst. Got it. Loud and clear."

"That's not fair."

I gave him a look that said *really?*

"Who stole Dad's car when he was fourteen and crashed it? Who snuck out of the house countless times? Who emptied half Dad's liquor bottles and filled them with water?"

"That was high school. Look...you want to write me off, that's fine. I don't care. I left. You're the one who showed up here. And, just so you know, I don't even need that blasted inheritance. I did earn money on my own when I was gone. It's in offshore accounts at the moment. That's why I called Gabe, because he's helping me transfer funds." Gabe had set the accounts up for me a couple of years ago. I had one small account that I used for day to day, and I'd had larger payments sent to the offshore account, partially to minimize taxes, but my intention had been to put it to good use. Donate it or do something worthwhile with it. I lost all the account information when one of my phones went overboard, but I wasn't about to admit that to Gregg. All that would do is bolster his view of me as a delinquent.

Gregg exhaled loudly and stretched while the waitress picked up our empties and delivered fresh beers.

"You know, a guy called the house looking for you. A while ago. Said he was trying to locate you. Struck me as odd. If you were in trouble and needed my help, would you tell me?"

"Probably not," I answered. "But I'm telling you the truth. How long ago did that guy call?"

"A few weeks ago. It's what prompted me to reach out to Gabe."

I huffed. *Traitor*.

"Don't go getting mad at him. I dug into him before he'd share anything. And even then, he didn't share much."

The bubbles in my fresh beer floated to the top.

"My old boss knew about the inheritance. Was there an article or something?"

"Little snippet in the Hartford paper, I think. Laura mentioned it."

"Do you know if dollar amounts were specified?"

"No. Wouldn't take you long, though, to Google and read whatever he found."

I gulped my beer, aiming to down it quickly, pay for dinner, and say goodbye.

"Hey, it's late. What do you say we pay here and pick this up tomorrow? I'm here through Sunday. Besides, I'm sure your girlfriend is sitting at that bar getting hit on."

I chuckled. "If we were anywhere else, that would be true. On this island, this time of year, it's all married people or old people. I'm pretty safe."

"I like her."

"I do, too."

"So, you say she's in grad school?"

I couldn't hold back my grin as I shook my head at

him. "I have to give it to you. It took you hours before you got that question back in for round two."

He held his hands out and lifted his shoulders in his classic you-got-me move.

"She's twenty-two."

"I would've guessed twenty."

"You think I'm wrong to date her, right? She's too young for me?"

"Nah. You remember my buddy, Dalton? He came around some. He was on my lacrosse team?"

"Yeah, kind of. Big guy, brown hair?"

"Yep. He lives in our neighborhood, on my street, actually. My age, thirty-seven or eight. Guy just left his wife and young twins for his twenty-two-year-old assistant. Now, he's a total schmuck. His wife gained weight after having twins, and he said he was no longer attracted to her. To me, he's despicable. Curls my stomach. Laura's good friends with his wife, so I know a lot."

I sat back, waiting for him to get to his point.

"In that case, age plays a part. It just adds to the whole sordid picture. In your case, you're not married, no kids, in some ways you're starting a new life just like she is. Age is just a number. Fourteen, fifteen years isn't that much. And you guys are both environmentalists. You'll both spend your weekends picking up litter and planting trees."

"You are such a fucker." He laughed. "She can do better than me. You're right about me starting over." He nailed that one. "But...she's me when I was twenty-two. Optimistic, believes she can better the world. I've lost that. And I don't want to dampen her...everything. She's pretty incredible, and I feel..."

"Hey, maybe you'll balance her. She'll inspire you.

Show you that you can plant enough trees to improve the oxygen count or whatever…or, what does she do?"

"Right now, she's focusing on sea turtle conservation."

"Perfect. You guys can save hundreds of sea turtles together. You'll help her see that shipping across the world might not be the best choice for a young woman, and thereby save her from the ocean underworld. And she'll maybe inspire you to get a job. It's a win-win."

"It's amazing how you can annoy me even when you are trying in your own way to be supportive."

"Nah, seriously, you've never met Laura. You've missed a lot." He paused, giving me a pointed stare, casting blame. "But I do believe finding a partnership is a good thing. Laura…she's my world. And you and Luna, I could see her being that for you."

I didn't argue. We paid and headed out. While I agreed she could be great for me, I failed to see me being anything for her long term. Not that it was an issue. Luna wasn't worried about the long term. At twenty-two, she was all about the now and life experiences. As she should be.

In the morning, I woke with Luna sprawled out over the bed like a starfish. The sheet fell around our feet where she'd no doubt kicked it. She'd been up several times during the night getting water. She and Poppy had had quite a bit to drink by the time we met up with her at Jules. When we got home, we'd had drunken, sloppy, loud sex. I had every intention of encouraging her to go out with Poppy more often.

I kissed her shoulder and caressed her bare buttocks.

The rough pads of my fingers against her smooth skin caused her to stir. She groaned and pressed a hand against her head. She wasn't so young that she was impervious to the after-effects of alcohol. I found her some Advil and refreshed her water, then went downstairs to get the coffee started.

I picked up my phone to check email and news and discovered a text from Gregg asking about morning plans. I'd gone so long without using the phone much, or even having family in my address book, that I responded with a smile. Ludicrous. Luna came up behind me and pressed a kiss to my shoulder.

"What are you guys going to do today?" she asked, reading the message over my shoulder.

"I don't know. I suppose he'll want to go to brunch. He's into that kind of thing. Maybe I can get him to go out surfing. He used to be good. But I'd bet he hasn't been up on a board since high school." I circled so my back pressed on the counter and I could pull her against me. "How are you feeling?"

"Oh, I'll be fine. I just need some OJ."

"I don't have any, but I can run get some. The market should be open by now."

"That's okay. I have some at home, and I think I might crash. Sleep a little later and then spend the day working on a paper."

"You know, you're welcome to take your nap here, even work from here. I have plenty of room." Even when I asked, I knew I sounded like a clingy lover, and maybe I was evolving into one. I didn't like the idea of her being away from me. Even if we weren't going to spend the day together, I'd prefer for her to be in my space.

She stood on tiptoes and pressed her lips to my chin, then patted my chest. "You need to spend time with your brother. And I've got work to do. But, you know, you've got to actually text him back. That's how the phone works. Once you read the text, you type a response and hit send."

I pinched her smart ass, and she grinned as she slipped on her flip-flops. I followed her outside like an obedient seal and leaned down to kiss her when she got behind the wheel.

She smiled and drove away, waving goodbye with her golden hair flying out behind her, carefree. The farther she drove away, the more she looked like any one of the teenagers who zipped by on golf carts, young, easygoing, and free.

twenty

TATE

"Hey, sweetie pie! I miss you. I'm here with your Uncle Adrian, and he says he's going to come up and visit with you soon." Gregg grinned at me.

A few heads turned our way out on the deck of the Sandpiper, mainly because Gregg almost shouted into the phone in an entirely different tone as if he was talking to a dog. When he hung up, he shrugged his apology.

"Sorry. I'd offer you the phone to speak to her, but she's three. It's kind of a one-sided phone conversation. She's much better on FaceTime, but the signal out here, it doesn't work."

"No worries." I couldn't imagine I'd have anything to say to a toddler I'd never met, anyway. "What you said, about me seeing her soon, you want me to visit?"

"That's one of the reasons I'm here. Williams told me I

shouldn't be handling this through the courts. He pointed out our parents wouldn't want this."

"I would've never hired a lawyer, but your lawyer told me I needed to get one. You get that, right?" I ask, completely exasperated.

"Yeah. And we'll still need lawyers, most likely, to wrap this up. But you and I can work out the specifics on the business. Because of the timing of your return, I assumed the worst."

"You always do."

He sipped his coffee as he looked out over the marina, giving no hint he heard me. When he set his mug down, he slid it back and rested his arms on the table.

"You think one day you might have kids?"

"Save the speech."

"No. I was going to make a point. Once you have kids, you're going to understand so much more about what I did and why. The company isn't just about me, it's about them. It's about their future."

I crumpled up a napkin and leaned back in my chair. "Actually, I've applied to adopt."

His jaw dropped open.

"I doubt the application will be approved. Or I don't know. Maybe it will be. I have a lawyer working with the adoption agency on it. One day I think it'll happen, the next I don't think it will." The adoption remained the one thing out there that might be me making a difference. It would mean my time away would be for something.

"I'm so lost right now. Why would you apply to adopt a kid? You're living out here like a…"

"Vagabond? Loser? Where are you going with that

one?" We'd been having a good conversation, but his judgment always set me off. My muscles tensed.

"No, it's…" He scratched his neck with his mouth still partially open, then he pushed his chair back and sat straight, looking me in the eye. "You seem like you are trying to find yourself. When I think of someone adopting a child, I think of someone who is stable and maybe married. I suppose that's not required, but…you don't even have a job right now."

I wanted to fight him, but he wasn't wrong. "I didn't apply the way people here in the States apply for a kid, because for whatever reason I can't have one of my own. I applied because when I was in Somalia. This girl is in a bad situation. Adopting her is the best way, I think, to help her. But it's not clear cut."

"So, it's a specific child you've applied to adopt?"

"Yeah." I leaned forward and copied his position from earlier, arms folded on the table. "She ran up to me in this open-air market. 'Caawin,' she kept repeating, which means 'help.' I don't know the language well, and really, her eyes, you could see the panic. I don't know why she came up to me, the one white man in the market. I think maybe she thought I was a doctor? But I followed. Her sister lay in this area between two stalls. They weren't buildings. It was just divided areas. Remember some of the more rural markets when we were in Morocco?" Gregg hadn't been to most of the places I'd been, but he and I had trekked to Morocco one summer when we'd decided to explore outside of Spain. He nodded, his brow furrowed, probably tallying all the bad decisions I'd made, and following a strange girl through a third world market being top of the list.

I exhaled. "I couldn't do anything to save her sister. She died while I held her hand and told her in English, a language she didn't understand, that she would be okay."

"What was wrong with her?"

I gritted my teeth at that phrase. I hated it. "She was bleeding. Gushing blood from between her legs. Her sister was a little older, and I suspect she'd tried to give herself an abortion. But there was nothing I could do. I grabbed some filthy rags lying on the ground, wrapped them in my cleaner shirt and applied pressure, but..." That whole scene was just one more image I couldn't force out of my memory bank. I pinched my nose and closed my eyes.

"I tried to get her sister help. She didn't seem to have parents. She didn't want to go back to wherever she and her sister had come from. I took her to an orphanage and convinced them to take her in. Then I spoke with someone there, and she talked about the process. I don't know. It's not like they can make it easy for someone to walk off the street with a kid, claim it's an orphan, and try to adopt her. My lawyer is working on it."

"How old is she?"

"Twelve. Practically old enough to start having kids over there. I want to bring her back here, help her learn English, and give her a different life."

"Does she not have anyone? Friends? Family?"

"She doesn't seem to. Honestly, I think she's hiding from someone. Another reason to bring her here."

"That's huge. I have to admit, when you said adopt, I was envisioning a baby. You know, she could have a lot of issues? Even though you won't be dealing with diapers, it could be...do you know what you're getting into?"

"*If* I get into it, yes, I do know. The adoption agency

helps you with a lot of that. Telling you what to expect and how to handle adjusting and bonding."

"And English?"

"The agency says kids learn pretty quickly. Far faster than adults. At least, that's what they say."

"Wow. This is…unexpected. And I take it she's…" He dipped his head and paused, waiting for me to fill in his words.

"What?"

"She's black?"

How the hell this guy and I were from the same two parents sometimes blew my mind. "Yes, she has a lot of melanin. She's from Somalia."

"Hey, I don't have a problem with it. It's just one more thing you're gonna have to, you know, deal with. How's Luna feel about it?"

"Luna? What does she have to do with it?"

"Your girlfriend is, what? Ten years older than the child you're trying to adopt."

"Luna wouldn't be…it's not something I need to discuss with Luna. She's going back to Florida for her second year in her program. And then who knows where she'll be. She's not…she's a kid herself. She's not about to settle down with an old guy like me. Adopted kid or not."

"So, this is just an island fling? Kind of like one of the one-week romances you used to have when you spent summers out here?"

"Don't be an ass. I like her. She's a great girl. But if you're thinking she's my Laura, then you're off base. And I don't even know why I told you about the adoption. It's not gonna happen, or at least, if it does, it's going to take years."

"Well, since it's out there as a possibility, have you thought about getting a job?"

I huffed out a half-chuckle. "Yes, dip shit. I'm trying to decide what I want to do. As for today, you want to help me paint?"

"I'll give you money to hire painters if you need it, but I'm not spending my Saturday at the beach painting. Let's go get those surfboards and try surfing."

By the time we reached Access 42, the waves were rolling smoothly in, and the ocean reflected the sun in almost glass-like formation. Gorgeous, but not at all what you want to see when you're planning to surf.

"Hey, should we set the boards in the sand and let you practice getting up?" It's the classic first step for surf lessons and a total dig at my big brother. He shot me the bird and continued into the water, stopping when it hit his knees.

"Shit, it's cold. I thought you said it's warm in October?"

"It is. This should be balmy compared to what you're used to up north."

"Ah, it's been a while since I've been to anything other than a pool."

"You and Laura don't take many vacations?"

"We have kids." He spewed the words as if that was all the explanation I need.

We both eventually dove under the soft, rolling waves, then straddled our boards. The sun glistened off the water, scattering billions of stars across the smooth rolls. By myself, I probably wouldn't have even waded out today. But it wasn't like Gregg and I had other things to do. Gregg and golf meshed, but I wasn't a member at the clubs. And we'd both rather hang out in the water than on the beach. The sun beat down on our backs, and the only sounds were an occasional crash of a wave and the squawk of a passing seagull.

"So, did you have to deal with COVID where you were?"

"It was a global pandemic." He gave me that 'don't be a fuckwad' look that he perfected before graduating from high school, and I grinned. "Yeah, it was around, but we didn't deal with it like you. Fishing boats kept fishing. Without a pandemic, no one gives a shit about fisherman's lives. What's anyone gonna care if they get the flu?"

"It was more than the flu." His lips flatlined.

"I know that." For some of that time, I was staying in a hotel near the orphanage. I had access to the BBC. I knew what was going on. I strummed my fingers through the water. "What I meant is that the fisherman on the boats in much of Asia aren't particularly valued. No one lined up to offer them masks."

"It probably pays well, right? I watched some reality show once about the men in Alaska. I thought of you and the crazy shit you must be doing."

"Those men in Alaska do get paid well. It's dangerous work, but they get paid. But the men in other parts of the world…they're lucky if they get paid at all, and if they do, it's shit pay."

"Why do they do it?"

"The promise of money. Or maybe to pay off a debt. But, on a lot of those ships, once they're on them, they're on them for life. Or until they lose a limb and can't work anymore."

Gregg leaned his arms back on the board, balancing,

soaking in the sun. "I suppose it all comes down to financials, right? The fishing boats barely make any money, so they need cheap labor. And what seems like low pay to you is probably a windfall for a lot of those men coming from whatever slum or tribal land. So, it seems off to you, but really, it's a win-win. And it keeps the whole world going with affordable fish."

"That's not a win-win, you dipshit. Subpar working conditions, indentured servitude. Put the barbaric treatment of humans aside, later generations that don't have fish won't find it to be such a winning situation. When Earth's ecosystem is crumbling because our generation cared more about present-day bank accounts than the future, it's not gonna seem like such a winning proposition." I gritted my teeth and breathed deeply. My nostrils flared in my peripheral vision.

"I think maybe we should agree to not talk politics. I have friends at home who we had to come to that agreement with, and something tells me that would be better for us." He slapped the water and peered up at me with a look I knew well. It was the one that said *I've had enough of this fight. Can we move on?*

"Fine. One thing you need to understand, those men go onto those boats under false pretenses. They live in horrible conditions, sleeping below deck in grunge with rats, working almost all their waking hours, and sometimes they're in chains. They aren't free to go. There's nothing winning about their situation."

Gregg dove off his board into the ocean, kicking his board closer to me. I reached out for it and held it as I watched his broad stroke cross the waves. After a few minutes, he changed course and returned to his board, pulling his body over it like a raft. He wiped his eyes then grinned up at me.

"You know, brother, it occurs me that if we were alive during Civil War times, we'd be one of those families fighting on each side of the war."

"Are you saying that because you live up north and I live down south, or are you saying that because you're actually going to try to make a case for slavery?" My muscles tensed, awaiting an answer that might really piss me off.

"No. I don't believe in slavery. I wouldn't have supported slavery. Ever. But I probably would've understood the economic argument the southern states were trying to make. Regardless, I would've fought for the preservation of the union. And so, I suppose that means we would've been on the same side. Now, granted, after it was over, I would've been one of the first guys down there looking for business opportunities, taking advantage of some good deals, and you would've been one of the guys working at the camps of homeless freed slaves, maybe teaching them to read and write or something. Trying to give them job skills. That's who you are, and it's nothing to be ashamed of. It's something you should be damn proud of, actually."

I squinted into the sun, his words ricocheting inside me.

He smiled broadly, his white teeth shimmering over the water. "I guess what that means is my house on planet Earth will always be nicer than yours, but you're gonna have a better cloud in the afterlife."

"You are such a schmuck." He laughed as I scowled at him. The fact that he could so blithely overlook others suffering or the plight of those less fortunate drove me nuts. But I'd never change him. And, like him or not, I'd always love him. "Come on, Richie Rich. Let's go to Mike's Ice. You can buy your professionally challenged brother a hot dog."

twenty-one

LUNA

"Knock, knock," I shouted from Poppy's doorway. As I entered her kitchen, the almost empty coffee pot and crumb-laden plate on the counter told me there was a good chance she was still home.

"Hello?" I called.

Loud thumps cascading down the stairs announced her presence. She landed with a thud on the bottom floor, a kimono wrapped around her. She had a noticeable amount of make-up on, and her hair sported hot roller bounce.

"Working?" I asked.

"Yeah. Saturday can be kind of busy. What're you up to? Why aren't you out with your new hot boyfriend?"

My facial muscles stretched with my smile. "Boyfriend? You mind if I have the rest of your coffee?"

"No, help yourself. You might need to pop it in the

microwave, though." She slid onto a stool and watched as I reheated the nut-brown liquid.

"I'm not sure men Tate's age have the girlfriend-boyfriend discussion. Do you think they do?" He and I definitely hadn't, but I'd chalked it up to it all being new and it being a mature post-college relationship.

"He's not ancient. From what I can tell, men in their thirties, even forties and fifties, aren't much different from men in their twenties."

"You interact with your clients?"

"Yeah, via messages. If you went out on a date with someone else, do you think Tate would be upset?"

"Who would I go out with?"

"It's a hypothetical." She stretched out her arms. "Would you be upset if he went out on a date with someone else?"

"Who would he go out on a date with?" We were in the offseason. Unless a person went to the mainland, there were few dating options on the island.

"Don't be dense." Poppy's brow furrowed. "You know what I mean. Would you be upset?"

"Yeah. It would hurt. If I walked into Jules and saw him at dinner with someone else, it would hurt. But I'd be okay." At least, that was what I wanted. For us to be casual enough that if we woke up one day and felt differently, we could easily move on.

"I'm not saying you wouldn't be okay. I'm—never mind. You guys are dating even if you haven't had the conversation. So, back to my original question. Where's your boyfriend?"

"He's hanging with his brother today. I wanted to give them space. They haven't seen each other in a long time."

"What're you gonna do? I'd offer to hang out, but I have a client upstairs I've got to get back to."

"I thought you just sold photos?"

"Well, yeah, that's the crux of it. But some clients like to correspond."

"Sext, you mean?"

She grinned. "Yeah, like that. But some I think are just lonely. Anyway, this one guy wants to meet me in person."

"I'm not so sure that would be smart. I don't like that idea." Fully aware I sounded like a parental, I aimed to play it cool, but my parents had thrown too many stories about Snapchat fatalities to feel good about a friend meeting up with a guy who bought her nude pics.

"Duh. I'm probably not going to agree. But he says he'll come to Wilmington if I say yes."

"That's not a good idea, Poppy."

"Yeah, that's what Gabe says, too."

"You're still in touch with Gabe?"

A slow smile spread across her lips, and her eyes took on a happy haze. "He's been texting me. Tate gave him my contact info."

"He did?"

"That's what he said. But he's been coming across like more of a big brother. He doesn't like the idea of me meeting up with anyone at all, but I get the sense he doesn't like me modeling in general."

"I can kind of understand."

"Well, it's not for him to decide. He's a random friend of a friend. And, as for you, I'm sorry, but I've got to get back upstairs."

"Are you on video?" I still didn't have a great sense of exactly what her job entailed.

"Only with some clients. Get out of here. Go enjoy your day."

"Yeah, cleaning up the bunkhouse and preparing for guests. That'll be fun."

"Why are you doing that?"

"Researchers. They arrive Monday morning."

"Fun, fun, fun. See ya later." She paused with her hand on the stair railing. "Has Tate mentioned if Gabe is coming back to visit any time soon?"

"No, he hasn't. But he didn't even tell me his brother was going to be visiting."

"I'm sure you guys had other things to talk about—or, I mean, do." A beeping sounded upstairs. "Ah. That's the warning it's about to disconnect. Gotta run."

She bounded up the stairs, and I cleaned her kitchen. I thought about sneaking up the stairs to see exactly what she did when she worked but decided against it. *She's a grown woman and she said she's happy doing what she's doing. That's all that should matter.*

As I left Poppy's house, I checked my phone. No text from Tate. As it should be, given he was with his brother. And no matter what term accurately defined us, we weren't the couple who texted nonstop when apart, anyway. The silent phone reminded me I should call my family, so I did.

"Hello." My mom's voice through the line shocked me enough that I double-checked which number I called. I hadn't meant to interrupt her on a busy weekend morning. "Hello? Is anyone there?"

"Mom?"

"Luna? Is that you?"

"Mom, what are you doing home? Is Dad okay?"

"He's fine." Her voice rang with amusement. "It's our anniversary today, so I didn't go to the diner. We're going out on the boat in a little bit. How're you doing?"

"Ahm, I'm fine. Everything's good. Happy anniversary. I'm…that's awesome you took the day off."

"Honey, I take our anniversary off every year."

"You do?"

"Yes. Have been taking it off for about the last twenty years. Ever since I worked late and missed a dinner your dad prepared."

"I didn't know that."

"It's true."

"Huh. Well, you should take more time off, anyway. You work too much."

"You sound like your dad. Who, by the way, has been itching to come up and visit you. This older man has him on edge."

"Mom, please don't let him come up here. That's ridiculous."

"Well, you're in luck. He's not making that drive anytime soon with a broken hip. How are things going? Are you still with him?"

"Yes, since the last time I spoke to you, what, a week ago?"

"Does he make you happy?"

"It's early days, Mom. Too early for those kinds of questions."

"Nuh-uh. Not at all, missy. Happiness matters from the get-go. It's years in that it might not be as relevant."

I decided to overlook her relevancy comment. "What I meant is, it's too new to tell if anything is going to come of it. It's fun for now. And besides, you're the one who told me a person can have many loves in a lifetime, and each one touches our soul and shapes us." The first time she said this, I'd been twelve and Brandon had hurt my feelings over something. I couldn't remember what he did, but I remembered my mom being there for me.

"That's right. So, in this moment, he's touching your soul. I want to know that at this moment he's making your soul happy." The grin she wore could be heard through her words, and I grinned right back at her. As I twisted the stacked rings on my finger, the mood ring transitioned to blue-green.

"It's all good. Really, it is. I mean, I'm trying hard not to get ahead of myself, you know? To keep it all reasonable and rational and to remind myself that we're still getting to know each other. But, Mom, he is incredible. Unlike anyone I've ever met. And it's not just because he's older. He's like, if I were to sculpt and create a man just for me, I'd make him. Does that sound crazy?"

"No." She sighed into the phone, creating a momentary wind funnel. "Just remember, honey, go with the flow."

twenty-two

TATE

"Good to see you." Gregg pounded my back, his voice gruff.

We'd returned his rented golf cart, and the ferry pulled up to the dock. Only a handful of passengers gathered around, waiting to board.

"Thanks for coming out. I'm glad you did. Next time, don't stay at the Inn."

"You're coming up to visit soon, right? Like in a week or two?"

"I'll book the ticket today and let you know."

"And you'll respond to my text and email? That's why we have the rectangular devices. Communication."

I grinned through unexpected emotion. I was shit at texting and emailing. Found it way too easy to shut things off. I'd see a text and plan to respond later and not get around to it.

"I'll text you my travel plans." I wasn't going to promise I'd ever be good at texting, because I didn't make promises I couldn't keep. Maybe with time I'd be like all the other people tied to their phones, but right now, half the time I left my phone back at the house or forgot to charge it.

I shoved my hands in my pockets and watched him board the ferry. Then I hopped in my cart and found myself at Luna's door. The cottage the conservancy provided rested high on a hill overlooking the ocean, and breeze blew the pampas grass along the dunes. The tiny cottage may not have offered much in the way of space, but you couldn't ask for a better view of the Atlantic.

She opened the door with a hand sheltering her eyes, squinting from the sun behind my back. She wore an old t-shirt that hit above her bellybutton and white cotton panties. Christ, she looked delicious.

"You answer your door like that?" I asked, cringing at how old I sounded. I stepped inside, kicking the door closed.

She glanced down as if she'd forgotten what she was wearing. "It's no different than if I was wearing a bathing suit. You forget, I spend most of my free time in less than this out on the beach."

Rationally, I understood what she was saying. But, somehow, white cotton panties felt different than bathing suit bottoms. But I wouldn't argue with her. Just like differences with my brother, some things weren't worth the argument. Especially when there were other things we could do instead.

I backed her up to her bed, easy enough to do in the one room. My lips found hers as I pulled her to me, cupping her ass then dipping beneath those soft cotton panties to her silky smooth skin.

"Do you have plans today?"

"I have to welcome a few of the researchers."

"When?"

"Later this afternoon."

"Good. This morning you're mine."

I lifted her t-shirt over her head and tossed it on the end of the bed. She removed my tee and let her fingers wander over my chest, my abs and farther down. She looked at me like she could devour me. Such a turn on.

She wrapped her long fingers around me and stroked, and I sucked in a breath. Then I pushed her back on the bed, intent on giving her pleasure, on making her chant my name. I kissed my way across her body, worshipping her. We'd only spent one night apart, and yet I missed her. Craved her. Needed her.

When we collapsed beside each other, sweaty and spent, she spread one leg over mine, and her fingers explored. I lifted her hand and kissed the pad on each finger.

"Hm," she hummed. "You want to go surfing this morning?"

"No."

I leaned over her and kissed along her neck, over her collarbone, and down to her breasts.

"I want to do this all morning. I want to lie in bed with you, naked, and listen to the ocean. That sound okay to you?"

Her gentle smile told me she approved of this plan. She stroked my back in a light massage, and I relaxed into the motion.

"What did you do last night?" I flipped over and positioned myself on a pillow then pulled her next to me.

"Nothing, really. School work. Met up with Poppy." She sank her teeth into my chest.

"Ow." Her tease didn't hurt, but she held a serious expression when she raised her head to look at me.

"You never texted me back."

"Crap. You and my brother."

"Weren't you with him?"

"Yes, but I mean, you're all over me about texting."

"Do you not like to text?"

"I just don't check it."

"Where's your phone?"

"Back at my place."

"You don't even carry it with you?"

"No. I don't. But I'll try to get better. How's that?"

She kissed over her bite mark. "That works."

"So, Poppy. I've been thinking about her. Is there something I could do to help her, so she doesn't have to, you know, sell photos of herself?"

"She doesn't need help."

"Did she not like bartending? She could go back to it." I twisted a long blonde strand around my finger, enjoying the feel of her naked body against mine and the intimacy of talking this way, spread out on her bed.

"Yeah, she could, but she seems to enjoy her current gig."

"Really?" I'd seen too many brothels in my time filled with women who didn't have a choice to compute someone having a choice and choosing that. Not that selling nude photos was the same thing, but it sounded like more than photos.

"I think so. She's thinking about meeting up with one of her customers."

"That can't be—"

"I know. I told her. But she's going to do what she wants to do. It's her life. Her choice."

"If she goes, you need to make sure you know how to get in touch with her. Where she's going. Can you track her phone?"

"Hhmm, we have friends, so I can locate her on that app. But all he'd have to do is turn her phone off. That's hardly a safety guarantee. I don't like her going."

I tilt her chin up to me. "I don't like her doing it at all. But I'm not one to get judgmental. Just promise me it's not something you'll do."

She sank her teeth into her bottom lip and studied me, then pushed forward to kiss the tip of my nose, dragging her body along mine as she moved. My dick twitched.

I rolled over onto her and intertwined her fingers with mine and kissed her slowly, taking my time, enjoying this. Everything between us felt so easy. No expectations. The perfect lazy Sunday. Just enjoying our time together, without the weight of the past or worries about the future interfering.

After Luna left to greet the researchers, I stopped by the post office on my way to the business center with a goal of following up on a lobbying position I'd applied to. The lone post office sat across from the lighthouse and serviced the entire island. As I approached the wall of mailboxes, I ran into one of the island realtors. Our conversation went on and on, then wrapped up with, "If you ever decide you want to sell your grandmother's cottage, let me know. Spring would be a great time to list it if it's something you're considering." He reached into his pocket and handed me his business card.

I slipped it into my shorts pocket and pulled out the tiny metal key for my mailbox. They'd crammed so much mail into it, I ripped the first catalog I pulled out. The unwanted catalogs and junk mail I dropped directly into the nearby blue recycling bin. One thick official-looking manila envelope remained stuck in the narrow box. The heavy weight paper reminded me of a college acceptance package filled with important documents. With effort, I pulled it out intact. My skin tingled when I read the return address. Washington D.C.

I ripped it open and skimmed the letter, then headed over to the business center. My lawyer worked magic. Or maybe the Somalian adoption agency case worker had. Whoever did it, it didn't matter.

The next few hours passed in a hazy whirl. Phone calls to my lawyer, to the adoption agency, to the U.S. Embassy. While I normally purchased airline tickets online, this time I used a travel agent as a double-check to ensure I followed all procedures and could bring my daughter home without issue.

My daughter. When she'd looked at me with those scared eyes, I'd known I had to help her. Adoption wasn't my first thought. But when the caseworker at the orphanage suggested it, it seemed like a reasonable solution. Plus, applying ensured the adoption agency would keep her in the orphanage and she would be safe.

The agency had said to expect the adoption to take

years. Everything I read online corroborated what they said. My lawyer warned it would likely not be possible. Less than one year ago I sat in a chair at Humanity Without Borders and waited for an English-speaking case worker to arrive. One year.

In that time, it seemed the girl I paid to protect had been smuggled into Kenya and paperwork created that would allow me to adopt her. I had told my lawyer I'd pay whatever I needed to. And I would. This girl, to me, stood out as a tangible personification for all the wrong I'd seen that I'd been powerless to correct. My opportunity to make a difference. Not in a whole classroom, like my mother, but in one life. My lawyer had told me how much it might cost, but I didn't expect the total fee would exceed his original outlandish cost estimate. But it wasn't like I was going to turn around and tell him money meant more to me than her life.

I listened to my voicemail, and sure enough, I had voice messages dating back since last week from my lawyer. In an old email account I hadn't been using, I found emails. My lawyer had kept me apprised, I'd just been on my own little island vacation.

The adoption agency provided me a list of everything I needed to do to prepare. For her, not for me. I'd fly to D.C. first, then Kenya.

By the time Tim tapped on the door to let me know they were closing up the business center for the night, I'd put an ad out for a tutor and emailed Gregg to let him know my nieces would now have a cousin. He responded within seconds. Of course. I promised to stop in Connecticut on my way back with her. He suggested I stay for the holidays with them. And, I had to admit, it wasn't the worst suggestion. I didn't have a clue how to be a father. And I owed it to him to get to know his wife and kids. No matter what, he'd always be my brother. Family would be good for my daughter. *My daughter…*

As I cleared out of the business center, an unease settled over me. The kind of unease that said you'd made a poor decision. That you weren't up for what was coming down the pike. I pulled up Luna's contact information on my phone but couldn't bring myself to press her name.

My twenty-two-year-old surfer girl. *What the fuck was I thinking, letting myself be with her?* I'd thought we were short term. She'd leave to finish her master's, or for another one-year research gig. I'd expected we'd part ways long before anything like this came to fruition.

And Luna, she'd probably grow attached to my daughter, maybe even do something stupid like consider not completing her degree or come back to a nothing job at the conservancy center so she could stay near us. I knew nothing about being a parent, but I knew what it was like to be twenty-two. I knew a twenty-two-year-old had no business carrying the burden of an adopted twelve-year-old girl.

I'd always hated goodbyes. Never liked emotional communication. The idea of saying goodbye to Luna, of tears welling up in sad brown eyes, it crushed me. I couldn't do it. I liked how I said goodbye to her this morning, with an expectation we'd be together again. We hadn't made plans. We had assumed it. We'd been happy.

If I met up with her and told her we had to end things, she'd fight me. She'd argue we could still see each other. That she wouldn't be sacrificing anything. But she would, and I knew it. A letter struck as the most reliable method of ending things. There would be no risk of my caving. Maybe it would stir up a little righteous anger in Luna. Anger would be good. Someone else would ask her out, and she'd move on to the next guy.

I scribbled in my journal. I might not make it off the island without running into her, but I could try. I liked my plan. Leave with happy memories. No painful goodbyes. No begging for more.

Thoughts of Luna surrounded me as I packed up my papers. Her giggles, her coconut sunscreen and her strawberry shampoo, her optimism. Her hair flitting behind her as she sped along. I closed my eyes and focused on my mental image of her flying down Wynd Road, surfboard strapped to the top of the cart, and memorized it.

I left the business center uncertain, with a half-baked plan, clueless. I left the island with a book from the adoption agency on what to expect, and an itinerary to become a father.

twenty-three

LUNA

A few of the researchers staying over for the week excavated the last remaining turtle nest on the island. We didn't find any remnant eggs, but we joked around and got to know each other. The research team comprised senior members of a volunteer conservation group. Most were professors at various universities around the country. I'd stumbled into a potential career-making networking event, just by doing my job.

The scientists invited me to join them during some of their work sessions. Exhilaration carried me through the afternoon like a full, smooth tidal swell.

I texted Tate. They offered for him to join us. Networking opportunities in our field had to be seized. Even if he had no interest, they'd love to hear his stories. But I didn't expect a return text. Phones and Tate mixed like oil and water. I rushed around the center, sweeping sand into a pile, eager to close up the center for the night and find Tate.

"Hello, child." Alice's kind voice preceded her into the large room filled with aquariums.

"Hi. What are you doing here? It's after ten." I set the broom and dustpan against the wall and scanned the room for any remaining things to do before turning off the light.

"I've been looking for you."

"Oh, is everything okay?" I gave her my full attention. Her braids fell around her shoulders, and she wore a multi-colored dress that flowed with the current of the air. Well-worn brown suede Birkenstocks adorned her feet, and her collection of toe rings glinted in the light.

"I have something for you." She held out a milky white envelope. "The tide ebbs and flows. The sun sets, but it also rises."

I played her odd riddle over in my head.

"Tate asked me to give that to you." She spoke so softly I stepped closer, unsure I heard her correctly. "He had to leave."

"Is he in danger? Did that man come back?" She'd told me to put out that bucket of water. And I did. I'd hidden it beneath his kitchen sink. I hid it so Tate wouldn't laugh at me, but I did as she said.

"He's finding his way. He'll be back." She took my hand. "You focus on you. All will come to be."

She turned and disappeared down the hall, her long dress flowing in her wake. *What the fuck?*

I ripped the letter open.

Luna,

I suck at goodbyes.

Please know that I've loved getting to know you. You've reminded me of what I used to be.

I'll always think of you with your golden hair flowing behind you, zooming along the island paths. I'll remember you on your board, catching a wave with grace.

I don't know if I'm returning. Do not wait for me. Live your life. Change the world for better.

One day when my feet are on the ground and I've figured out a plan, I'll reach out. Connect. Maybe I'll become a texter. When I do, I want to hear all about what you've done and what you've accomplished.

Maybe we can compare notes.

Love,
Adrian Tate
P.S. If I were twenty-two, I'd never let you go.

Eraser dust covered the postscript notation, but the indention in the thick stationery paper left the words clear on the page.

I sat down on the floor in the conference center room and held the letter in my hands. Confusion swarmed. *He just left?*

Numb, I drove over to his cottage. No lights were on, and the door was locked. I followed the moonlight down the narrow path along the side of the house to the back porch and found the screen door locked. I pressed my face against the window. Fog formed on the glass pane as I strained to see inside.

I drove to the ferry terminal. No one waited for the next ferry.

I curled up in bed, holding the letter. It felt surreal. I just couldn't believe he would leave and not say goodbye. It didn't make sense. We were happy. Concern for his safety surged. The only logical explanation I could come up with was that he was in danger and left.

Over the next several days, I sent several short texts.

Are you okay? Are you in danger?

Tate, what the hell? You don't just leave with a letter.

I know you don't like to text, but this is ridiculous. Where are you?

I'm not going to hunt you down. I promise. I just want to know. Are you safe?

Every day, I drove by his cottage. I don't know why. But I thought some part of me needed to see he was gone. Because I just couldn't believe it. My emotions crashed around each other. Concern crashed over anger, then annoyance rose and crashed over sadness. It all leveled out into unexpected grief. I hurt, a deep pain like none than I had ever felt before. This was what it felt like to have someone break up with you. This was what I'd done to Brandon. Maybe this was karma.

I spent my nights on the beach, tears streaming down my face, when no one could see. I spent my days working alongside the scientists, keeping my head up and focusing on my tomorrow. Poppy drank wine with me on a few evenings while we watched mindless television, and she pushed ice cream on me. Alice checked on me daily, bringing me dried herbs to hang in my home and for tea. Every time she left, she told me to have faith.

After a week of silence, I sent Tate one last text.

> When I look up at the stars at night, I think of you. I love knowing that somewhere, you too are staring up at the same guiding lights. Those suns guided sailors for centuries. Chance crossed our paths. Did I ever tell you I considered three other internships? If I'd taken one of those, we'd have never met. Even if our paths never cross again, a part of you remains within me. We weren't yet at the stage where we told each other the deep stuff, but you imprinted on me. You altered my chemical make-up in a fundamental way. That means… I'll never forget you. Wherever you are, may you be safe. And know you are loved.

The next day, Poppy had me send one more text.

> Don't take my last text to mean I'm not pissed. I'm mad as hell. Who the hell leaves with a letter? FUCK YOU!

"There's my moon pie." My dad's deep voice thundered through the one-story ranch I grew up in. In a flash, he surrounded me, picking me up and twirling me around until—"Jimminy."

"Dad, are you okay?" He hunched over like an elderly person, his face contorted.

"It's just my damn back."

"What are you doing picking me up?" I guided him over to a chair and forced him to sit.

"What good am I if I can't pick up my little girl?" he moaned.

"I'm not so little anymore. And you're still recovering, aren't you?"

I stood back, taking him in. Gone were the broad shoulders and wide biceps, replaced by a narrower frame, thinner hair, and much more gray. He gazed down on the floor, his right hand glued to his side.

"Can I get you something? Advil? A heating pad?"

"Advil. That should do it. Good thinking."

I brought the Advil bottle and a glass of water to the table. He popped the pills, with no water, as if they were candy. I pulled out a chair and sat down at the table.

"We missed you at Thanksgiving."

"I missed you guys, too."

"How'd the boil go?" The low country boil fundraiser had kept me busy straight through November. The island always drew a good crowd of homeowners on Thanksgiving weekend, and the Saturday event had been a hit.

"Good. We raised almost fifty thousand dollars."

"Nice. I suppose that's worth missing Thanksgiving."

"Dad." He'd already let me know he wasn't happy I didn't come home to eat turkey. I suspected Mom had been relieved she didn't have to create tofu turkey for me. "Where's Nova?"

"She's at the diner, helping your Mom."

"How're things going there?"

He let out a pained sigh. "Always seems busy to me. Your mom always worries it's about to go under. My damn back. If I could get back to work, she wouldn't need to be so stressed."

"Dad, you've worked most of my life and she's been stressed the entire time." Stressed was Mom's standard state of being. Growing up, they'd always been a study in contrasts. Mom worried over every little thing, every dollar spent, and Dad didn't worry about anything at all. If he felt like the fish might bite, he had no qualms about taking off for the day. He never worried about getting fired or paying bills. He never saved to take the trips Mom dreamed of. As a kid, I thought Dad was the most amazing adult on the planet. Now, as a bill paying strapped grad student, I wondered why Mom hadn't left him yet.

"One day I'll win the lottery, and she won't need to stress." If he'd saved all that money he'd spent on lottery tickets over the years, by now she probably wouldn't be stressed. But there was no point in pointing that out. Besides, Dad's lottery ticket habit replaced his nicotine habit, and I had to believe lottery tickets were cheaper than the cartons of Marlboros he used to buy back when I was little. "So, how many nests did you end up with this year?"

"One hundred and fourteen."

"How many babies you think made it? Not just into the water, but out into the ocean?" Those statistics weren't so promising. Tiny turtles faced a world of predators. "Probably the same odds as my lottery tickets." He pounded the table with his fist, and his smile stretched across his face, entertained by his own humor. "But you still keep trying."

"Dad. It's not something to smile about."

"I know that, baby cakes. Those turtles are key species...that's what you call 'em, right?"

"Keystone species." If turtles became extinct, it would cause declines in all species whose survival depended on healthy seagrass beds and coral reefs. But I didn't need to go on about it. My dad played the I'm-not-so-smart card, but he taught me. I owed my love of nature and passion for conservation to him.

"That's right. Keystone." He grinned. "Brandon stopped by. Dropped off some material for a few events going on over the next few weeks. It's all up there on the counter. There's a Christmas Eve Manatee Run."

"Oh. That'll be fun. A 5K?"

"Yeah. Like your Turtle Trot you do over there on your island."

"Those events are great fundraisers. Did Brandon get it going here?"

"I believe he did. He's working for some group..." He scratched his head.

"Sanibel Island Conservation."

"Yep." He sighed. "He also mentioned some job opportunity he thought you should apply for. Something in the Virgin Islands. Don't know what he's thinking. If he wants to win you back, sending you off to a gig in the tropics doesn't sound like a good plan. That boy never was right in the head."

"Dad, Brandon and I broke up two years ago. I think he's accepted we're not getting back together."

"Yeah, I'm sure you're right. He comes by here every week 'cause he likes to see my smiling mug. Has nothing to do with keeping up with you."

I glanced around the kitchen, searching for a topic to change the conversation. A calendar hung on the side of the fridge, and I noticed Mom's handwriting in all caps and multiple exclamation points. *Therapy. Do not forget!!!*

"Do you have physical therapy today?"

"Oh, shit. Your mom is gonna to be so mad at me."

"What time is the appointment?"

"I don't know. Doesn't matter. I'd rather be here with my little one."

"Dad, they charge you when you miss." I huffed out my frustration as I searched for his phone and the calendar app. An alert rang out, which helped me to find his phone under the kitchen towel.

"Your appointment is in thirty minutes. Come on, let's go. I'll drive."

Later that evening, Nova returned home. She had flour remnants in her hair and over the front of her jeans, and dark stains dotting her jean skirt, t-shirt, and even the leather straps of her Birks.

"Does Mom have you working in the kitchen now?"

She proudly put her arms up in the air and pointed down at herself. "Pastry chef. Right here. Promoted."

I laughed. Growing up, we helped at the diner counter, bused tables, and cleaned dishes.

"Where's Dad?" she asked, looking around. I had the pamphlets Brandon dropped off spread out on the kitchen table.

"He went back to rest after his physical therapy."

"He made it this time?"

"Yeah. I think it's hard on him. You know, painful. I made him ice when we got home. Now I think he's avoiding me in case I make him do something else he doesn't want to do."

"Sounds about right." She plopped down at the kitchen table with me and picked up a brochure.

"How's Mom?" I asked.

She dropped the paper and fell back against the chair. "She's Mom. Powerhouse." She lowered her voice to a whisper. "I think she's close to leaving him."

"Really?" We'd thought this so many times in the past. More than I could count.

"She hardly ever comes home. I mean, I bet, even with you home, she won't make it home until, like, eleven at night. She's back up at four a.m., out the door before five."

"She can't maintain those hours."

"No, but I think when Dad's not working, it drives her crazy and she can't bear to be around him. Either that or their financial situation is precarious, and she picks up extra hours at the diner to supplement Dad's missing income."

"But Dad's getting workman's comp, right? He was injured on the job."

"If that's true, then he drives her crazy."

"Well, we know that's true."

Our eyes met across the table, and we both half laughed. The state of our parents' marriage was both funny and not funny at all. We worried but couldn't do anything about it.

"Hey, did you ever hear from Tate?"

"No. Still no response. One letter. I still can't believe it." The ache in my chest remained. An odd mix of emotions swirled day to day, ranging from hurt over being discarded so easily, to concern over what could be going on, to guilt for hurting Brandon when I broke up with him, because now I knew the pain of being on the dumped end of a break-up. It sucked.

"You doing okay?" she asked. I didn't miss the tilt of her head or the way her eyes squinted, focusing in, analyzing me.

"I'm fine. Sad, you know?" Sad wasn't an accurate description. I'd cried buckets. It hurt before when relationships ended, but never like this, this ongoing ache.

She gave an understanding nod and waited for me to say more.

"I thought we had something real. And he seemed so different from all the other guys I've dated."

"You mean Brandon?"

Brandon was actually a younger version of Tate. Only he wanted to stay right in Florida. He never wanted to leave. And I always struggled to explain it, but I wasn't attracted to him anymore. We grew apart. He liked different kinds of parties than I did. He found friends I didn't really like. He liked to drive around in his ridiculously loud car.

We drifted apart. It happened. You could look at my

parents, married for almost twenty-five years, and see it could happen even if you lived in the same house.

"We were kids, Brandon and I. Tate, he's so different." I'd thought we had a mature relationship, whatever the hell that was supposed to be.

"You mean because he's old?"

"Mid-thirties doesn't make you old." I rolled my eyes at her naivety.

"Eh. I bet his balls sag."

"Oh, my god." I kicked her under the table, and she laughed. "Actually…"

"They do sag."

"Stop it. Even though he's in his mid-thirties, he's still figuring things out. Trying to decide what he wants to do with his life. No, what I meant is there's a depth to Tate. He's lived enough to know that there are more important things than weekend plans or video game rankings. He's lived hard. And he's…I don't know. None of it matters. He ghosted me."

I looked off to the corner of the room as my eyes burned. I refused to cry in front of anyone, especially my little sister.

"If he doesn't realize what a catch you are, then he's not worth it. End of story. Move on. Next."

A knocking at our back door interrupted us. The door swung open seconds later.

"I heard you're back." Brandon filled the doorway, and a wide grin spread across Nova's face.

"As I was saying." She raised her eyebrows and rapped the table. "I'm gonna go get a shower." She waved as she backed out of the kitchen, eyes locked on Brandon. He smiled his warm, familiar smile.

With a nod, he stepped inside and opened the refriger-ator and retrieved a water bottle, then asked, "You want one?"

People talked about deja vu. That moment felt like that, or more like it had transported me back in time to high school, when Brandon came over every single day. Like maybe graduation lay in our future, not in our past.

twenty-four

LUNA

Three months later

I blared the radio at deafening levels the entire drive from Florida to North Carolina, drowning out thoughts while singing along to the classic greats. After buying my ferry ticket, I called my parents to let them know I arrived unharmed.

"Honey, you go knock it out of the park with the rest of your assignment, okay?"

"Yes, Mom."

"Honey, I love you. I know you're hurting, but you're strong. I raised you to roll with rogue waves. You can do it." One thing about my parents, I might question how their marriage worked every single day, but I would never again doubt they were both in my corner.

"Love you, too, Mom." Dad came on the phone, and we exchanged love, too.

The ferry horn bellowed out, warning a smaller craft. The choppy, dark whitecaps hinted of frigid waters. I huddled against the bone chilling February breeze on the wooden bench at the ferry terminal, my bare fingers ice cold.

Myself, a family, and an older couple handed over our tickets and boarded the ferry to return to Haven Island. I found a window seat below deck and stared out over the whitecaps as the ferry sliced through the wake.

Four months had passed since I'd last seen Tate, and I still bore a dull ache. I missed Tate. One night, I told Brandon all about him and how he left.

"If he doesn't see you for all you are, then he doesn't deserve you." He proved himself a great friend, coming around every day to check on me. My parents were concerned him being around so much was responsible for my sad face, my dad's words to describe my mood. For years, I'd thought my dad preferred Brandon to me, but he proved me wrong when he asked Brandon to not come around. I smiled as I remembered Nova tentatively knocking on my bedroom door and fiddling with the throw on the bed nonstop as she explained that she hadn't meant for anything to happen, but she and Brandon were secretly dating. Secretly, because they didn't want to hurt me. I laughed because, really, it couldn't have been more perfect. Brandon and I had a history, sure, but all I wanted was for him to be happy. And maybe it was a little odd for my sister to be dating my first love, but Brandon and I had stayed together so long because it was easy, not because we were in love.

Brandon and I had a long talk. He'd missed the *idea* of us far more than us. He found himself leaning on Nova more and more while I'd been gone. Together, they concocted a scheme to see if him dating an old friend would upset me. It became clear to them both I really was over him, and he began to accept it. Without even realizing it, he fell for my sister, who had become his first call in the morning and his last call of the day.

Alice had been right. Things did have a way of working themselves out.

The captain swiveled the boat around the corner and up against the pilings with practiced ease. I deboarded with a handful of other passengers, and we all congregated in front of the baggage claim, cold and impatient. The clatter of the luggage cart banging the metal ramp reassured us of a short wait. Exhilaration stirred—a new season, a new spring.

"Look who's back!" Tony bellowed from across the asphalt parking lot.

"Hey, Tony. How've you been? You working today?"

"Half day. Headed home now. As soon as the contractor ferry decides to show. You have a good holiday?"

"I did. It was good to be with my family."

"You've got a nice tan. A glow."

"It's a lot warmer in Florida."

He looked me up and down and licked his lips. I pulled my coat tighter around me.

"You know, your lover boy is back."

"Back...Tate's here?" I didn't think I heard him right.

"Yep. Must've gotten in with the help 'cause he came back with a daughter about a month ago. Looks like he knocked someone up when he was pretty young. Something must've happened to her ma, and now he's saddled with her." He clucked his tongue and whistled. The contractor ferry horn announced its impending arrival and overshadowed Tony.

"What've you been up to?" he asked, nudging me to regain my attention. "Thought you'd up and left for good. Dr. Wilton has been back since January."

"He gave me permission to work from home. After all, no one's really here in December and January. I've been working on building connections for the conservation center with a few of the Florida universities…" I trailed off as Tony's focus centered in on his phone.

If Tate returned here, then he wasn't hiding from me. He never responded to my texts, but knowing Tate, he might've lost his phone and had no way of even finding me. I'd written him off. Assumed he'd gone back to Asia to deal with his exploding boat issue. Maybe he did. Maybe he saved someone and came back. No matter what Tony assumed, I couldn't believe he had a daughter. The notion sounded absurd.

A tram driver approached, breaking me out of my thoughts. "Ma'am, is that your luggage?" He pointed.

"Yes, it is. I'm sorry, I just…" spaced. The uniformed man ignored me and gathered up my luggage, throwing it into the back of the truck bed.

The blue trams transported visitors and luggage to their cottages. I climbed into the back of my assigned tram and before long zipped past Tate's cottage. Two rusted beach cruisers leaned against the outside of the golf cart shed. The open garage door exposed his golf cart and the small grill he wheeled in and out.

I threw open the doors to my little cottage, dumped my luggage inside the door, and sprinted down the hill.

Alice had assured me he'd be back. I hadn't believed her. There'd been no sign or evidence he'd return. I'd believed his letter. I'd believed I wouldn't hear from him for years—maybe not ever again. And he was back. He owed me answers. Did he come back for me? Had he expected me to be here?

I jumped up the steps to his porch and froze in front of the screen door. A woman with long dark hair stood before a clean cut, short-haired version of Tate, her hand on his shoulder. He gazed intently down on her.

I watched. Comprehension filtered through my pores. A crushing pressure around my chest cavity made it hard to breathe. *So naive. So stupid.* In all my what-if scenarios, never once did I think he'd found someone else. Or would bring her back to Haven Island.

My eyes stung, the world blurred, and I spun around and ran.

twenty-five

TATE

"She'll be ready to go to school in the fall. She's dedicated. She works hard. It's like I told you, kids learn a language through immersion so much more quickly than adults. Keep talking to her in English. She'll get it." Cali spoke to me like a patient teacher repeating herself. We had some form of this conversation almost every day. The idea of pushing Jasmine, my adopted daughter, into the U.S. school system terrified me. When Cali responded to my ad for a tutor on the island, and she was available to work with Jasmine full-time, and was fluent in Arabic, it had seemed too good to be true.

"I hear you. But if she's not ready, will you consider keeping her on through next year?" I wasn't paying Cali enough to live on, but she was recently divorced and didn't seem to be worried about her income. I needed her to remain here, helping us. I didn't like having a deadline for Jasmine.

Cali laughed and slung her backpack over her shoulder, signifying the end of the conversation. "That's, what? Eight months away? You're going to be blown away by her progress. But of course, if you need me, we'll talk about it when the time comes."

Jawaahir had asked about an English name. Actually, I wasn't entirely sure she came up with that idea on her own. I thought Laura might have planted the concept. Nevertheless, through a disjointed conversation pointing at photographs and drawings, I got the point across that my grandmother's name was Jasmine Pearl Tate, and she and I agreed she'd go by Jasmine, or Jazz, for short.

I fell in step behind Cali and halted when she unexpectedly turned. "Have you arranged for Jasmine's therapy yet?"

"I'm working on it." We'd been back for less than four weeks. Any therapy options were on the mainland, and I hadn't had time to do the appropriate amount of research.

Cali placed her hand on my shoulder and lightly squeezed. She meant it as a comforting gesture, but her questioning me felt like censure. I couldn't blame her. My parenting was hardly a safe bet.

"Hey, I'm not criticizing. You're doing a great job with her. But it's easy to put off scheduling therapy. Sometimes there is fear it will hurt more than help. But I suspect she's experienced a lot. Talking about it, or even her emotions, will be good for her."

"Will a therapist even be able to help her if she can't speak English?" The chances of locating a Somalian or Arabic speaking therapist on the coast of North Carolina were slim. Callie spoke five languages, and she didn't know Somalian.

"She's going to be learning English more quickly than you think. If you find the right therapist, it can be more of a language lesson to start, and they can build a relationship, and as she becomes fluent, she'll have a trusting relationship with someone. I'd expect the chances are good she's been raped, or witnessed a rape, based on how you met her. Even if she hasn't, watching her sister die, and then moving to another country—I can't begin to imagine all the emotions she might have. At the very least, therapy will be one more tool in your arsenal to help her adjust to life here."

"Thank you." I didn't know what else to say. She wasn't saying anything new to me. The adoption agency also recommended a therapist. Cali had been a godsend for me. Gratitude for her help, for having someone else to weigh in, overflowed. I said thank you to her every single day. The word felt woefully inadequate, but I didn't know what else to say. I squeezed her hand that rested on my shoulder, trying to silently convey all the appreciation I felt.

Movement outside the screen door caught my attention, and I looked over Cali's head in time to see Luna running. Her hair whipped in the wind as she sprinted away. A heavy weight held me in place. I hadn't done right by Luna. In typical Tate fashion, I'd closed the door and not looked back.

Cali patted my shoulder and inched away, her movement bringing me back to the living room.

"We'd better get going if you're to make the next ferry."

My thoughts ran rampant as I drove to the marina. When I returned to the island, I'd expected she'd be dating someone else by now. Life at twenty-two went like that. Or, well, twenty-three. I'd missed her birthday.

But twenty-two and twenty-three were both the same. One door closed and another opened. Sometimes all in the same week. Hell, more than once I'd said goodbye to a girl on a Saturday, moped around on Sunday, and discovered a new girlfriend on Monday. That was life in a place with summer renters on constant rotation.

It wasn't like Luna and I were meant for forever. But I'd be lying if I said relief didn't fill me when I found out she hadn't yet returned. I didn't want to see her with someone else. I also didn't want to have to face how I'd left her. Saying goodbye sucked. But hello after pretty much running away had the potential to suck more.

When I pulled up to the marina, Cali tucked her hair behind her ear as she stepped off the cart. "Are you okay?" she asked.

"Sure. So, I'll pick you up tomorrow morning?"

"I'll text you confirmation when I'm on the ferry, but my plan is to catch the nine a.m."

"See you tomorrow."

I didn't wait for the ferry to dock. I drove straight to Luna's. The way she turned and fled bugged me. She deserved an explanation.

As I drove up the familiar Long Wynd Road, it occurred to me she might have thought something was going on with Cali and me. I was sure if I walked up to her cottage and a man was standing close to her, I'd assume the same thing. But Luna and I...we were supposed to be carefree. A relationship in the moment. She could be upset for how I left, but not if I were dating someone else. Not now. Months later. But that didn't mean I didn't owe her an explanation.

Once she learned about my new responsibility, she'd understand. She wouldn't want a part in raising a teenage daughter. She'd broken up with her first love because he wanted to settle down, and that wasn't the life she wanted. I saved her the pain of having to be the one to end it. Because, without a doubt, settling down with a kid in tow wasn't anywhere on her agenda.

The ache that had become my normal lessened as I approached her home. Nerves fired off. My breathing quickened through the bite of the bitter cold wind. I had missed her far more than I'd anticipated. More than I'd missed anyone, and given my past, that said something. A day didn't go by that I didn't think about her. We weren't building toward forever, but we were more than a series of hook-ups. I owed her more than my cop-out note. I owed her both an explanation and an apology. The way I acted, you'd think I was the twenty-two-year-old in our relationship.

I'd known this day would come—if she returned. Haven Island was too small for avoidance to be any sort of solution. Even if it had been a metropolis, Luna deserved more.

I parked in front of the lifeless board and batten cottage. I'd walked by it almost every day since my return. The garage shed remained closed. I bent down and tugged on the silver handle. The door stuck, and with an extra heave, it lifted, exposing a dusty golf cart.

I knocked on her doorframe. The screen door remained shut, but the heavy wooden door was ajar. I peeked inside.

Two suitcases and an open tote bag with towels spilling out rested against her bed.

I ventured along the sandy path out to the ocean, searching. Far down the beach, close to the point where the ocean and the inlet crashed together, I found her. Her long blonde hair blew behind her, just as I'd remembered for these months away. The frigid ocean air gushed down the beach, and she gripped her coat tightly around her, huddled as she rambled along the water's edge.

I caught up to her and slowed, letting my feet fall into her sand indentions.

Sensing a person approaching, she glanced back. Her hair whipped around in the wind, flowing toward me and partially covering her tear-streaked face. Her honey brown eyes raised to meet mine. Deep inside, warmth and remembrance surged.

I shoved my hands in my pockets to prevent myself from reaching out to her and pulling her against me. My throat constricted, and my eyes burned. My chest ached. An urge to crush her against me and breathe her in, to comfort her and dry away those tears grew, and I fought it. I hunted her down to explain, not to reunite.

"Who is she?"

It took me a moment to place her question. "A tutor."

Her forehead wrinkled, and she stepped back.

"My daughter's tutor," I amended. I looked around the vacant beach and gestured to a dry location closer to the shelter of the dunes. "Sit? I'll explain."

She crisscrossed her legs, taking a space about a foot away from me on the sand. I fought the desire to pull her onto my lap. I tried to not remember how she felt against me, how it felt to hold her close as we talked. I shoved it all down. I pressed against my sternum, seeking to alleviate the building pressure. *Get on with it.*

"Do you remember when I told you about the girl in Somalia, the one who died?"

She nodded.

"I adopted her sister. I wanted to give her a different life."

"Why didn't you tell me?"

"I didn't think it would work out. I couldn't legally adopt her from Somalia. The U.S. doesn't allow it. My lawyer had some ideas. She pulled some strings. In some parts of the world, with enough money, anything is possible. I knew this, but I didn't think it would really apply to me. I thought by pursuing the adoption I was keeping her alive and safe. And, I mean, it's good it all worked out. It probably sounds like I'm not happy about it?" I questioned. Her blank expression reminded me to get on with it. "I'm just trying to explain that it didn't really feel like something that would really happen. Not any time soon. And then it did."

"Why leave like that? With a letter?"

A white seagull flew overhead, squawking high above us.

"I...I don't like goodbyes."

"That's a shitty excuse." She pushed her shoulders back. Her hands lay still in her lap.

"It's not an excuse. It's the truth. And besides, telling you...how was I supposed to tell the twenty-two-year-old girl I'm seeing that I adopted a twelve-year-old girl?"

"Just like that."

"It was a nail in the coffin. There was no point in hashing it out."

"Why? Because I'm twenty-two? I'm actually twenty-three, but…" Her hands waffled in the air for a moment. "Why are you so caught up on age? Why does my age matter so much to you?"

I scooped sand into my hand and let it filter through my fingers. My throat tightened, and swallowing became a chore. I gazed out over the ocean, seeking the calm it brought me, matching my breaths to the roll of the inbound waves.

"It's not your age, per se…it's that you have so much in front of you. It's all that you have in front of you. I refuse to get in the way of that."

"So, your fear is that I'll fall for you so hard I won't finish my master's? I'll follow you around in hopes of becoming your stay at home wife? Something like that? Is that your fear?"

Shame threatened to drown me. I'd never put it in words, but hearing it said made me feel foolish. Egotistical. Conservative.

"I'm a single father. You need to be out having fun with kids your own age." Even as I said the words, I hated every single one of them and on some level recognized them for what they were—an ineffectual defense.

"Right," she said, drawing it out, calling me out with one slow word. She stood and dusted the sand from her legs. Tiny grains flew at me, biting my raw skin as they hit. "For the record, how you treated me was incredibly immature. At a certain point, age becomes a number and nothing more. I'd say I've been the more mature party in our relationship." I bowed my head and dug my toes into the sand. "When I got that letter, I didn't know what to think. I assumed you were in danger. That you had to leave. I would've been beyond panicked, except Poppy spoke to Gabe, and he told her you were safe. But he didn't think you were going to return."

I hadn't planned on it. But Gabe also told Poppy what I'd wanted him to tell her so Luna wouldn't be scared. So she'd move on. The kind of thing I'd do in high school, letting a friend talk to a friend.

The words "I'm sorry" were on my lips, but I couldn't force myself to say them. Those words might be a bridge to reconciliation, and that wasn't the answer. I stood by my decision. How I handled it might not have been the best, but as much as I wanted Luna, she and I couldn't be together.

"Why did you return?" Her question held anger, the emotion I'd hoped for when I decided to leave a letter behind.

"Jasmine, my daughter. This seems like a good place for her to adjust. I also…just, practical reasons. I didn't want to continue living in Connecticut."

"You spent the holidays with your family?"

"With my brother. His wife and kids. We spent Christmas and New Year's with them."

"That must have been nice."

"It was good. It's hard to be a guest for too long. Hard to have a guest for too long…"

Luna wrapped her arms around herself, her lips in a firm line, stoic. The air between us blew cold and hard. I hated it. My Luna was warmth and sun and the stars and the moon. A guiding light. The cold wall in front of me, that wasn't my Luna. But it was what I created.

"If Jasmine wants to come to the center, I'd be happy to

spend time with her. We have a number of teen science programs." Her professional demeanor sliced me.

I swallowed and forced a response. "She barely knows English."

"It would be good for her." She held her chin high.

There was no reason to fight her. "A teen science program...I'll talk to Cali about it. I'm sure you're right."

The topaz in her light brown irises held an icy glaze. All her warmth gone. I'd done that. And dammit, that was never my intent.

twenty-six

LUNA

"There's my Luna. I've missed you, sweet one. Come out and have some tea with me."

"How've you been?" I wrapped my arms around Alice and soaked up her warmth. I could bask in her grandmotherly aura all day. True, she spoke of spirits and pails of water and owned an ungodly number of cats, but in her presence the kookiness dissipated.

"I've been good." She grazed her thumb over my cheek, tilting my face up, measuring me. "Come."

We both sat down on her back porch, overlooking the marsh. The golds and greens mixed, and the wildlife staccato vibrated around us. Winter covered the southern island with a tender stroke. The days were chillier, and some nights brought frost. A sweater combatted the chilly air on most days. The reddish-brown hues displayed prominently along the landscape offered the predominant evidence of our distance from the sun.

She passed me my tea, and my fingers warmed around the ceramic mug.

"Your family is good?"

"Yes, they are." I smiled. "They will release Dad to work again within a week or two. That'll make Mom happy. It drives her a little crazy when he's just sitting around, even if it is doctor's orders."

"And she's working so hard? Understandable. He's going back to roofing?"

I sighed out my disappointment. "Yeah, I think so. But this time he's returning as a manager, and he'll be over-seeing several sites. He's been offered a supervisor role before, but he's always liked being one of the workers. Says sweating in the sun makes him feel worthwhile. But I think this latest fall made him face the fact he's getting older."

"There aren't many things in life that are harder to face than getting older. But it's as certain as the sun rising. And the alternative, well, once we're nourishing the soil, our conscience is no longer." She paused, her dark ebony eyes honing in. "But this sad face. 'Tis not for your family, no?"

"Maybe. I always thought my parents would divorce once my sister and I left home. And they haven't yet, but…"

"You believe they should?"

"Sometimes. It's not what I wish for them, but I'm not sure they make each other happy."

"How long have your parents been married?"

"Twenty-five years. They've been together longer."

"Relationships ebb and flow, like a sea through the

marsh. Maybe you're right, or maybe they bring each other a happiness you can't easily see. But it's not for you to concern yourself with. The only two people who know the rhythm of a relationship are the two banging those drums and spinning the music." She paused and placed her weathered hand over my knee. "If they decide to part, their love for you won't change."

"Oh, I know that. I do. I spent so much time thinking they stayed together for us, you know, me and my sister. And yet they're still together. Maybe I was wrong."

"Or maybe on some days you were right, and some days you were wrong. Ebb and flow. But this sad face. It is not for your family. Tell me."

I sipped my tea. Her kind eyes and gentle words tempted me to unload. Poppy still hadn't returned from Las Vegas where she'd gone to get certified in restaurant management. I'd thought about calling my sister, but she'd already written Tate off as someone I needed to forget. Nova wanted me to focus on my next gig, and she seemed particularly keen on me traveling the world like I'd always wanted. Alice's ebony fingers squeezed mine. *What to say?*

"I liked a guy more than he liked me." I lifted my shoulders and exhaled loudly enough to blend in with our surroundings. "A tale as old as time, right?"

"Are we talking about my Adrian?"

I kicked at a dried, shriveled leaf on the step, masking my smile with my hair as I bent my head down. Very few people ignored Tate's wishes and called him Adrian.

"Darlin', take it slow. All you need is patience."

"Patience? He left months ago, leaving me a letter. Didn't respond to any of my texts. And now he's adopted a daughter. It's over. And he's hired this…" I stopped myself. I wouldn't go there. I refused to spew jealous hate.

"Adrian is a good man. He's healing. Sometimes when we heal, we have to protect the wound until it scabs. This girl he's adopted, she's part of his healing. He's a little lost, but he'll find his way. It'll come together fine." She put her left hand flat on my forehead, then reached for my right wrist and placed her palm over my pulse. She closed her eyes and hummed, weaving left and right. The vibrations of her song soothed the deep sadness rooted in my chest. When she opened her eyes, concern flashed momentarily across her features. She let me go.

"Sit. I'll be right back."

She rattled around, opening drawers in an old dresser left outside on the back porch. She stepped down and disappeared behind the brick altar. She came around the corner, her hips swaying as she sang in a rhythmic mix of Spanish and English. Mesmerized, I observed. Her bare feet crunched the leaves as she returned, holding out a woven necklace with a piece of shell for a pendant. "You wear this. Keep the good spirits with you, *si*?"

My fingers clasped the smooth shell, and I nodded my submission. I didn't believe in the world of spirits Alice succumbed to, but I'd never dispute it. After all, her world version was far more colorful than mine.

She uttered one last word to me before I drove away. "Patience."

The next day, I stopped by the Sail Shop and picked up a big, hooded sweatshirt. I rummaged through my shell collection and found an unblemished starfish and a sand dollar. Then I stopped by to bring the welcome gifts to

Tate's daughter. It felt like the cordial, southern thing to do.

Even if Tate didn't want a relationship with me, there was nothing that said we couldn't have a friendship. And surely his new daughter could use an extra friend. There weren't many of us locals on the island in the offseason, and in the height of summer, the vast majority dropped in and out for a week or two at most. In such a secluded environment, the year-round residents banded together.

When I arrived at Tate's, I found him outside pumping air into a bicycle tire. His friend Gabe leaned against the wall of the shed, chugging a bottle of water. Gabe smiled in recognition. Tate remained crouched on the ground, testing the tire.

"I brought a few things for Jasmine, to welcome her." I scooped them up and brought them over.

"She's out walking on the beach," Gabe offered, not moving from his spot. "How've you been doing, Luna?"

"Good. What about you?" I asked him while I locked eyes with Tate. Chills washed over me.

"No complaints. Have you heard from Poppy?"

"A few days ago. She's enjoying Vegas."

"Is she thinking about staying?"

"In Vegas? No, I don't think so."

Gabe muttered something and turned to head inside. Poppy claimed he had no interest in her, but that wasn't what it seemed like to me. He paused at the door. "Good to see you, Luna."

Alone, an awkwardness settled between Tate and me. His windblown hair fell around his face, and he pushed the unruly, curly strands behind his ear. My heart pounded with the force of crashing waves, but I

226

contained the turmoil. I refused to present as anything other than calm, refused to be anything other than mature.

I held out the gifts for Jasmine. "You can give your daughter these. If she'd like to stop by the center, I can take her through some of our educational presentations. Even if she doesn't understand the words, she'll comprehend what I'm showing her."

"Thanks." He reached for the sweatshirt and covered the shells with his palm. "Luna..." His eyes pleaded with me. "I didn't mean—"

"It's okay," I interrupted, not wanting to hear what he didn't mean.

"Is it?" He swiped the beads of sweat off his brow, his back to the distant afternoon sun.

"No." My gaze locked on those aqua blue eyes, and my ribcage contracted. I forced myself to breathe. I forced a calm normal. "But it will be."

I left Tate behind and continued on my way to meet the new scientist who joined the team. Whereas I had accepted a one-year term, William Walker had accepted a permanent position. I had considered applying for his position, but for me, this place served as a steppingstone.

When I entered our group room, William and another woman sat at a picnic table in the middle of the research lab, eating orange Italian ice.

"I see you've already found one of the best things the island has to offer."

William smiled. "I'm gonna gain weight. This stuff is delish."

"Pina colada is my favorite."

The woman sitting at the table, a petite redhead with

freckles all across her face, spoke up. "I'll try that next time. This mango is a bit too sweet."

"Hi. I'm Luna." I extended my hand, curious who my fellow scientist had brought with him for our initial meeting.

"Oh, hi. I'm Tegan, William's wife." I glanced between the two of them. The dark-skinned William who I had thought from his resume wasn't that much older than I was, and the young, almost albino looking girl, who I had to believe was younger. Tegan twirled her spoon in the cup, her gaze down at the floor.

"You both look so young."

William flashed a wide set of sparkling white teeth. "We got married while Tegan was still in undergrad. We're used to people being surprised, right?" he asked her, grinning. "It's not like our life ended after marriage."

A flush covered her pale skin, and she bowed her head.

Dr. Wilton entered the room and greeted me with a hug.

"Luna, welcome back."

Tegan excused herself, and Dr. Wilton, William, and I discussed plans for spring. Our meeting ran long, as Dr. Wilton had a lengthy list of items for us to work on preparing for the upcoming board meeting. William glanced at his watch with increasing frequency the longer our boss talked.

"William, do you need to be somewhere?" I asked.

"Yeah. I'm sorry. I'm supposed to meet Tegan back at the ferry. I didn't know our meeting would run this long. I promised Tegan we'd do some shopping for the new apartment."

"William, always feel free to interrupt me. If you need

to get out of here, go. We're relaxed around here. Right, Luna?"

"You couldn't ask for a better place to work. Or for a better boss." A look of surprise flashed across Dr. Wilton's face. "You know you're great to work for, right?" I explained myself to William. "He gives you a substantial amount of independence but involves you in the research. You'll learn a ton under him, and you'll get to spearhead your own projects."

Dr. Wilton said nothing, but his soft smile told me he appreciated my outspoken compliment.

"I'll update you in the morning on anything you miss," I told William as he gathered up his files and notebook.

When he departed, Dr. Wilton dove back into the presentation. From my perspective, anything to get my mind off Tate served as a welcome distraction, so I didn't care how late we worked.

"Luna, I think we should include a couple of slides on the contacts you made in Florida."

"Oh, I can do that. I can also include a summary of some similar research coming out of the University of Miami."

He chewed on the end of his pen thoughtfully. "Would you be up for grabbing dinner and working through this? We can bring our laptops and finish this up. I'd like to get the first draft done tonight, so Barbara has a couple of days to review and make changes."

"No problem at all."

twenty-seven

TATE

The screen door slammed behind me, and I closed my eyes, attempting to unsee Luna driving away. I hurt her, and the fucked-up thing was I hurt, too. Our little carefree whatever-happens-will-happen relationship had morphed into more. In another country, I could package it up in a box and ignore it. Here, I couldn't box anything up. She picked out the paint colors in my house. Every fixture, the vents, she even found the flooring I walked on. I couldn't shut the door on her because memories lived and breathed on every surface.

If the adoption had come later...we'd probably be living together by now, in an idyllic vacation from reality. Resenting the adoption and the impact on my life was wrong. Didn't make the emotions any less real.

"You okay?" Gabe asked from the kitchen table. File

folders covered half the surface, all part of the reason for his visit.

"Fine."

He scratched his head and resumed typing. I leaned against the kitchen counter, staring through the long room to the ocean, seeking equilibrium. All these fucking emotions leaked out, and I'd plug the hole, and it would work for a while until they found another break. I needed to go for a run, or a swim, or something to clear my head. I had to save my ship, keep it above water. Re-focus.

"All right. I'm about to complete these transfers and close out these accounts. Are you sure this is what you want to do?"

"What are you worried about?" My mind wasn't anywhere near my financial affairs.

"If anyone is tracking you, these kinds of deposits and purchases are going to hit your FICA, your social. Legal title changes. It's kind of like not using a credit card when someone's tracking you. You're about to use some pretty big credit cards, so if anyone out there is trying to locate you, well, they're gonna."

"No one is tracking me." No matter how often I insisted to my brother and Gabe I wasn't on the run, they didn't believe me.

Over the holidays, I'd worked out the business logistics with my brother. He dropped his suit contesting the will. He insisted he'd pay me over time for a percentage of the business. Now I just wanted to get my financial affairs in order.

I'd set my brother up as executor of my will should anything happen to me, with everything going to Jasmine. I wanted to get everything set up so if something happened, say the random Great White off the coast of NC struck or I had a stroke, she'd be taken care of.

Adopting a young teenage girl hadn't been easy—no fault of Jasmine's. On some days it felt like I had a stranger in my house, or maybe I was babysitting someone else's kid, but this bit of logistics, I could take care of.

"Do it," I told Gabe.

He tapped some keys then folded his laptop. "Okay, it's done. Now, what do you want to do for the rest of the day?"

"I don't know. Bike ride? Jasmine should be done in thirty minutes or so. We can go for a nice ride and grab a late lunch?"

"She's pretty determined to listen to those tapes you got her every day, isn't she?"

"Yeah, she is. She spends so much time upstairs in her room. She's always studying. But sometimes I wonder if she's up there to avoid me."

"I don't know, man. She looks at you like you hung the moon. Reminds me of the way my mom's cat used to treat us after we adopted her from the shelter. I think she's a hard worker. You've given her a chance at a completely new life, and she wants to do her best."

"I can't imagine. Moving to a new country, not knowing the language. I mean, the adoption agency gave me lots of info on what she's going through, but I still can't imagine it."

He rapped the table with his fist, then gave me the drop-the-bullshit look he perfected in undergrad. "Why'd you end things with Luna?"

"I didn't end anything." His facial expression stopped me short. "Technically," I muttered.

"Dude. You left her a Dear John. Then didn't respond to any texts."

"I lost my phone."

"Seriously? You lost your phone when you went out of the country?" Lost wasn't quite the right word. I left it at the hotel, charging in D.C. Didn't realize it until I touched down in Heathrow on my connecting flight. I bought a temp phone and had the hotel return my phone to my brother's house. There was something about disconnecting. I found it easy to do, but a shade of guilt chased me for it.

"Whatever. Look, the only reason I'm saying anything is that I know from Poppy that Luna was pretty hurt."

I flinched.

"Poppy and I don't talk a lot about you guys, but it's come up."

"I didn't even know you and Poppy were in touch."

"We text."

"Hmm."

"Shut it. Look, my point is, I think I get why you cut her off. Knowing you, you have it in your head you can't date her now that you've adopted a kid."

"She's young."

"If you're not into her, fine by me, man. My point is adopting a kid doesn't mean you have to live like a monk. I mean, I know single parents sometimes feel like not dating is part of putting the kid first, but in your case, you've adopted a girl who has seen a lot. She's not a young child. I think she can handle seeing a healthy adult relationship. It might even be good for her."

"She's only thirteen." If her birth records were correct, she was barely thirteen.

"You and I both know she's mature for her age." I glared at him, hating the truth, not him, and he put his hands up in the air. "Look, I don't know shit. But it seems to me, making yourself miserable will not help Jasmine in any way. She's a part of your life now, so in my opinion, you need to focus on living a full, healthy life. Because she's part of it. Sequestering yourself from the world might be something you get off on doing, but it's not healthy. You need to force yourself to open up to others, date and such, so you create a healthy environment for her. Your personal life doesn't end when you become a parent."

"You've been thinking a lot about this."

"Some. I had nothing to read last night, so I picked up some stuff the agency sent you. It got me thinking. I get why you brought her back here. I know Gregg disagrees, but I agree with you that a tutor for this first part will be an easier transition than entering middle school without knowing the language. Especially entering a very white middle school." His eyebrows rose with the word *white*. Yeah, the Connecticut private school we went to, and the one my brother planned to send his kids to, qualified as extremely white. Didn't mean the students wouldn't accept her, but her skin would be one more difference. Regardless, when I met with them, the school encouraged me to take this route as they weren't set up to take on a foreign student like her.

I had nothing else to say, so I unpacked the dishwasher, effectively terminating our conversation. Gabe didn't get the hint.

"The tutor you hired. She's pretty hot."

"Hmm." I hired Cali for her educational experience,

sight unseen. Plus, her willingness to come out to the island, as opposed to me having to bring Jasmine to the mainland daily, was a big win. In all the time I'd spent with Cali, I hadn't thought of her as anything other than my adopted daughter's educator.

"It sucks Poppy isn't here. I'd been hoping to spend some time with her. Unlike you, I don't like to be lonely, if you know what I mean," he droned on. "But you know, she's not the only young hottie on the island. Maybe I'll reach out to Luna, see what she's doing tonight."

A slick plate slipped out of my hand and shattered on the tile floor.

He laughed. *Mother fucker.*

twenty-eight

LUNA

> Any interest in joining Jasmine and me for
> dinner tonight? She'd like to meet you.

The text taunted me for hours before I responded. Three days had passed since I dropped off my mature, I'm-an-adult-and-above-all-of-this gift for Jasmine.

Dinner wasn't what had me hesitating. It was more of whether I was willing to move forward as if nothing had happened between us. I debated showing him how I felt by responding with a snappy "no" and proceeding to give him the cold shoulder, a sure sign I wasn't really okay with how he treated me. But something about that felt juvenile, and I worried playing that game would prove his fears about my youth correct.

So, I put on my big girl panties, as they say, and went to dinner with a cherry pie from the market tucked beside me on the seat and a bottle of wine. I spent at least twenty minutes perusing the cabernet selection, debating if bringing wine meant I expected more than a friendly dinner. I concluded that almost all adults brought wine to dinner, and even if they didn't, I needed the fortification.

Through the screen door, I could see into the kitchen. Tate sat at the bar, working on his laptop. I knocked lightly, and he smiled that slow grin. My insides plummeted and swirled. He pushed the screen door open, holding it wide for me to enter.

"Hi." I held up my dinner contributions. "For you."

"You didn't need to do that." He lifted the items from my arms and placed them on the counter. "Thanks for coming."

"Where's Gabe?"

"Back in New York. He only came down for the day. He needed my signature on some documents. Easy to do when you have your pilot's license."

"Must be nice." I leaned back on the counter and stared down at his white socks. "Oh. I should take off my shoes."

"Nah. No worries. We track sand in all the time. You're probably better off keeping your shoes on so you're not stepping in it." *We.* I looked around for Jasmine, but there was no sign of her.

He wore an off-white cotton sweater and faded blue jeans. Bare feet would have made him model worthy, but in February, thick socks made sense. His new hair cut, short and trim, leant him an older, mature vibe. The small fire in the den filled the living area with a woodsy campfire aroma.

"I didn't realize that fireplace worked."

"I had someone clean out the chimney. It's one of those

convertible chimneys that could be used for gas, but I had it set up as wood burning." He shoved his hands into his back pockets, and an awkward silence fell between us.

My cheeks burned. I had nothing to say. A familiar pull, an invisible connection between us, flowed. I rubbed the center of my chest and scolded myself. *He doesn't feel it. It's in your head.* I stepped closer to the fire, feigning the need for warmth. Then I remembered my purpose. "Where's Jasmine?"

"Oh, she's upstairs. Let me call her down." He climbed a few steps and shouted, "Jasmine. Come on down." Faintly from up above, a door clicked.

"She took the third floor as her room," he offered as he gazed up the stairs.

"That's a great space." The third floor offered panoramic, unfettered views of the ocean. The ceiling matched the roofline and created alcoves. When I'd been helping him renovate, we'd put in window seats in the alcoves and built-in bookshelves below them. It made an ideal girl's bedroom, and it had an attached full bathroom.

"Yeah, maybe you can help her decorate it? I put a mattress and bed frame up there, thinking she could pick out what she likes. But every time I show her something, she shakes her head and says, 'No, thank you.'"

Just then, a tall shadow filled the space behind Tate. He turned and smiled at her. "There you are. This is my friend, Luna. Luna, this is Jasmine."

I held out my arm, and her gaze fell to my outstretched hand. She placed her slender ebony fingers in mine. My skin appeared ghostly, almost luminescent, next to her raven color. High cheekbones gave her a regal appearance. Her short hairstyle, trimmed close to her scalp, offset her mahogany irises beautifully. Like her adopted father, she wore a cotton long sleeve sweater, jeans and socks, only her socks were multi-colored and looked to be handmade. Her toes wiggled, raising the yellow and red threads.

"You like the socks? Alice made them for her. Did you know she knits socks? That woman can do anything."

Jasmine stood tall, shoulders back. I had no idea how much she understood of our spoken words, but something told me she could read any situation, and as her gaze flitted back and forth between Tate and me, she might sense more than I wanted.

"I love the socks," I offered.

Jasmine licked her lips then spoke. "You." She swallowed then licked her lips again. "Do. You. Know. Alice." She spoke with perfect pronunciation and her head bobbed slightly with each uttered word.

"I do." I smiled the same smile I used when a child at the center exhibited shyness. Remembering how frustrated I got when I'd visited a friend in Mexico City and her family spoke at lightning speed in Spanish, I pointedly slowed my words. "Alice is a good friend. I love her." I placed my hand over my heart with the word love, and she beamed, flashing white upper teeth that were mostly straight, other than one incisor that tilted at an angle.

"Here, you two sit down." Tate had already set out three places at the kitchen table. I followed the two of them, waiting for a cue for which seat to take.

Jasmine stood two feet from the table. Her poise struck me as both remarkable, and a sign she wasn't yet comfortable in her new home.

"Which seat do you normally—?" Confusion flashed, and I started over. "You. Sit."

Tate brought a platter of crackers, cheese, and grapes over to the table.

"Jasmine sits here. I sit here. You can sit here." He placed himself between us at the rectangular table, with himself sitting at the head.

There were so many questions I wanted to ask Jasmine, but I didn't want to put her on the spot. I'd been in a similar position, where I was learning a language, and knew how frustrating it could feel, trying to decipher every word and feeling like a conversation was nothing more than a verbal test of skill.

Something told me Tate felt similarly, as he spoke more slowly when talking to her, and took care not to put her in the spotlight. But he spoke more fluidly than I did, and she seemed to understand him.

I thought back on some initial phrases you learned when studying a language and put some of those to use. "How old are you?"

"Thirteen."

I already knew the answer and smiled at her enthusiasm. She could pass for eighteen. If I'd met her on campus, I would have assumed she was a freshman, or maybe even a sophomore.

"Do you like it here?" I meant in America, but the moment I said it, I knew Tate interpreted the question differently.

"Yes."

Tate spoke up. "She's doing great. She meets with her tutor Monday through Friday. And Alice has taken her under her wing. She spends time with Alice every weekend and some evenings." With his head turned to me, and in a rapid side comment, he added, "I half expect her to come home chanting."

I traced my fingers over the charm Alice gave me. Jasmine's gaze followed my movement, and she smiled.

"Alice. Is. From. Africa. Like. Me."

I remembered what Alice once told me, and I repeated it. "Alice has roots in three countries. Cuba. The United States. And Somalia." Jasmine beamed. "You are both from Somalia. What a small world, huh?"

Confusion flashed, and I knew I'd spoken too quickly. I tried to think of an easier way to convey the small world concept and gave up.

"Nice," I said and then realized I'd said it like I was talking to a deaf child.

For dinner, Tate had roasted a vegetable mix and tossed a fresh salad. Within minutes, we finished the meal, offering tight smiles to each other. I got up to serve the pie.

I watched as Jasmine tentatively dipped the prongs of her fork into the pink filling. She placed the tiniest amount on her tongue and tapped it against the top of her mouth. She seemed to like it somewhat and ate about half of her slice. Something told me she was far too polite, or too grateful, to turn down any food, even if she found it horrible.

After dinner, Jasmine and I got up to clear the dishes, and Tate shooed us out. "Go upstairs and check out her bedroom. Maybe you'll get some ideas for furniture or decorations?"

She led the way up to her freshly painted room. The crisp white we painted the whole place in had worked to brighten the space and create a calming guest room. But now that a young girl would live in the room, the plain white struck me as far too barren for a teenager's room.

Books were placed on the bookshelves in perfect alignment, tallest to shortest. On one shelf, notebooks filled the shelf in tidy stacks. Clothes folded in neat piles on the floor lined one wall. I knew without checking her closet would hold an orderly line of shoes and hanging clothes.

"I can bring over my laptop, and we can go over some ideas for bedspreads, or art for the walls, maybe some posters or frame some photos. Get you a dresser for your clothes."

Her eyes crinkled around the corners. I'd talked too fast. I also suspected my word choice might be beyond her current English level. It would be easier to show her pictures.

"Nice room. We can make it pretty," I said.

She looked around the room, then at me. "The. Room. Is. Beauty. Full."

"Yes, it is."

"I. Study. You. Be. With." She hesitated, then added, "Father."

She stood, poised, while discreetly massaging the right side of her jaw. She cast a wishful glance to the bookshelf.

I got it. Sure, most other thirteen-year-olds would climb on the bed and grab an electronic device of choice and act like I'd already left the room. Jasmine wasn't like that…yet. But she'd get there.

"Would you like to come to the research center one day this week? I'll show you shells? Fish? Turtles?" She smiled and nodded, but I didn't feel confident she knew what I'd said. It didn't matter. I'd see her again.

When I joined Tate downstairs, he was wiping down the counters.

"Her room turned out nice." The last time I'd seen it, it had been a shell of white walls and built-ins.

"She needs furniture. I think my idea to get what she likes wasn't a good one."

"I think she'll like anything you get her right now. She seems so eager to please. If you want, I'll show her a dresser and bedspread, maybe a bedside table and lamp? I can line up several options. Get her to point at what she likes best? I don't think she'd ever ask for anything. If I were to guess, she's probably overwhelmed with all she has now."

"Yes, the adoption agency warned about that. Said to not overwhelm her with gifts."

"I think you're doing a good job."

He wrung out the cloth and hung it over the side of the kitchen sink. He exhaled, and his shoulders rounded. "Thanks. I don't know what I'm doing. It's good to hear you don't think I'm bungling it too badly."

I laughed. "Well, let's be real. I know nothing about it. But she seems happy. She's healthy. Focused and determined. Those are all good things, right? And she referred to you as father."

"She did?" he asked, incredulous.

"Yeah." I didn't get the sense she felt he was her father yet, but using the word was an undeniable start. "She was massaging her jaw, though. Do you think she might need a dentist?"

"Oh. No. She's been thoroughly examined by all the doctors, including a dentist. She's healthy. They said to expect her jaw muscles may be sore as she uses different muscles…you know, learning an unfamiliar language."

"Interesting. Do you give her Advil or something?"

"I haven't yet, but if she needs it…" He paused, leaving his incomplete thought hanging, and rested his palms on the counter. "Want to go for a walk?"

"Sure."

He walked over to the stairs and shouted up the stairwell. "Jasmine, we're going out for a walk."

He stood three steps up, waited, glancing between me and the top of the stairs. After a beat, Jasmine answered with her own yell. "Okay. I. Read. Then. Go to. Sleep."

"Good night," he shouted.

Then she called, "Good. Night."

I smiled at the scene, and his gaze washed over me. "What?"

"I think you two are making excellent progress toward being a family. I like the new hair cut." I had liked his hair longer and wavy, but he looked just as attractive. The trim cut wiped out the sun's highlights, leaving only dark strands. He reached into the hall closet and pulled out a long winter coat.

"Thanks. Here. It's cold out on the beach. But it's a clear night."

All bundled up, we made our way down the wooden boardwalk, our hands buried deep in our coat pockets. The stars lit the night sky, a million brilliant pinpricks over an enigmatic sea. In the distance, lights from the oil rigger off the coast danced. One ship traversed the coast with a spotlight combing the shore.

"You think they're fishing?" I asked.

He stopped and studied it. "In February? Here? I don't

think so, but…they're close. Maybe it's just a yacht traveling down to warmer waters."

"Judging from the marina, it seems there are many of those. Still, February's a bit off season." I scrunched my nose, trying to remember when yachts from far away showed up in the marinas at home. It seemed like they were there year-round.

"Those yachts are the kind that hire someone to make the trip. Wouldn't expect the owners to head out in undesirable conditions."

"That's true. Spring breaks are around the corner. Someone might move their yacht down to the Keys so they can enjoy it in the upcoming season."

"It's kind of nice thinking about what a ship is doing out there, right? I used to do that all the time when we'd see lights. Of course, in the South China Sea, you're also looking for signs it might be pirates or…" He trailed off.

We walked silently and passed several dark, oceanfront homes, before I gathered up my courage.

"Tate, when you were away, did you ever think of me?"

He found a place to sit on an enormous piece of driftwood beached near the dunes. I joined him on the log, placing a couple of feet between us, and waited, hoping he would give me answers.

"Every single night when I looked at the moon."

"Yeah, I suppose my name sort of does that to people."

"And every single day."

"But you couldn't call? Or text me back?" I didn't want to sound like a whining kid, but sitting there, I needed to understand.

"What would be the point? An awkward hello that

reminds us not only of the distance but that we're in two different places in our lives? I'm a parent now. And you… you're…a kid."

"A kid? I'm a kid? You're unbelievable, you know that?" I stood and brushed sand off the back of my pants. "It's not like you thought I was a kid when you had your dick crammed down my throat."

"Luna, that's not what I meant, and you know it."

"Do I? I don't think I do. Why don't you spell it out for me? After all, I'm a kid, so better speak slowly and with extreme care."

"You've got your entire life in front of you. That's what I mean."

"Oh, then by all means…go away for months, don't get in touch." I glared down at his bowed head. "I mean…I don't know what I mean because I don't know what you mean."

He pulled his hair back and looked past me at the ocean, then stood and finally faced me.

"You know what I think?" I shook my index finger at him as anger surged. "I think you're too chickenshit to put yourself out there. I think you hate missing people, so you wall yourself off. I think you don't know how to express your emotions, so you don't even try."

"Maybe you're right. Missing people, it hurts, and I hate it. But you're wrong. I'm not afraid to try. I just…why would you even, at your age, want to date a guy like me? With a thirteen-year-old adopted daughter? Stop and think about it."

"Why wouldn't I want to date a guy like you? Look at what you've done with your life. You've devoted years to stopping illegal fishing practices in areas of the world where almost no one else gives a damn. You've helped women who couldn't get access to the medical care they needed. You adopted a stranger because you knew she was in a dangerous place. And now, Poppy spoke to Gabe. She told me what you're doing now as a lobbyist."

"Those are all reasons to want to work with me, not date me. I'm more than willing to write you a stellar recommendation for your next job, or graduate school."

I clenched my fists in my coat pockets and looked out over the ocean and up into the constellations.

"Okay. You want to know why I want to date you? My dad always told me I should find a guy who gave me butterflies and who shares my passions. You do that for me. Not that it matters. But, with you, I feel more." I could have gone on and said more, but my cheeks burned. Embarrassment choked my words. He'd made it clear he didn't feel the same.

"Did you feel more on your date the other night?"

"What date?"

"I saw you walking into the Shoals Club for dinner." He buried his toes in the sand.

"It wasn't a date."

"He seemed interested," he said, skeptical.

I huffed. "No. Not a date. Work."

He puckered his lips thoughtfully then took a couple of steps forward. I followed along, and he pointed into the night. "See those bright stars? The ones that are a little brighter than the others? It looks like a W? Or an M?"

A million tiny pricks of light hovered far above. I didn't see a letter, and I didn't feel like hunting for constellations. "Yes, I see it," I lied.

"It's Cassiopeia. Have you heard that story?"

"It's the one where she's super vain and gets thrown up to the stars as punishment by Zeus's wife. And Cepheus loves her so, and begs Zeus to be thrown up with her, and he does." I'd spent enough time under the night sky to have heard a good number of stories about the stars.

"Those stars there…that's Cepheus." He pointed into the sky, but I gazed at the ship, anchored across the way, its light brighter than any of the stars above. Tate continued. "His wife, Cassiopeia, wasn't perfect, but he loved her so much. And now they spend an eternity together, in love."

For me, the beauty of the night sky lay in the collective whole, not in attempting to piece together bright spots and historic designs. I did not understand how my conversation with Tate turned into a constellation discussion but had no desire to continue talking about the stars.

"Thanks for dinner."

He reached out, and I stepped back, out of his grasp. I couldn't bear his touch, not when he didn't want me. "See you later."

"I'll walk you home." He gave the offshore floating light one more thoughtful glance before guiding me up the trail to my place.

twenty-nine

TATE

When we arrived at her cottage, she turned to face me on her front doorstep. This was where a friend would say goodnight. She fidgeted with the strap on her pocketbook. The moonlight reflected on her golden strands and cast an opalescent glow.

"Good night." I didn't move away. She leaned closer. I pressed my hand against the door, caging her in, surrounding her. Her honey brown eyes darkened to a mahogany in the shadow. The eyes I never wanted to forget. The familiar light scent of coconut wafted through the breeze. I bent closer, breathing her in. She remained still, but her chest lifted and fell at a more rapid pace. I hovered over her, the inches between us serving as a barrier between what I should do and what I wanted. Her tongue flicked over her bottom lip, leaving a sheen over the full pink curve.

"God, Luna, I've missed you."

Her palm pressed against my chest, holding me away.

"Really?" The whispered question cut across the winter night. "I've missed you, too."

Those dark eyes met mine, and her fingers grazed my jaw with a light touch. My restraint snapped.

My mouth claimed hers. Familiar and warm. I kissed her slowly, remembering. My heart pounded, and my body quivered, as emotion I'd locked down leaked through the cracks.

A frantic urgency swept over us. She tugged at my sweater and explored beneath it, roaming over my bare chest, the winter air nipping the exposed skin. I lifted her shirt and tweaked her nipple, and it hardened beneath my touch. We couldn't get close enough, couldn't bare enough.

She wrapped her legs around my waist, and I pressed her against the wall, dry humping her like a horny teenager until the squawk of a nearby seagull reminded me how exposed we both were. I reached down for the doorknob, and we tumbled inside.

I kicked the door closed as she lifted her sweater and threw it across the room. I followed suit, then began unbuttoning my jeans, eager to be free of them. She did the same. I paused, taking her in. She stood before me in white silk panties and nothing else. The moonlight coated her skin. The lines of her flat, smooth belly were accented by night shadows. Her nipples peaked above the pearly curve of her breasts and her hair cascaded down her shoulders, wild and unkempt. She was gorgeous and wild, and a better man my age would stay away.

I stalked toward her, intent on claiming her as mine.

Screw being right. I angled her head up, my fingers tangled in her hair, and kissed her. As our tongues tangled, she gripped my cock, and the unexpected touch and pleasure almost sent me over the edge. I groaned, breaking our kiss, as the base of my spine tightened with need.

I pushed her down on the bed and crawled up her delectable body, kissing and sucking and biting my way up those long, toned legs to her apex. She lifted her hips to allow me to remove those prim and proper panties. And then I tasted her. Fuck, it had been so long. So long since I'd made her come with my tongue. Seen her body squirm as my fingers worked away on her. Heard her moan and twist and felt her quiver. So long since she chanted, "Th, th, th, th…Tate." Our acoustic musical melody.

I grinned as she fell apart, then kissed my way up along her body, bit her nipple until she squealed and spread her legs wide, wrapping them around me, welcoming me in. Her warmth and tightness encapsulated my throbbing cock, and fuck, she felt like home. We felt too fucking good, too right.

"Fuck, Luna. You feel so good, so tight. If you keep moving like that, I'm…" And then she tilted those hips up more as her fingers slid down and coaxed right above our joining. The sight of her working her clit combined with her moans and the tremors kneading my cock was all too much, and I exploded, pulsing deep into her.

I collapsed onto her, gasping for air. Kissed her shoulder, her neck, the soft skin below her ear.

"That was too fast. Sorry."

"I came, too." She ran her fingers to my hair and brushed her lips against mine. "It was perfect."

We held each other, with soft, slow touches. Relearning

our way around each other, as if neither of us could believe we were once again tangled together.

Once our heartrates had calmed, I pulled a light blanket over us and settled her onto my chest. I combed her hair with my fingers. "I've missed you. So much."

She lifted her head, studied me, then bent down and bit me.

"Ow."

"Could have fooled me," she scolded. "What the fuck, Tate? A note? No text? How is that remotely okay?"

A weight fell heavily over me. How to explain the detachment I fell into when away? As if I slipped through a portal to another world. It felt monumentally difficult to communicate to the other side. She waited for my response.

"I thought the note was best."

She pinched me, and I squirmed then caught her hand. "In retrospect, it was selfish. Cowardly. I didn't want to say goodbye to you, Luna. Not ever. It felt too difficult. And then, when I was away, I missed you too much. It felt easier to shut it down and block it out."

"Block what? Emotions?"

I teased her hair, combing out the knots.

"Yes…I suppose. You're the best thing that's happened to me in a long time, Luna." I wanted her forever, but I loved her too much to lock her down when she had so much to live for, so many choices to make.

"You know that goes two ways, right?" She raised her head so she could look me in the eye. I loved looking into those eyes, observing the varying shades, from day to night. Holding her in my arms, a contentment fell over me, an ease and warmth I'd missed. For me, she was perfection. But, for her, while it might feel good to her, I had no business destroying her dreams.

"That's a point we'll need to agree to disagree on. One day, you'll see. You're going to want to be with a younger guy, someone who is free to do everything you're supposed to do in your twenties. You have no business being saddled down with an old guy and his teenage daughter."

She slapped her hand against me, and the loudness of her skin against mine in the quiet of the cottage startled us both. "Shit, did I hurt you?"

I lifted the offending hand and kissed her fingers. "It didn't hurt."

"Good." She dropped a kiss to my chest. "Now, as far as this notion of yours that I'm going to dump you for a younger guy…I don't know what to do with that. But I was with a younger guy while you were away, and I still wanted you."

"You dated someone?" I wrapped a long strand of hair around my finger as I absorbed her words.

"My high school boyfriend. Brandon. He moved back home. To Florida."

My lungs deflated. Jealousy twirled. An irrational response. We were apart. I had known, had been aware, at her age, she'd move on. A faint light glinted across her ceiling.

"Brandon and I…" I froze. "I haven't had sex with anyone else since you. If that's what you're worried about, you know, since we just, you know, without a condom."

That hadn't been where my thoughts had gone at all. I hated the idea of any other man touching her.

"Brandon, he—"

"Stop. Don't tell me."

"I couldn't forget about you. Brandon and my sister tried to get me to go out on a date or two, but I had no interest."

Conflicting emotions swirled. A caveman desire to tell her she couldn't date anyone else, she couldn't be with anyone else, fought with a childish impulse to push her away and punish her for dating. But her naked form pressed against mine. The internal and the external clashed. Too much to take. "I've got to get going."

She draped her leg over mine and straddled me. Comprehension of my emotional state eluded her. The proximity of her still wet center had my cock twitching.

"Don't do that."

"I need to go."

"Don't block me out."

"That's not what—"

"Listen." She blocked my words with a finger pressed to my lips. "Too many relationships end because there's too much worry about what will be. Don't do that. Give us a chance."

I flipped her over onto her back to gain control. Those dark eyes glistened. I dipped my head and traced kisses down her neck, over her beating heart. She skimmed her calf along my thigh.

"Do you agree?" she prompted. I'd almost forgotten what we were talking about.

"No worry? Focus on now?" I asked. She grinned. God, to be that young and optimistic.

"You'll be gone in less than a year, right?"

She reached between us and tugged on my half-erect cock. "That's a year away. Who says you and Jasmine won't move with me? She's going to need a bigger community and friends. Let's take it day by day. See where life takes us."

I watched the magic of her hand, pressing my hips into it.

"Tate?"

"Yes?"

"Look here. In my eyes." I tore my gaze away from her hand. "I fell in love with you. I don't know what it will be like a year from now. But how about we take each day as it comes? Together, okay? And I wouldn't try to be a mother to Jasmine. But I've thought about it, and I can still be an important person in her life. I can be a mentor or a friend. I can be a woman she can rely on. You care about her, and you are giving her a new life. And I can be there for her too. No matter what happens between you and me, I can be there for her too. For both of you."

And fuck if I didn't explode in a completely different way.

Some time later, I kissed my girlfriend goodnight, promising to deliver her golf cart to her in the morning. My girlfriend. It felt like a juvenile label, and clearly the hormones had engulfed my head, because I felt a strong urge to magnify that descriptor.

It wasn't until the gravel ground beneath my feet as I made my way back to Jasmine that the reality of what I'd agreed to weighed down on me. Taking it day by day made all the sense in the world at twenty-two. But in my thirties, with an adopted teenager, it didn't. Did it?

My phone glowed on the countertop as I closed my front door with care. I tiptoed inside, overly cautious given Jasmine slept three floors above.

I picked up the phone, expecting a goodnight text from Luna.

My entire body froze. Ice.

Photo after photo. From an unrecognized number. Jasmine on the golf cart. Jasmine eating an Icee. Jasmine on a surfboard. Luna on the path beside my cottage. Luna and me on the beach. Earlier tonight.

thirty

TATE

I dropped my phone. Plastic cover on tile. The thud shattered the dark's stillness. Three by three, I ascended the stairs. With a shaky hand, I twisted the knob on the third floor. A body lay sprawled out on the bed, covers kicked off.

I gasped for air. Relief overflowed. Her chest rose and fell in peaceful slumber. I closed the door. Stopped by the second floor and locked my balcony door. Double-checked the locks on the double-hung windows overlooking the bedroom balcony. Reason informed me the lock on the door and the windows were essentially useless, as all someone would need to do was shatter the glass and step right through. Downstairs, I repeated the futile process, locking the windows we opened and closed throughout the day and never locked. But with that text, everything changed.

We weren't safe here. But we'd be safer together. I jumped on the cart and pressed the accelerator flat down, garnering as much speed as one could on an old battery-operated golf cart. The faint hum of the battery engine blended with the shrill cry of crickets and the dull, constant beat of waves.

As I ascended the hill to Luna's, the beacon light from the ship offshore caught my attention. I shivered. I rammed my fist against Luna's front door while simultaneously twisting the knob and discovering it unlocked. She popped up in bed, rubbing her eyes.

"Come on. Get your stuff. You're coming back with me."

"What?" she asked, dazed.

"You're in danger."

"Huh?"

She wasn't moving. Panic flooded my thoughts. I had to get back to Jasmine. An empty suitcase rested in the corner, and I flung it open, then one by one, opened the six dresser drawers and threw items in.

"Grab your toothbrush. Whatever you need."

She sat on the bed, head cocked sideways.

"Now. We're going. Now!"

She flinched. Then moved. She exited the bathroom with a toothbrush wrapped in toilet paper on one end. She threw it in the open suitcase, and I zipped it up.

"Let's go."

Barefoot, in a t-shirt that fell mid-ass, she followed me out to the golf cart. I turned and almost lost it.

"It's winter. Shit, Luna." In a flash, I re-entered her cottage, snatched up her coat, and threw it at her.

The icy wind penetrated as we sped back home to Jasmine. Luna's sleep fog lifted.

"What's going on?"

"They're on the island."

"Who?"

"Zane's men." The ship's beacon seemed to follow us along the street. An eerie awareness lingered. The panic gripping my ribcage eased as the street sloped downward behind the rows of houses dotting the shoreline.

"What do they want?"

"I'm going to guess money. I don't really know." But those photos. I knew his tactics. We used them in ports to grease negotiations. He wanted something. Those I loved were collateral.

"What...I'm so confused." She ran a hand over her face.

"He texted me tonight. Photos of you and Jasmine."

Understanding dawned. She slid closer and held on. I wrapped my arm around her shoulder and pulled her into my side.

When we arrived at my cottage, all seemed as I had left it. I unlocked the front door, and we tiptoed in. I pointed to the stairs and followed her up. On the landing, she turned, awaiting my direction. I pointed to my room. Then I remembered the balcony and grabbed her wrist, forcing her to change direction to the guest room on the other end of the hall.

Fuck. I didn't know what to do. The guest room didn't have a bed. Only a desk. I'd been using it as my office. Jasmine's room had twin built-in beds. That high up, they'd be safe from anyone breaking windows to get in.

Once again, I changed course and redirected Luna.

"You'll stay with Jasmine tonight," I whispered.

"What about you?" She circled my wrist, tugging to slow me down.

"You and Jasmine sleep. I'm going to make some calls first. Then I'll come up." I lied to her. I'd be up all night, on guard.

I stood in the doorway as Luna pulled back the bedspread and climbed into Jasmine's second bed.

I blew her a kiss from the tips of my fingers, then blew one to Jasmine for good measure. It was something my mom used to do from my doorway every night. A silly action that delivered a rogue wave of emotion, choking me.

I pulled the door closed and wished for a lock. A deadbolt. Or some heavy furniture to push against it. I had so little furniture. Had kept everything so sparse.

On the second landing, I opened my bedroom door wide. I positioned the bedroom chair so I could see both the balcony and the landing. I didn't have a gun or any way to fight anyone. With that thought, I ran downstairs and picked up the kitchen knife block and carried it back up with me to my chair.

With the chef's knife in easy reach, I dialed my one friend with connections.

Gabe didn't pick up. Not on the first call. Nor the second. By the fifth time I called, hanging up each time voice mail picked up, I was about to lose hope, assume he had it set to not ring at select hours.

"Tate?" Gabe answered, his voice heavy and throttled.

"I need your help."

"Shoot."

"Do you remember the repo guy I told you about?"

"Yeah. Let me guess. He got wind you have money."

"He sent photos of Jasmine and Luna."

"What'd he say?"

"Nothing. Just photos. Photos that show he's on the island. Or his goons are."

"No threat?"

"Nope. Just photos."

"That's…no threat? No demands?"

"No. But I know him. It's a first step. He's going to ask for something. He wants money. Can you help me access it quickly?"

"Don't fall for scare tactics." Shuffling sounds came through the line. "Man, I told you transferring shit out of offshore accounts might not be a smart idea."

"I'm not running from anyone. I just…"

"Yeah. It's what time in the morning and you're calling me?"

"I shouldn't have."

"I'm up now."

"So, what do I do?"

"I think you have to wait. Until he sends a request. Lets you know what he wants. It's an intimidation tactic. But whatever it is, don't worry about. We'll get it covered. Pay him off. It's gonna be fine."

"But with a guy like this, what's to say he's not gonna come back and ask for more money later? Or what if he doesn't even want money?" *Fuck. I could go to the police. Once he did more than send me photos. Or, no…* "Wait. What if I threatened to share all I know about his business? There's sick shit going on in Asia. I can share all I know about his illegal fishing practices."

"Does anyone really give a flying fuck about that?"

No, the answer was not really. Sure, some people tried to buy farm-raised fish and tried to make a difference, but irresponsible fishing practices rang like old news. "What about his slave ring? Indentured slaves? Slave trafficking? That would get attention, right?"

"Maybe. If you had photos. Where's this guy based?"

"He's American. Who the fuck knows where his businesses are legally located."

"Send me the names of his businesses. The proper names. I'll find country of origin. But you might be on to something. You put some heat on him, and he might decide you're not worth messing with."

The dark hallway beckoned.

"Or he'll end me."

"Shit, Tate. What have you gotten yourself messed up in?"

"He'll probably want more than I have. That's his MO. How he traps people."

"Nah. I've had some gangbuster years. I'm not worried about paying the douche, I just don't like recurring payments. I want one and done for you." Keys tapped through the line. "Send me over those business names. We'll start there. We'll know more once he makes his demands."

"Right."

"Do you have a gun?"

"No." True to my liberal roots, I hated guns. At the same time, I felt like a foolish schmuck sitting next to a wooden block of dull kitchen knives.

"I'll try to get some to you."

"What? I wouldn't even know how to use them."

"I'll bring them down and give you a lesson."

"Guns aren't needed."

"Don't be a fucking idiot. I'll come down this weekend. I'll figure it out. In the meantime, stay calm. If he wants something from you, he needs you alive. Those photos were just meant to get you to take him seriously since you blew him off before. It'll all work out."

I sat in the chair, clutching the black handle of the chef's knife until the hint of dawn. Luna found me asleep in the chair. She removed the knife from my grip and urged me to bed.

"No one's coming in at five in the morning," she told me. "My parents used to always say that anyone coming into the diner early morning were hard workers, good people. All the partiers and druggies were passed out somewhere. These early morning hours, when the sun is rising, you can relax." She closed the wooden plantation shutters, shutting out the rays from the rising sun.

"Jasmine's still asleep?"

She nodded. I wanted to pull her into my arms, to fall asleep holding her. But I felt better knowing she was with Jasmine. Soon, I'd have to explain to Jasmine what was going on. Unfortunately, I didn't expect it would be too hard for her to comprehend that there were bad men in the world, and some of them might be coming for us.

thirty-one

LUNA

I woke, aware a person watched. The pinprick sensation followed along my spine, and I lay still, attempting to get my bearings. The window frame near my legs looked familiar; the wall next to my head did not. The lavender sheets hinted of fragrant fabric softener…Jasmine's room. I stretched and rolled away from the wall. Jasmine sat straight, her back as rigid as a flagpole, and the whites of her eyes gleamed in the morning light.

"Morning," I mumbled, my mouth dry and icky.

She waved one hand then blinked, and with perfect pronunciation, "Good morning to you."

"You must wonder what I'm doing here?"

Once more she blinked. I reminded myself to slow my speech.

"Tate asked me to sleep here in your room." Then I sat up quickly. "Has Tate been up here?"

"Tate?"

"Stay. Here." I commanded.

I took the stairs two at a time. In the middle of Tate's bedroom, the empty chair remained, his bed where I placed him in the early morning hours empty, the bedspread smooth, freshly made.

I ran down the hall and down the next flight of stairs, slowing once I saw him, coffee cup in hand, leaning against the kitchen counter.

"Coffee?" he asked.

My shoulders rounded in relief. "Did you sleep?"

"Some."

"Jasmine's up. I think she was confused finding me in her room."

A stair creaked. Jasmine's legs came into view as she slowly descended the stairs, one by one, scissors gripped in one hand and held out like a weapon. She visibly softened when she found only Tate and me in the kitchen. She held out the scissors with a sheepish expression.

"Scare," she offered.

Tate glossed over her comment. "You want coffee?"

"Thank you." She might only be thirteen, but she already liked coffee and hot tea.

"Sit. Both of you." Tate gestured to the breakfast bar.

I excused myself to go brush my teeth and to find a hair band to pull my hair back. When I returned, a steaming cup of coffee awaited me, and Tate stood in front of the stove, coddling a mixture of scrambled eggs. His t-shirt strained around his biceps, and his longish hair was pulled back. He didn't normally wear it back, but I suspected he was too wound up to handle the distraction of hair blowing around his face.

"I want to take both of you over to Alice's this morning," he began, his back to us. "Can you both hang there today?"

"Why Alice?"

"There are some things I need to do today." He spun around, brandishing the spatula like a presentation pointer. "And I feel like you are both sitting ducks here in this house." Jasmine's gaze batted back and forth between the two of us.

"Tate, this island isn't big. If someone is here, they can just as easily find us at Alice's as here. Or at my house."

He shook his head. "No. Here we're on the beach, exposed. Alice lives on the inner island. No one from a ship can see through the tree canopy. Plus, Alice knows this island better than anyone. If someone came looking for you, she'd know where to hide."

I slowly shook my head, not buying it. Anyone could be found here.

"Remember that cat?" he asked.

"Yeah."

"There are places to hide."

Truth. The only reason we found that cat was because he came out by choice. If he'd remained hidden, well, he probably would've been gator food.

"Are you sure you want to bring Alice into this?"

He returned to the business of stirring the eggs on the heat. "It's either that or send you guys to the mainland. Maybe to Florida? But...I don't like you being so far away from me."

His gorgeous blue eyes met mine at his admittance, and a warmth surfaced. I didn't want to be away from him either. Thoughts of last night at my place surfaced. Heat emanated off my face.

If Jasmine wasn't with us, I'd wrap my arms around him. Hold him. His smoldering gaze made me suspect his thoughts were along the same lines as mine.

Jasmine remained poised, watching us both. The scissors lay on the table, resting near her right hand.

I cleared our plates, rinsed them, and set them in the dishwasher. Jasmine excused herself to pack for going out for the day. I joined Tate by the back door where he stood staring out at the ocean. The skyline cast a scarlet hue over the horizon.

"Is it supposed to storm today?" I asked.

"There's a storm over the ocean. Last time I checked, it shouldn't come inland, at least not until it hits the Northeast."

"I don't like this."

His thumb grazed my lips, and he caressed my cheek, then bent me back and kissed me with a searing intensity that left me leaning against him for support.

"It'll be okay. Trust me?"

I answered without hesitation. "I trust you. But I'm scared. You are scaring me. Let me come with you and help."

"Luna, by helping with Jasmine, you are helping me. This is my problem. My mistake to fix. If I seem scared, it's only because they found my weakness."

"Which is?"

"You." He placed a soft kiss on my forehead. "I can't let anything happen to you. I'll take care of this. Pay them what they want. Put this behind us."

A creak on the stairs announced Jasmine's return. He kissed me softly, and I let go.

When we arrived at Alice's deep green cottage, she stood by the front porch railing, watching out for us.

"Come inside." She welcomed us with a boisterous smile. Her loose dress cascaded down to the ground and skimmed above her purple leather sandals. Her stacked toe rings glistened in the morning sun that filtered through the tree limbs.

Tate followed us inside and scanned behind him before pulling the heavy wooden front door closed. I didn't know exactly what he feared, or what he was imagining would happen. I didn't know how bad these men from his past were. But his unease unsettled me. I paced the room and fidgeted.

On Alice's stove, a mixture brewed. I hovered over it, inhaling. It smelled like cinnamon. Granules of her seasoning floated on top. Using a ladle, she spooned the hot liquid into mugs for each of us. Then, almost ceremoniously, she tied woven bracelets on our right wrists, then methodically clipped the extra string, chanting a nonsensical series of letters.

Tate and I locked eyes as she bent over my wrist, administering her odd gift, and he smirked. I refused to mock her. Yes, we all thought of her as the island eccentric, but when push came to shove, we found ourselves on her doorstep.

Jasmine fingered her bracelet and beamed. She'd been given so many new things since she arrived in the States, but gifts were still new enough that every single one touched her. I pressed my forearm against hers, so we could compare the bracelets. They reminded me of the friendship bracelets I once wore in middle school, only Alice had woven in small pieces of smooth sea glass, and the beads glistened like jewels.

"Alice, these are amazing," I gushed.

"For safety. Needed, no?" she asked Tate.

"Maybe." His Adam's apple shifted as he swallowed. "Thank you for letting Jasmine and Luna stay with you today while I take care of some business."

"Of course. My home is yours. This, you know, dear child."

Tate hesitated then stepped up to me and brushed his lips against mine. I immediately glanced at Jasmine. She watched us, but I couldn't discern her opinion.

"Walk out with me?" Tate asked, so I did.

As soon as the heavy wooden door closed behind us, Tate pulled me against his body, his muscles tense and tight. The wrinkles around the corners of his eyes highlighted his worry.

"Stay here until I come back for you?"

"Do you really think we're safe here? If you're right, Tate, and those men aim to kidnap us or hurt us, we could put Alice in danger." I'd weighed the risks this morning, but Jasmine's proximity prevented me from fully venting my concerns.

"You're safer here than anywhere. There's nothing to indicate whoever took those photos is on the island. The angle of all the shots makes it look like they were taken from a telescopic lens, possibly from a boat. Chances are, I'm responding exactly how they want me to respond. Freaking out enough to do whatever they ask. It's an old negotiating trick we used to use. Chances are, whoever sent those photos, they don't intend to actually harm you or Jasmine. And you'll spend an entertaining day at a crazy old lady's home."

"Where are you going?"

"The business center."

"Why there?" He had an entire office set up at his home now. Even Jasmine had a student desk and laptop.

"Faster internet. Anonymity." He kissed the top of my forehead. "Luna." He pressed his forehead to mine. "I love you. Stay safe."

He opened the door and pushed me back inside, as if locking me in a vault. His first time saying *I love you*. And my stomach dropped to the ground because it rang like a last rites statement.

thirty-two

TATE

On ships, we relied on radar. Radar told us not only what was below us, but what was near. We tracked the currents and both cold- and warm-blooded objects. Ships also tracked weather systems through sophisticated satellites. Without adequate data, one could find themselves in a deadly situation fast.

I built a plan without a radar system in place. After tucking Luna and Jasmine away, I stopped back by the cottage to get my cell. Forgetting that thing had become a force of habit, but I needed it for the contact list.

The front door banged into the wall after I flung it open. The loud noise shattered the quiet, and the door reverberated. "Fuck." A black mark and slight indentation into the wall marred my freshly minted paint job.

Movement out the window flitted through my peripheral vision. A man wearing a long, dark wool dress coat traversed the dunes. Islanders crossed the wooden board-walk all the time, but this man didn't fit in with the beach scene.

Leaving the front door open, I crossed the downstairs floor and peered out the back for a better view. He was an older man, with thin, dark hair and a noticeable pouch. As he came closer, I grew more certain. I stepped out onto the porch. Breeze blew through the cottage and slammed the back door behind me.

An eerie smile spread across Zane's pock-scarred face. His heavy black work boots pounded on the wood planks, the volume of the beat increasing with each step. I stood in the doorway, blocking his entrance to the porch.

"Tate, my man. Long time, no see." He held out his hand, and I looked down on it, two wooden steps higher and a world more ethical than the conman below me.

"What do you want, Zane?"

He turned his hand to display his palm and stuck his lower lip out.

"Is that anyway to greet an old friend?"

"No games. What the fuck do you want?"

"Since you're asking…" He shoved his hands into the front pockets of his dark jeans and ground the heel of a boot into the plank. "Why don't you invite me up, and we can have a chat about it?"

"You're not coming inside."

He turned his head, looking up and down the beach. Cottages surrounded us. We were alone outside, but someone could conceivably be looking out any number of windows.

"You know, I don't think that's the way you should treat a friend. Especially a friend who you owe."

"I owe you jack shit."

"Now, that's not true." He wagged his finger in the air. "And I happen to know you've already taken your fuck toy and that nigger and tried to hide 'em away."

I peered over the dunes. The same cargo ship from last night docked offshore.

"That ship's yours."

He licked his lips and grinned. "Let's go inside."

I sat down on the top stair and glared up at him, my hands balled into fists. "Nope. Tell me what you want. Out here."

His trench coat had long slits for pockets, and he thrust his right hand into the pocket as his nostrils flared. His beady, angled eyes reminded me of a shark, circling, debating the best attack point. He pivoted, casting glances at windows once more, then lifted his hand partially out of the deep pocket, enough to show me the butt of a pistol.

"Inside. Now."

I debated my options. If he killed me, he'd get nothing, so flashing a gun was nothing more than an empty threat. I didn't know what he wanted. All I wanted was to get him to leave us alone.

I huffed loudly, spit at his feet, just to show the pissant I wasn't scared, and let the screen door slam behind me.

He followed me inside. Scanned the place, taking stock of the interior like a thief. Translation workbooks and Learn to Read books sat in a neat stack on the kitchen table, along with pens. Jasmine's flip-flops rested near the back door. Several throw blankets lined the sofa. A framed photo of Jasmine and my brother's family in front of a lit Christmas tree decorated the side table.

The photo grounded me and reminded me of my purpose.

"What do you want?"

"I need your help."

"So you sent threatening photos?"

"Wanted to grease the wheels. You know how it works."

"I told you, I don't work for you anymore. Plus, I've got a family now."

"Thought you might say that." He scratched his jaw and pivoted on his boot. "Are the rumors true? Did you torch *Rising Tide*?"

"No."

"Don't believe you. Transfer ten million to my account, and we'll call it even."

"Ten million? Are you out of your mind?" I'd expected he was after money, but…

"You blew up a fucking ship. Native Shipping figured out who did it. They're coming after me now since you were my employee. You can work it off or pay it off."

The god damn fucker. Same logic he used on the indentured slaves they kept on ships. Yeah, the ship might have cost ten million, but I knew his game. He pegged numbers high enough that he'd think I had to work and find ways to keep me in his employ. Maybe not as long as the men sleeping with rats, but he'd find something. To a guy like Zane, I was only a means to an end, and that end was money in his pocket. I glared at him, hating I'd ever gotten wrapped up with this guy or that world. The dark underbelly of the manmade lawless ocean.

He traced a finger over my television and lifted it,

examining the pad of his finger as if checking for dust. "Why'd you do it?"

"What?" I barely heard the question, he said it so low, under his breath.

"Why'd you blow the ship up? You delivered it. Did your job. What the fuck happened? Did you decide you had to go all martial law? Did something happen on that ship?"

"Native Shipping has slaves on those ships. *Rising Tide* wasn't a cargo ship. And you know it."

He shook his head, slow and sure.

"Unless you're counting humans as cargo, it wasn't cargo."

"You didn't think it was a wee bit suspicious that you quit right after the ship you returned mysteriously blew up out in the harbor?" I'd known it was suspicious. That was why I'd dumped my cell before returning to the States. That captain had men in chains. Someone had to do something. The Haitian officials were corrupt. Options were limited.

I rubbed my forehead. There was no point in debating anything with a guy like Zane. He saw himself as a good guy. An arbiter on the seas. Sometimes, the term repo man probably did fit. The times he reclaimed ships for banks when the shipping companies fell behind on payments. Other times, he was in deep on bilking schemes. Corrupt local officials fined boats in port and effectively captured them. Sometimes he instigated the charges. Other times he escaped with the ship and took it out to the twelve-mile line, out of the jurisdiction of local authorities.

"Ten million, and you leave me alone, for good?" I asked. Going back to work for him wasn't going to happen. The whites of the eyes of the men on those boats visited all too often.

He stepped back, studied me. He ground his teeth as if he had a small wad of chewing tobacco tucked into the side of a cheek. His expression shifted, and I could tell the moment he decided his first number hadn't been high enough.

"You'll transfer the funds to the account I give you?"

"Yep."

"Today?"

"I'll get my laptop. Do it now."

"There's no way to get you to come back out and work with us?"

"No."

"Do it." He pulled out his cell and opened it to a screen with account information to a bank in the Seychelles.

I flipped open my laptop and debated my next move.

I stood to find my phone.

Zane pulled the gun out of his pocket and held it casually by his side, pointed at the ground, watching me. The shark circling prey.

"I need to call someone. I don't have that kind of money sitting around."

"Didn't think you did."

The way he said it gave him away. Somehow, he had access to all my accounts. Gabe had been right. He'd been monitoring me.

"Hey, man, what's up?"

Zane's thumb rubbed up and down on the butt of the gun.

"Gabriel, I need you to transfer ten million for me. I

don't have it in my accounts. Is there any chance I can borrow the funds from you, then pay you back?"

For Gabe, ten million was the equivalent of loaning Taco Bell money back when we were in high school. Still, I hated the idea of borrowing money. My brother had set up a payment plan to pay me back for my shares of our family company, so no matter what happened, I'd eventually pay Gabe back. Plus, I had some gigs in play working as a consultant.

A door closed on Gabe's end. "Is someone with you right now?"

"Yes." Zane glared at me, tracking my every move, but he'd relaxed enough to return his gun to his coat pocket. I backed up and leaned against the far wall, hoping I was far enough away he couldn't hear Gabe.

"Are you in danger?"

"To some extent. Can you help me out? I'll pay you back."

"You know if you do this, chances are this won't be the end of it."

"Yep." Gabe wasn't saying anything I didn't know. Guys like this were sharks. Blood in the water, and there was a good chance they'd come back if they got hungry again.

"No problem, man. I made a lot more than that yesterday. Plan G in effect. My contact at the *New York Times* got back to me. I think he's gonna want to meet you."

I smashed the screen against my ear, uncertain what Zane could hear.

"Let me send you over the account details for the wire transfer." I ended the call then texted the details Zane provided while looking over my shoulder. Gabe texted back a transfer confirmation. The money wouldn't immediately transfer. There would be a temporary hold on an amount that large. Zane requested the wire details, and he sent the information off into the ether. Deal done.

"Can you give me a ride back to the marina?"

"You have a boat there?" I'd assumed he had a dinghy or something up on the beach.

"Small craft."

"Sure. Come on." The sooner he got off the island, the better. Then I could go pick up Luna and Jasmine and tell them everything was okay.

Left down Wynd Road would be the most direct path, but Zane pointed right. "Can we go that way? I've been watching this island, and I'd like to see the middle. I'm curious."

Turning right then driving down the middle of the island would add maybe five to ten minutes, tops. I didn't see any harm in taking the longer route. I also didn't have a choice.

"Sure." I turned right.

He shifted in the seat to study the beach houses that lined the path. Pretty much standard for anyone going this way. The cool breeze stung my cheeks, and my tension eased. Those fucking photos had had me edgy. The unspoken threat terrified me, as intended. All I needed to do was borrow from a friend who had more money than a small country. Problem solved.

"My sources say you're thinking of downloading info on Native Shipping. You do that, you'll make enemies." There was no threat in the statement. He dropped the comment in an offhanded, casual manner.

"Not sure what your sources are saying, but I wouldn't be that stupid."

"Really? No plans to share information with the *New York Times*?"

I felt his eyes on me even as I stared straight ahead. We entered the shade of the middle island, the path covered by overhead tree branches. The hum of crickets, frogs, and birds surrounded us.

I swallowed. He waited.

"No plans. Besides, even if I was going to do something like that, it wouldn't make sense now, right? I've paid you. You and I are even. Native Shipping and I are even."

"Yeah, but you're one of those environmentalists. You probably have a problem with what they do."

"Oh, you mean illegal fishing? Or are you talking about smuggling guns and drugs? Or the human trafficking bit? Because, like you said, they're massive. Billion-dollar company, right? Have they ventured into all the areas of the trade? Or are they still staying out of piracy?"

"You publish any nonsense, and it means pressure from some countries might increase and make life difficult. Don't do it."

"What countries do they care about? Haiti? Liberia? Ghana? Somalia?" The list could go on and on. Ports of call to cater to the high sea criminals weren't exactly small in number.

"God damn. You're such a fucking bleeding heart."

My grip on the steering wheel tightened. "You know, I think people use the term bleeding heart because it's the only negative they can come up with for someone who wants to do good. And the only reason people like you don't like it is that doing good stymies your ability to commit crimes against nature."

A hard object jammed into my ribcage, and I twisted away from it, right as his large, gloved hand fell over mine. My attention zoned in on the black leather glove. The temperature hung in the fifties. Chilly, but not glove weather.

"Stop the cart."

I pulled to a stop. A bone deep chill penetrated my hands, then deep within my chest.

I'd paid him. Now, his only remaining objective would be to shut me up. Another rogue wave, never entirely unexpected. *Keep your head and ride it.*

"It's not like what I know matters. Plenty of articles about crimes on the high seas exist. TV shows, even movies. There's nothing in it for me to share what I know."

"Probably. But there's no reason to take on unnecessary risk. Tensions between China and the U.S. and Iran are sky-high. If a story breaks, impossible to say who'd try to use it to their advantage. Better to nip the small fires before they spread."

He pointed his gun down a nature trail through the marsh. "Walk."

I didn't move, and he walked around to my side and pointed the gun at my head.

I lifted my phone and dialed Gabe's number, said, "Cancel the wire transfer," and disconnected.

Zane's eyes bulged. "What the fuck? You have a death wish?"

"You're going to kill me anyway, right? That's the plan?" He raised his gun, and perspiration kicked in. I slipped into negotiation mode. He taught me how to do this. *Stay calm. Be in control.* "Where'd you want to walk to?"

He muttered a string of expletives. Called someone. Paced. Gritted his teeth. Cursed. Kicked a rock.

"Transfer canceled." The cold metal of his pistol pressed hard against my forehead.

"Go ahead. Shoot."

He cocked the gun. "Wire. That. Money."

"Your plan is to kill me. Why would I wire you the funds?"

"All right. Take me back to my boat. Then wire the money. I'll leave you alone. You have my word."

"Get in."

We drove back to the marina in silence. I ran through scenarios in my head as I drove. Negotiating with Zane would never lead to a win. Especially now that I had people in my life to protect. As soon as the marina came into view, I stopped the cart.

"You always said repo men aren't bad guys. You told me we make threats, but we don't actually break the law. No violence. No guns. That's what you said."

"And you were naive enough to believe me. Now, call your friend back. Wire that money. If you don't, you'll always be looking over your shoulder."

"See, here's the trouble, Zane. Even if I do wire the money, I'd have to look over my shoulder. As it stands, all that information has already gone out to the *New York Times*. There's a journalist there who's been covering ocean crimes for a decade now. It's done. Whether you kill me or not, I've shared everything I know."

"You're bullshitting me."

"No. I'm not."

"You just fucking told me—"

"I was scared." An island safety patrol pickup truck with lights on top of the cab pulled up behind my cart. I nodded to Logan, the driver and the island's police chief, and the strobe lights flicked on. "I'm not now."

Zane's hand gripped the butt of his pistol. I feared he'd use it, and held my palm up, instructing Logan to remain in the relative safety of the vehicle. A U.S. Coast Guard boat pulled into the marina at a speed that ignored all no-wake guidelines. Zane turned his back on the uniformed officer, his focus intent on the incoming boat.

"You're coming with me." He motioned for me to move.

"Why? Is that how you want to go out? With a hostage? You're smart enough to know no one ever wins with the hostage strategy."

"What do they know? What are they after?" His right hand gripped the butt of the pistol, but his focus centered on the marina. A police boat with flashing lights sped through the harbor entrance.

"I'm not sure. What account did you give me to transfer money into?"

Hatred spewed. "You motherfucker."

"I would've left you alone. But you came after my family."

He raised the pistol as his face contorted. The pickup truck door opened, and the officer raised his pistol into the air.

"Put the gun down. On your hands and knees."

"Game's over, Zane."

thirty-three

LUNA

Sasquatch, one of Alice's tabby cats, curled up on my lap the moment I perched on the papasan. To accommodate the large orange tabby cat with golden eyes, I had to sit farther back in the chair and eventually crossed my legs to create a comfy spot. Her purr grew into a soothing, rumbling engine. Alice draped a wool knit afghan around my shoulders and set a steaming cup of tea and a worn paperback romance on the side table. She set Jasmine up similarly on the futon against the wall.

A long-haired gray cat circled Jasmine's lap before cuddling up next to her. "Fresco will keep you company." She cupped Jasmine's chin and said something more, something I didn't understand.

I sat in a trance, lulled by Sasquatch, as Alice flitted about from the glass case filled with bowls and jars, out to the back yard, and then back in. She filled a small cotton pouch with white powder, then brushed her hands off on the front of her dress. The white powder floated through the air.

"You two are in good care. I'll be back."

"Where are you going?" I asked.

"To see to things. Stay here today. If you get hungry, you help yourself to anything you want in the fridge."

I would have asked more, but the door closed.

The whites of Jasmine's eyes glowed in Alice's dimly lit den. Here on the marsh, trees surrounded her cottage, and a golden glow transcended through the back windows, and inside the house, shadows gathered along the walls.

"Is Alice?" Jasmine paused and stroked the long-haired beast in her lap. "Is she?"

"What?"

"Voo. Doo?"

I rested my head on the back of the cushiony chair and laughed. In Haiti, voodoo priests were held in high regard. I wasn't sure if the same would be true in Somalia, or even if her understanding of the English word was the same, but based on her spooked expression, I imagined she had a fairly accurate understanding of the word.

"No. I don't think Alice does voodoo."

"Is she…witch?"

I had to think about that question before answering. Sasquatch's claws dug into my skin as he stretched. "Witch sounds bad. Alice is good." I tried to keep my words basic. "Alice is spiritual."

Jasmine licked her bottom lip but gave no sign as to whether she understood that word.

"Alice loves nature. Alice loves the Earth." I stopped judging people for their chosen religious beliefs long ago.

If Alice wanted to build an altar in her back yard to be closer to her chosen god, who was I to judge? If she wanted to go outside and pray and chant, which was what I suspected she had gone to do, why stop her?

Fresco climbed up Jasmine and put his nose to hers. She giggled as his whiskers tickled her. He settled back down on her lap.

I picked up my book, and Jasmine did the same.

"I like Alice," Jasmine told me, pronouncing each word with care.

"Me too. You don't have to share all of a person's beliefs to like them."

I pretended to read and look natural and unworried, knowing Jasmine watched closely. Tate wanted me to look out for her, and I could do that. Even though my insides roiled intensely to the point of nausea, I could act like all was well, for Jasmine. I refused to pick up my phone or text Tate to check in. He had things he wanted to get done in the business center, and I didn't want to interfere. But I wished he would text something…any kind of an update.

An awkward routine settled between Jasmine and me. I would stare out the window, feel her gaze, and I would quickly look down to my book and pretend interest, flipping pages to enhance my performance. She practiced her writing in a workbook, creating a flurry of eraser dust as she wrote, erased, and rewrote letters. My ringtone, a shrill cry of a seagull, shattered the silence. Sasquatch jumped off my lap, his tail twitching his discontent. An unknown number flashed on the screen.

"Probably a telemarketer," I said, answering her silent question. She squinted in confusion.

"Hello?"

"Luna? It's Gabe. I can't reach Tate. Have you seen him?"

"No. We're at Alice's."

"I know. I thought he might have made it back there."

"No—"

"Luna? Make sure he keeps his phone on him today. Plan G is rocking and rolling."

He hung up on me. Confused, I stared at the phone in my hand. He had some plan in the works and hadn't deemed me adult enough to share it with me. And no matter how much I wanted to leave this house, I couldn't. Jasmine didn't need a babysitter, but she didn't need to be left alone either. I didn't mind being there with her, but I minded Tate treating me like I was less. Like I wasn't someone he could share everything with. Like I wasn't an equal.

If he wanted a relationship with me, this crap would not fly.

I paced the room, trapped. Every now and then, Jasmine's gaze would lift from her workbook. Several old board games with yellowed cardboard and dented corners filled the bottom shelf of a shelving unit near the stairs. I lifted the Scrabble box and brought it over to the coffee table in front of Jasmine.

"Game?" I offered.

I spread out the wooden pieces and the board. Jasmine picked up on the game with ease, and we played out the game using three- or four-letter words.

An eternity passed, and the door cracked open. I scanned the nearest coffee table for a weapon.

Alice passed through the door, and I lowered the

wooden letter tray I'd been prepared to pummel an intruder with.

"You've got the jumps," Alice teased.

"Can you blame me? And Gabe called and said Plan G is in effect. Do you know what that is?" *She'd better not. If he told Alice and not me...*

Her gentle hand rested on my shoulder. "He wanted to keep the two of you safe."

"Well, that's—" Jasmine's wide eyes forced me to swallow my anger and frustration. I stood and stretched under Alice's watchful gaze.

Alice patted my shoulder then squeezed it. "Listen to me. No man is perfect. Talk to him. No relationship works if you don't."

thirty-four

TATE

I shook hands with the FBI agent who seemed to oversee the entire operation. I had to hand it to Gabe, the man had contacts. Boats with flashing lights filled the marina. Small groups of islanders hovered around the marina, looking on and talking. I'd seen more than one finger pointed my direction.

Gabe and I alternated between texts and calls. There would be no need for him to fly down. We'd somehow concocted a plan that worked. I kept checking the time on my phone. Luna would wonder what was going on. Every time I had a second free, another uniformed man would approach, wanting to ask questions. The FBI, US Coast Guard, Homeland Security. Logan directed officers, one by one, to me. I had only seen the guy in passing before this, but he'd taken me seriously this morning when I stopped in and met with him. I owed the guy. Prior to today, his biggest worry had been speeding golf carts. He handled it all like a seasoned pro.

Gabe texted and asked the same question, with different phrasing, multiple times. "Do you need a lawyer?"

A man in khaki shorts, a badge, and a gun holster approached. I'd stopped paying attention to the badges over an hour ago.

"Do you know an Alexandre Gueirrero?"

"No."

"He was on the offshore ship. There's a warrant out for his arrest."

I slipped my hands in my pockets and shrugged. I wouldn't put it past Zane to be hauling a felon into international waters. The man would do anything for a fee. But I had no information to offer.

Zane would face multiple charges, not the least of which included carrying an unregistered firearm. The more significant charges, as I understood them, would include blackmail, extortion, wire fraud, conspiracy to commit wire fraud, and tax evasion. He unwittingly led the feds to an entire network of offshore accounts. Prosecutors sought a minimum thirty-year sentence.

Hours passed before I escaped all the men with questions. Alice's house came into view through the wooded lane. Jasmine and Alice swung on the front porch.

"You get everything taken care of?"

"Yes, ma'am. Where's Luna?"

"Once we got word that we were in the clear, she took off."

She probably had work to do at the center. I climbed

the two porch steps and rested my hand on the back of the chair I planned to sit in.

Alice shook her finger and clucked her tongue. "No, sir. Your day's not done. You've got some making up to do."

I glanced around the porch, clueless.

"Get on with it. Jasmine and I are all good. You got a lot to learn about communication. And partnership."

You have to be fucking kidding me.

"Uh-uh." She snapped those fingers, and Jasmine smiled like she was in on a joke. "Drop that attitude. Would you like it if the shoes were reversed? If Luna left you in the dark? Treated you as less? You got some wallowing to do. Now, get to it."

I gritted my teeth as an argument brewed. Alice's eyes leveled on me, and the fight deflated.

I found Luna out on the beach and sat down beside her. She threw a shell fragment out into the wake. We both looked straight ahead, out over the crashing wake. Farther down the beach, a dog rushed the waves, its owner trailing behind.

"Everything's okay now." Luna leaned forward to pick up another shell fragment, acknowledging my comment with a slight nod. Tension radiated, and I didn't like it. But I refused to apologize for keeping her safe. I gritted my teeth, debating how to best address her.

"It's not going to work with us if you treat me like I'm not your equal." She wiped the sand off the shell fragment, her focus so concentrated on her task it took me a moment to be certain I didn't imagine her words. I picked up a smooth gray shell and rubbed it between my fingers, thinking. "Or have you decided you don't want it to work?"

"Luna, I want us to work more than anything." I told her the truth, but she sensed my hesitation.

"But I'm young. Right?"

"It's wrong to tie you down." *No matter how much I want to.*

"Is that the way you see relationships? Once you commit, it's a done deal? Every decision made? By the man?"

"No." I tossed the shell, and it landed near my big toe. Her questions knocked me back. What was my expectation? That if we were together, she'd sculpt her life to fit mine? But that was what would happen, right? That was what couples did.

"Why don't you ask me how I see a relationship?"

Because that's an odd question. What does that even mean? I dug my toes into the cold, heavy sand. "All right. Tell me."

"I've watched my parents my whole life. For years, I wasn't sure they'd make it. Can't tell you how many times they called us down for a family meeting, and I expected them to tell us they were getting separated."

"That sounds...awful." Admittedly, my mother died when I was a teenager, but I never recalled ever wondering if they would divorce.

"Awful? Yes, and no. Because you know what I realized when I went home over the holidays?"

A seagull dipped into the waves and a second later flew away with a slim, silver fish.

"You're not even listening."

"No, I am." I shifted on the sand to face her and

crossed my legs. She continued staring straight ahead, but acknowledged I'd given her my full attention by continuing. "Every day, they wake up and decide. Will they keep trying, or won't they? So far, each day, the answer has been yes. That's twenty-five years of yes. Next year, one of them may decide it's a no."

"That sounds unstable."

"I suppose. But it's also the reality of any person in a modern-day American marriage. None of us are locked into a marriage. We always have options. Every day, we decide. I didn't always see it that way."

The sun glistened in her hair. I thought about the meaning of her words. "When you went home…your ex. He'd be a better—"

"I don't want Brandon. I had thought I didn't want him because what he offered was too similar to my mom and dad. Being trapped in the same small town for the rest of my life. But I realized I didn't want Brandon because he's not right for me." She shifted her gaze. My reflection shone on her shades. "I believe you are. I want to give us a try. But if you can't get past my age, and you can't treat me like an equal partner, then you're not right for me either."

She stood and wiped the sand off her bottom. Gobsmacked, I remained sitting. As she walked away, understanding dawned. I chased her down and matched her pace once I caught up. The wind whipped her loose hair around, covering a portion of her face, and I tugged on her arm for her to stand still. I tucked her unruly strands behind her ears and cupped the back of her head, angling her chin upward. I kissed her, gently, deeply, and with promise. I broke the kiss and lifted her shades, forcing her to look me in the eye, so she could see.

"Luna, if you are open to us, I want to try. You're the best thing to happen to me. I don't see you as less. I see you as so much more. Jasmine, she's in the picture, too. She's a part of me now—"

"I care for her too, you know? She's a remarkable person. I want to be there for her. Help her with her new life. She's stronger than you give her credit for. And she'll be off to college in four years."

I grimaced at the notion, unsure. "Not if she's not ready—"

"You'll be there for her if she needs you."

"What about you?" My thumb grazed her smooth, flawless skin, and she looked up at me, silently questioning. "Are you thinking you want to pursue your doctorate?"

"I still don't know. But my options don't change because of you and Jasmine. It's something I'm exploring. We can make it work." She pressed her palm against me, pushing for space. "But not if—"

"Luna, this morning, I didn't know what I was dealing with. I didn't know how it would play out. When I dropped you off, I still didn't have a cohesive plan. I didn't know Zane would be on the island today, not for certain. It's luck Logan was in his office when I stopped by the police station." Station was a generous description. It was more of an attachment to the fire station that housed the only two fire engines on the island. "If anything happened to you...I had to keep you safe. Can you understand that? I love you."

"Okay."

"Okay?" She nodded and pulled at a wisp of flyaway hair, her eyes glassy with emotion. I held her close and kissed her forehead. *I will try harder*. Her cheek. *I want you in my life*. The corner of her lips. *Please let me be enough*. Her lips. *I need you. I treasure you*.

"I love you too." Her softly spoken words filled me like wind against a sail.

I clasped Luna's hand, weaving her fingers through mine. When I arrived on this island, I'd been on the brink of a fall line. No more.

"So, how do we do this? Where do we start?" I looked to her for direction.

"We take it day by day."

"Together?"

"That's the only way." Her determined gaze locked on mine, and all doubts evaporated.

epilogue

LUNA

6 months later

> Find the hidden pond & follow the
> instructions.

I'd heard about this hidden pond before. Tate had once
suggested we go there to skinny dip. An insane suggestion, that one. Here on Haven Island, we were surrounded
by the Atlantic, ergo plenty of snake-free skinny dipping
options.

The leaves crunched beneath my sandals as I gripped
my phone. The prior two clues had required I send photo-
graphic evidence of my location, then additional instruc-
tions arrived. Jasmine and Tate loved these games.

The hidden pond left much to be desired. Interior inlet,

or sunken area in the middle of the island described it better in my mind. A yellow piece of fabric tied around a skinny pine marked my destination. With great care, I stepped through the underbrush.

Once again, the paper scrawled in Jasmine's textbook elementary handwriting read

TAKE A PHOTO AND RECEIVE YOUR NEXT SET OF INSTRUCTIONS.

I snapped a photo, sent it into the ether, and repeated the careful stepping process back to my golf cart. My phone vibrated.

> Find the island's highest point. From there, me you shall see.

I took off for the lighthouse. We'd used the highest sight line in more than one of our games. In order to enter, you had to make a donation to the lighthouse conservation fund. Joni, the lighthouse volunteer extraordinaire, waved me through when I stepped up to the cash register inside the tiny museum next to the stone structure.

"He's already donated for you."

"That means I've really got to walk up all those stairs this time?" I asked, and she smiled and pointed the way. She got a kick out of our trail map games.

The inside of the centuries-old lighthouse held a dusty smell. Remnant spiderwebs coated crevices as the stairs to the top became steeper and narrower. A faint layer of perspiration rose as my heart rate increased.

At the tip top, the stairs transitioned into more of a ladder, and I crawled into the six-foot round space. Deep windows let light in. There was a sign propped against one of the windows.

LOOK THROUGH THE WINDOW AND SEE THROUGH MY EYES.

The thick, ancient glass didn't provide the best view, but all around the tower, the ocean could be seen. The mainland, not so far away, appeared as green trees. The marsh line could be seen in closer proximity, up until the ocean laid claim. I searched every angle along the three-hundred-and-sixty-degree circumference, but I didn't see.

My phone vibrated.

Marina side.

Treetops and buildings blocked the view of the bulk of the marina. The sun set against the mainland's horizon, casting rose and golden hues over the line of trees. Closer by, near Jules, lights twinkled over the outside deck. Farther out, in the marina, a sailboat with an oversized flag hung between the sailboat and a nearby post. It read, 'Come Sail Away.'

He'd done it. Tate had gone and bought the small sailboat.

I texted back *OTW* then took the stairs two by two, jumping down as I went. I found my cart and floored it to the marina. Jasmine beamed as she saw me approaching and scrambled onto the deck, running toward me.

"It's the *Luna*! Or, he hasn't decided what he's going to name it. He might name her the *Jasmine Luna*. Or the

Jasmine Moon. Or *Sweet Moon*. He's brainstorming. He wanted you to have a say."

As predicted, she'd become fluent and now could speed talk and text like any other teen. Her accent gave her what I thought of as a sophisticated advantage.

"I see."

Along the opposite side of the boardwalk, Poppy approached. She carried an ice bucket in one hand and a champagne bottle in the other. She leaned off the dock, and Tate reached over and took both items from her.

"Ah, fun. Are you coming out for her maiden voyage?"

"Oh, no, lady. Jasmine and I have a girls' night planned. Movies and all."

Jasmine bounced on the back of her heels and clapped her hands.

Gabe shouted out from the deck of the *Will o' the Wisp*, a tiny restaurant overlooking the marina. "Love the boat, man."

Poppy wrapped an arm around Jasmine's shoulders. "Jasmine, it's time for ladies' night to commence." She smiled at Gabe and waved to him.

Gabe waved back then picked up his beer and returned to his bar seat overlooking the marina. He appeared to be in deep conversation with Logan.

Tate held the boat close to the dock for me to board. As I stretched over the water gap, I pointed an index finger Gabe's way. "Is everything okay with those two?"

"Gabe and Logan?"

"No. Gabe and Poppy."

"How would I know?"

"Didn't you go surfing with him this morning?" I'd missed out on dawn patrol because Jasmine and I went for a run. She was considering joining the school's cross-country team, and we'd started building up her endurance, although she'd need to start running with Tate soon. Like most things, she approached running with a singular focus, and she improved rapidly.

"The waves were decent this morning. Not much talking."

"Ah."

A white tablecloth lay over the small table on the back of the boat. Champagne glasses rested in the ice bucket, and a cooler was below the table.

"Look at all this. Is there an occasion, or is this the sailboat life?"

"Welcome aboard. I thought we'd take a romantic sunset cruise."

"That's so sweet. But you didn't want to include Jasmine?" She had to be excited about us getting a new boat.

"You don't know what today is, do you?"

I shook my head. End of summer. *No birthdays…*

"One year ago, you zoomed by in a golf cart. You didn't know it, but you reeled me in. Jasmine helped me with the surprise. When Carter decided to sell me his old sailboat, it all fell into place."

"I'm impressed you remember the date."

He wrapped an arm around me as the boat tilted and we fell against the side. "It's also the day I arrived on the island." The corners of his lips skewed up, creating his signature tease of a smile. "And I remember this young girl, gliding by, so carefree."

I leaned up and kissed him, pressing against him until

that deep moan of his mixed in with the shrill cries of the sea gulls.

He pressed his forehead against mine. "I'm crazy in love with you, you know that?"

"Ditto."

There were a lot of unknowns in my life. I decided to extend my contract with the conservancy for one more year while I finished my master's remotely. I still wasn't entirely sure what direction I wanted my career to take, but Tate assured me he and Jasmine would follow me no matter what path I chose. Any option I chose needed to work for Jasmine, so schools for her factored into any decision, but we were exploring options as far away Costa Rica. This fall, she would start school in South Port. A first big step and one I constantly questioned, knowing it would be a major adjustment for her.

Tate and I both worried about her, not that she gave us cause. At fourteen, she studied so much I worried we hadn't done enough to build her social world. Cali said to give it time. Jasmine's therapist assured us she was adjusting well. Still, I worried. But I held no doubts about Tate.

"Would you rather have dinner while we're docked here in the marina, or do you want to take her out?"

"I want the full sunset cruise experience. Let's head out to the causeway and sip champagne as we watch the sun go down."

We drifted slowly, puttering out into the glasslike water. The sun hung low, casting shades of gold over the dark water. The silver steering wheel spun as Tate guided us expertly out of the harbor.

THE END

Would you like a glimpse into the future?

Sign up for my newsletter and get a FREE bonus epilogue... Visit bit.ly/roguewavebonus to get Tate & Luna Five Years Later emailed to you.

Poppy & Gabe's story is up next in **Adrift**...

She's supposed to be my distraction while my life gets sorted.

Only, I make a mistake. Because while I'm focusing on the one-dimensional centerfold, her three-dimensional self knocks me on my ass.

The billion-dollar scandal doesn't hold a candle to the demolition the blue-eyed babe wreaks to my well-ordered, disciplined, successful life.

also by isabel jolie

Arrow Tactical Security Series

Better to See You (Wolf and Alexandria)

Sure of One (Jack and Ava)

Cloak of Red (Sophia and Fisher)

Stolen Beauty (Knox and Sage)

Savage Beauty (Max and Sloane)

Sinful Beauty (Tristan and Lucia)

Gilded Saint (Sam and Willow)

Scarlet Angel (Nick and Scarlet)

Prophet (Dorian and Caroline) - Releasing June 12th

The Twisted Vines Series

Crushed (Erik and Vivi)

Breathe (Kairi and David)

Savor (Trevor and Stella)

Haven Island Series

Rogue Wave (Tate and Luna)

Adrift (Gabe and Poppy)

First Light (Logan and Cali)

The West Side Series

Blurred Lines (Jackson and Anna)

Trust Me (Sam Duke and Olivia)

notes & acknowledgements

Haven Island is inspired by a real place—Bald Head Island, North Carolina. For obvious reasons, I couldn't go with that name. I have nothing against bald men, even dated one, but that word doesn't work for me, especially on repeat. Haven is the name on the island's magazine, so I grabbed that and gave it a twist. My family and I spend time each summer on Bald Head. I was married on the island, as was my brother. It really does feel like you're in a different country when you're out there. The absence of automobiles makes all the difference. If you ever get the chance to visit, I highly recommend it.

Tate's experiences prior to arriving on the island are largely inspired by Ian Urbina and his work covering the lawless ocean. My research included articles from sources such as the *New York Times*, NPR and *The Guardian*. But the work that has remained with me is *The Outlaw Ocean*, written by Ian Urbina. The issues facing our oceans are real. Sharks really are dumped to the bottom of the ocean after having their fins chopped off. The saying that there are no tread marks (to investigate) on the ocean is a real one. Tate's experience only brushed the surface of the dark world on the deep seas.

I wrote this during the lead-up to the American 2020 presidential election. Never in my life have I felt such division within my country. I tried to parcel out some of that division between Tate and his family and friends. The environment is only one example of an issue that can be divisive. So many times, when people see things differently, it all comes down to perspective. And we all have different perspectives. That's greatly oversimplifying everything going on right now, but I like to believe at its heart, even in divided families, at the end of the day, love remains.

Alice is a Santeria. She's not a real person, and she doesn't really live on the island, although I did model her home after one of the marsh facing cottages. A Santeria has special powers, and they come into those powers at varying times in their lives. She is religious, and spiritual, but her religion expands upon the major religions of our time—the ones I think of as the big five. The buckets of water to ward off evil spirits, that's one version of praying. It may or may not work, but she'll keep doing it.

The books in this series all center around redemption, taking a step out of the drum of everyday life to heal. I suppose that's what BHI has come to mean to me. It's a place to escape.

When I sent the original manuscript to Amy Claire Mager, I told her it needed work. And it did. She helped me to see areas that needed an overhaul. I'd also like to thank my beta readers, Carly Autumn and Evan Dave, for reading the whole manuscript and providing valuable feedback.

Rogue Wave marks my fifth book working with my editor, Lori Whitwam, and I am forever grateful for her guidance and continued efforts to improve my work. Heather Whitehead completed the line edit and searched to remove any and all comma errors, spacing, or any little thing that might have been overlooked.

Rogue Wave marks my first cover design working with Elizabeth Mackey, and I hope to work with her for a long time into the future.

I'd also like to thank my ARC team for sticking with me into a new series. And of course, thank you to all my readers for reading my books! Every review helps Indie authors, and I so much appreciate the positive words and recommendations- they help to keep me going. Thank you!

about the author

Isabel Jolie, aka Izzy, lives on a lake, loves dogs of all stripes, and if she's not working, she can be found reading, often with a glass of wine. In prior lives, Izzy worked in marketing and advertising, in a variety of industries, such as financial services, entertainment, and technology. In this life, she loves daydreaming and writing contemporary romances with real, flawed characters with inner strength.

Sign-up for Izzy's newsletter to keep up-to-date on new releases, promotions and giveaways. (**Pro-tip** - She offers a free book on her home page…just scroll down after arriving at her site.)

Buy ebooks and signed paperbacks direct from Isabel at www.isabeljoliebooks.com

Want to say hi? Email her through her website or reply to her newsletter…she loves to hear from readers.